'You _____ gising.'

The i_____ restored
Sophie_____aved in a
shame_____ssed any
decency at all he would have pretended to
ignore her eavesdropping!

'You go too far, sir,' she retorted with a
haughty frown. 'I am sorry if I have given
offence, but it is not your place to rebuke me.'

'No, that task belongs to your legal guardian,'
he agreed smoothly. 'But obviously he has
been shirking his duty.'

Dear Reader

We welcome back Gail Mallin who offers DEBT OF HONOUR set against the brooding backdrop of the Lake District, and in DEVIL-MAY-DARE Mary Nichols gives us Lydia, who walks a tightrope of possible disgrace. Our American offerings are STARDUST AND WHIRLWINDS by Pamela Litton, set in Texas 1873, and AUTUMN ROSE by Louise Rawlings gives us seventeenth-century France. Happy New Year!

The Editor

Gail Mallin has a passion for travel. She studied at the University of Wales, where she obtained an honours degree and met her husband, then an officer in the merchant navy. They spent the next three years sailing the world, before settling in Cheshire. Writing soon became another means of exploring, opening up new worlds. A career move took Gail and her husband south, and they now live with their young family in St Albans.

Recent titles by the same author:

THE DEVIL'S BARGAIN
A MOST UNSUITABLE DUCHESS

DEBT OF HONOUR

Gail Mallin

MILLS & BOON

MILLS & BOON LIMITED
ETON HOUSE, 18–24 PARADISE ROAD
RICHMOND, SURREY, TW9 1SR

*First published in Great Britain 1993
by Mills & Boon Limited*

© Gail Mallin 1993

*Australian copyright 1993
Philippine copyright 1994
This edition 1994*

ISBN 0 263 78243 3

*Set in 10 on 11 pt Linotron Times
04-9401-87334*

*Typeset in Great Britain by Centracet, Cambridge
Made and printed in Great Britain*

CHAPTER ONE

THE exotic figure standing outside the handsome-fronted shop caught Kirk Thorburn's attention as he strode down the Highgate. Wintry sunlight burnished the gilded feathers on the Turk's turban and danced down his red jacket and baggy green trousers to catch the upturned tips of his crystal-encrusted slippers. A long clay pipe was held to his lips and in his other hand he clasped a large plug of tobacco.

Kirk halted, his gaze going to the name painted above the wide bow-window. 'Fleming and Sons, Snuff-Merchants'. It seemed he had found the place he sought. Kendal had been a major centre for the tobacco trade for over a hundred years now, but Flemings was reputed to be the best. Perhaps he would find an answer to his questions here?

Involuntarily, his long fingers tightened around the leather pouch in his coat pocket, but as he made to cross the narrow street to reach his goal a tall young woman stopped outside the shop. She had her back to him, but he spotted the friendly pat she bestowed on the exotic statue before entering.

A brief flicker of amusement lightened Kirk's expression. There had been something decidedly pro-prietorial about that little gesture! For an instant he wished he had caught a glimpse of the girl's face. Then his curiosity died. He was not here to dangle after any petticoat, pretty or not.

Ten minutes passed.

'Damn the wench!'

His feet were growing numb and Kirk had the feeling that he might become frozen to the spot if he didn't move soon. Caroline had laughingly informed him this morning that his blood must have grown thin during his long absence from his native soil, and Kirk was beginning to think she might have a point. Certainly, he could do with a little of that fierce Bahamian sun right now!

Kirk stirred restlessly. He had hoped for privacy in which to conduct his business, but he had travelled over three thousand, five hundred miles to try and find an answer to a mystery, and his patience, never abundant at the best of times, was all but exhausted.

What the devil could she be doing in there, anyway?

'Why, Miss Sophie, what brings you here on such a cold afternoon?'

Sophie Fleming smiled at the thin, stooped figure behind the polished counter. 'I thought I might persuade my uncle to accompany me home, Mr Hoggarth.'

Behind his steel-rimmed spectacles Mr Hoggarth's faded grey eyes assumed an apologetic sympathy. 'I fear you have already missed him. He left a quarter of an hour ago, saying he had an engagement to meet Master Strickland at his warehouse to discuss that new shipment of port.'

'In that case there is no point in waiting,' Sophie announced ruefully, knowing that such a business might turn out to be protracted.

It had been something of a wasted afternoon. Against Nancy's advice, she had donned her warmest cloak and boots and ventured out in search of ribbons to trim her new gown for tonight's soirée, but the shade she had wanted proved elusive.

'Is Mrs Nelson waiting for you in the carriage, Miss Sophie? Only it won't do to keep horses standing in this weather,' Mr Hoggarth reminded her gently.

'Oh, I walked,' Sophie replied airily, 'and left Nancy

at home to toast her toes by the fire, since she viewed the prospect of any exercise with such repugnance.'

Mr Hoggarth looked scandalised. 'Then I hope you'll let me procure a chair to take you home, Miss Sophie. 'Tis blowing fit to bring the chimney-pots down! You shouldn't ought to be out in this weather, let alone walking.'

'It is very kind of you, but there is no need. Truly!' Sophie strove to keep her annoyance out of her tone.

It seemed no one could forget the childhood accident which had almost killed her. The fall from her pony while learning to ride had left her with a weak ankle, but she was not delicate!

'Then won't you at least take a glass of something to warm you before you leave?'

Becoming aware that her uncle's oldest and most trusted employee was regarding her with anxiety, Sophie curbed her impatience and nodded. Mr Hoggarth had known her ever since she was a baby and, like her uncle, he found it difficult to accept she was a grown woman of one-and-twenty.

When she was settled with a glass of sherry in the most comfortable chair that the shop could boast Mr Hoggarth enquired how she had enjoyed the recent round of New Year festivities.

'Very well, thank you, sir. Though Nancy swears she is tired of mending all the petticoat frills I have torn while dancing.' Sophie laughed. 'She is convinced I must have two left feet!'

Mr Hoggarth chuckled. 'You are teasing me, Miss Sophie. You are too light on your feet to be a poor dancer.' A beam of fond pride lit his wrinkled face. 'I am sure even an elegant London gentleman like Sir Pelham Stanton could not wish for a more graceful partner.'

Sophie merely smiled. There was a note of curiosity

in the old man's voice, but she had no intention of satisfying it.

Disappointed, Mr Hoggarth sipped his wine. Everyone in Kendal was agog to see if Sir Pelham's whirlwind courtship would come to anything, but he knew that he would get no hint from Miss Sophie. She was completely lacking in the girlish fluttering he felt appropriate in such momentous circumstances.

Rising to her feet, Sophie set down her empty glass.

'Thank you for the wine,' she began, but her speech of farewell ground to a halt as the door flew open with a noisy bang.

Turning automatically, she beheld a tall figure framed for an instant against the doorway, his dark cloak swirling in the icy wind. Then he turned to close the door behind him and the picture dissolved.

Sophie let out the breath she hadn't realised she had been holding as he advanced into the centre of the room. Politely he raised his high-crowned hat in her direction, revealing a head of hair that gleamed like a golden guinea.

'May I enquire if your business is concluded, ma'am?'

His voice was attractive, a deep, rich baritone, but with a curiously heightened sense of awareness Sophie caught the hint of sarcasm behind his question.

Colour flared into her pale cheeks. She was not used to being spoken to in such a fashion.

'No, it is not,' she snapped and, turning to the surprised Mr Hoggarth, she demanded to see a selection of smoking pipes. When a rack was brought for her inspection she viewed them with a show of concentration, but every now and then she allowed her gaze to flick triumphantly to the tall man impatiently waiting next to her.

Kirk restrained the impulse to curse. Unless he missed his guess, the baggage was being deliberately provoking. When she asked to see yet another rack of clay pipes Kirk was sure of it.

Sophie was aware of Mr Hoggarth's unspoken disapproval but her irritating behaviour owed its origin to more than her hasty temper. Something about this man had caught her on the raw! Only look at the way he was standing there, glowering at her. Over six feet tall if he was an inch, with broad shoulders to match, he reminded her of nothing so much as an angry giant out of a child's fairy-tale.

Sternly Sophie quelled the thought that without the frown he would have been devastatingly handsome.

'Ahem, while the lady makes up her mind, perhaps I could help you, sir?'

Mr Hoggarth could not fathom what Miss Sophie was up to, but it was against his principles to risk losing custom.

Kirk hesitated fractionally and then nodded.

'I'm obliged to you, sir,' he said. Delving into the deep pocket of his coat, he produced a leather pouch. 'I have here a snuff-box. Observe the motif on the lid, if you would be so good.'

Surreptitiously, Sophie glanced up at the object he handed over.

'Mmm, Odysseus blinding the one-eyed Cyclops, executed in *quarte-couleur* gold.' Mr Hoggarth studied the snuff-box. 'A very beautiful item, sir. Did you wish to sell it?'

Kirk laughed, and Sophie thought she had never heard a sound so devoid of mirth.

'Nay, it's not for sale. My purpose in bringing it here was to discover if you have ever seen it before. I have reason to suspect it may have been purchased in Kendal, but none of the other snuff-mills I've tried stock such fine goods.'

'It is indeed French workmanship of the highest order,' Mr Hoggarth murmured, turning the box in his hand and surveying it intently. 'We do stock such quality pieces on occasion, but I cannot recall one like this.'

'Are you sure you don't recognise it? It was bought some time ago. Think, man, think!'

The urgency in his tone caused Sophie to abandon her pretence of indifference. Staring at him in frank amazement, she wondered at the reason for the look of strain which marred his classically cut features. Hot-tempered herself, she sensed that something more than mere impatience lay behind his words.

'I'm sorry, but I cannot help you, sir. I would have remembered such a fine snuff-box had I seen it before, I do assure you.'

From the coolness of his reply, Sophie realised that Mr Hoggarth was somewhat ruffled. He took pride in running the shop like well-oiled clockwork and he plainly resented any implication to the contrary.

The stranger did not seem to notice he had given offence, but let out a low mutter, which sounded suspiciously like an imprecation.

Mr Hoggarth's disapproval deepened. He coughed and threw a warning glance in Sophie's direction.

'Will that be all, sir? Or did you want it filling?'

He flipped open the snuff box lid in one easy movement and sniffed cautiously at the interior. 'Kendal Brown. A popular choice, sir, but we can offer you a large selection of other blends or prepare one to your particular requirements if you would prefer some-thing a little more unusual.'

'Thank you. Kendal Brown will suffice.'

Sophie received the distinct impression that snuff was the last thing on the stranger's mind, but his casual assent brought a smile to Mr Hoggarth's face. He was clearly relieved to have matters back on a normal business footing again.

A grin curled Sophie's wide mouth. Plainly he did not

share her curiosity; Nancy was forever complaining that
it was her besetting sin! But, in truth, she had to admit
she was intrigued by this man. It was hard to tear her
eyes away from his tall, well-proportioned figure. There
was an air of purpose and a sense of energy about him
that was exciting, and somehow almost dangerous.
With a little shiver, Sophie suddenly decided he would
make a ruthless enemy.

Who was he and why was he here in Kendal? His face
was deeply tanned, but she did not think he was a
foreigner. What was more, his black caped cloak and
well-polished leather boots were obviously of the finest
quality. No doubt a dandy like Sir Pelham Stanton
would decry his lack of fashionable accessories — he
carried no Malacca cane and his cravat was plain — but
he was undoubtedly a gentleman.

Mr Hoggarth had reached down one of the many
glazed earthenware jars that lined the shelves of the
shop and begun weighing out the correct amount of
snuff on to his scales. His expression became creased
with annoyance when he realised that he was a fraction
short of the necessary amount.

'Your pardon, sir. I shall have to fetch a new supply
from the store-room. It will only take a moment,' he
announced, going red with embarrassment. Flustered
by this unusual mishap, he hurried out.

The snuff-box lay on the counter where Mr Hoggarth
had placed it, and out of the corner of her eye Sophie
could see that the upraised lid was decorated on the
inside with an intricate design.

What an odd sort of place to put such an elaborately
embossed initial, she thought to herself. That beautifully gilded letter would be constantly splattered with
snuff and difficult to clean.

Was it an S? Unconsciously, Sophie moved nearer
for a better look.

'You admire my trinket, ma'am?'

The cold voice made Sophie jump and then flush until she felt sure her face must be as red as her hateful fiery hair.

'I. . . I. . .that is. . .' Aware of her appalling lack of manners, Sophie could hardly bring herself to meet his gaze.

Viking eyes he had, as blue as the reflection off a sunlit sea. Her heart began to thump in the strangest way and to her intense annoyance she found she was tongue-tied, something that had not happened to her in years.

If only he would not stare at her in that sardonic way! The more she struggled for composure, the more those azure depths filled with a cool amusement that mocked her efforts.

'Sir, I. . . I hardly know what to say,' she stammered, ending the silence at last.

'You could always try apologising.'

The impudence of this remark restored Sophie's wits. Granted, she had behaved in a shameless fashion, but if he possessed any decency at all he would have pretended to ignore her eavesdropping!

'You go too far, sir,' she retorted with a haughty frown. 'I am sorry if I have given offence, but it is not your place to rebuke me.'

'No, that task belongs to your legal guardian,' he agreed smoothly. 'But obviously he has been shirking his duty.'

Sophie's big brown eyes widened as she digested his meaning. 'You are insulting, sir! No true gentleman would think of speaking to a lady in such a fashion.'

A short bark of laughter answered her. 'Then it seems we are quits, my girl, for no real lady would dream of trying to pry into matters that were none of her damned business!'

Sophie sucked in her breath, but before she could deliver a blistering reply Mr Hoggarth returned and she had to hastily school her expression into serenity. He would be horrified to discover she was quarrelling like a fishwife, and with a man she hadn't even been formally introduced to!

Deciding that the only dignified escape lay in retreat, Sophie smiled sweetly and bade the elderly shopkeeper farewell.

However, before Mr Hoggarth could extricate himself from behind the counter, the tall stranger said, 'Allow me,' and swiftly moved to open the door for her.

Gritting her teeth, Sophie inclined her head in a gracious gesture. 'Thank you.'

'My pleasure, ma'am.'

Nettled, Sophie glared at him. He was grinning at her, malicious amusement dancing in his blue eyes.

Quelling the absurd tug of attraction his smile provoked, Sophie swept past him with her chin held high.

A faint chuckle followed her out into the street.

'Lord save us, Miss Sophie, where have you been? Your uncle came home long ago.'

Sophie had hoped that the lengthy, roundabout walk she had taken would have restored her temper, but she had reached the Flemings' handsome Queen Anne residence in the Stramongate without being able to dismiss that hateful man from her mind.

Flinging off her fur-lined cloak, she dropped into her favourite armchair by the fire and held her chilled hands to the blaze. 'I am frozen to the bone, Nancy.'

'Well, you would go out,' the older woman scolded, rescuing the abandoned cloak and folding it carefully.

'So I would,' Sophie laughed, the tension draining out of her as she watched Nancy's plump figure bustle about, restoring order. There was something very soothing about the familiarity of her companion's action, she decided as she stretched out her long legs, revelling in the warmth and comfort of her boudoir.

It was a very pretty apartment adjoining her bedroom, beautifully decorated and large enough to hold
all the expensive presents her uncle had showered upon
her over the years, like the elegant rosewood writing-
desk that sat before the silk-curtained window. Sophie
knew she was very lucky to have been taken in by so
kind a man as Thomas Fleming after her parents had
been killed in a tragic accident when she was only a
baby.

'Your uncle wants to talk to you when you are
dressed, but shall I order some tea first? It might restore
you. You look as if something more than the cold has
upset you.' Nancy came to stand before her, her arms
folded in a manner that Sophie recognised as a sign of
anxiety.

'What nonsense, Nancy,' Sophie replied lightly, not
wishing to confess the reason for her ill temper. 'I think
I had best forgo tea if my uncle is already waiting for
me. Do you know what he wants to talk to me about?'

Nancy shook her greying head. 'He was pleased
about something, though,' she volunteered.

'Oh, well, I'll find out soon enough, I suppose.'
Sophie shrugged, moving into the bedroom. She surveyed the daffodil-yellow gown Nancy had already laid
out for her. 'I have changed my mind. I will wear my
blue brocade.'

'But the matching petticoat needs pressing.'

'Then be a dear and press it for me, Nancy, darling.'
Sophie smiled coaxingly. 'I couldn't find those yellow
ribbons I wanted.'

Nancy rolled her eyes, but did not argue. The gown
was well enough as it was, but stubborn as an ox Miss
Sophie could be when she had set her mind on something! She took the sapphire flowered brocade with its
sky-blue petticoat from the clothes-press and left her
young mistress to her ablutions.

The copper can of hot water Nancy had placed earlier

by the fire had kept warm, and as Sophie poured it into the rose-patterned china basin on her wash-stand her mind returned to the man she had encountered at the snuff-mill. Perhaps he was visiting friends in Kendal. She had lived all her life in the old grey town and knew everyone of note. Surely they would be bound to meet again if he was staying for any length of time?

A thread of excitement flickered through her slim frame at the thought. Provoking though he had been, she longed to know his name, and her heart skipped a beat at the prospect of meeting him in more favourable circumstances.

'What a fool you are!'

Sophie pressed her hands to her hot, damp cheeks. She whirled away from the wash-stand, scrubbing furiously at her skin with a towel, and caught a glimpse of her reflection in the ornate mirror above the mantelpiece. A hectic sparkle showed in her dark eyes.

'Perhaps I am coming down with a fever,' she murmured ruefully.

Forcing herself to sit down, she tried to be calm. If it wasn't a fever turning her brain, then it must be madness possessing her, for she could not rid herself of the image of a man she had barely spoken to!

A tiny laugh escaped her compressed lips. Perhaps it was his unusual height that had struck a chord. It had made her feel femininely petite, a deliciously novel sensation, since she was taller than most of her friends. Indeed, she towered over her uncle and even her most ardent admirer was only a scant inch or two taller than herself.

The thought of Sir Pelham brought a slight sense of comfort to her self-esteem. At least he would never address her in such a rude manner, unlike that provoking great oaf!

* * *

Thomas Fleming was comfortably ensconced in the parlour, reading the latest copy of *The Times*, a news-sheet brought up from London by mailcoach. The White Hart, where the stage stopped, boasted the best coffee-house in Kendal, and as he was a member of their reading-club the landlord was happy to order a copy for his private use. The news it contained, of the inevitable prospect of war with Revolutionary France and the unhappy position of the imprisoned King Louis, made his expression serious, but his plump face bright-ened as his niece entered the room.

'You look lovely, lass,' he said, surveying her with approval.

Sophie smiled faintly. Her doting relative held parti-san views! Still, she had to admit the dazzling creation of flowered brocade suited her, and her rebellious curls had been tamed for once. They fell in artistic disarray to her shoulders and she had used Spanish wool paper and pearl powder to draw attention to her clear com-plexion. Her long, slender neck was another asset and she wore an ornate necklace of opals and diamonds, a recent Christmas gift from her uncle, to emphasise it.

'Nancy said you had something to tell me,' Sophie remarked.

He nodded, his eyes shining with pleasure. 'Sir Pelham has asked permission to pay his addresses to you.'

Sophie's mouth fell open in sudden dismay.

Her uncle viewed her reaction with surprise.

'I thought you would be pleased. Don't you like the idea of marrying him, m'dear?' he asked, motioning her to sit down and resuming his own seat.

Sophie did not immediately answer and he waited for her reply with growing concern. 'Come now, am I such an ogre that you cannot tell me the truth?'

A faint smile touched Sophie's mouth. Anyone less

like an ogre would be hard to find. From the top of his silver head to his small feet, Thomas Fleming did not possess a mean bone in his short, rotund body. His generosity was matched only by his girth, and everyone who knew him admired the way he balanced his adroit business skills with a genuine compassion for those less fortunate than himself.

No, it was not fear that tied her tongue in knots, but a desire to avoid hurting her uncle's feelings. He was bursting with pride and plainly longing to boast of her conquest to all his friends. But I cannot pretend about something so important, Sophie decided, summoning all her courage.

'When Sir Pelham began to call on us last autumn I thought his interest in me would not last,' she began obliquely. 'I told myself it was just a harmless flirtation to while away a sojourn in the country.'

'Aye, I thought as much myself.' Uncle Thomas nodded.

'Then when he returned from London for Christmas there seemed to be a change in him,' Sophie continued slowly.

'I dare say he'd discovered that he had missed you, lass,' Thomas chuckled jovially. 'I'll own I am a little surprised he has asked for your hand so soon, but we should have known what was in the wind. A man don't dangle after a girl the way he has been doing unless he is serious.'

'But why, Uncle?' Sophie flung out her hands in a gesture of bewilderment. 'Why should he want to marry me?'

Thomas looked at her in astonishment. 'What a question, lass!' he exclaimed. 'Why should he not wish to marry you, eh? You are a considerable heiress and a fine, healthy girl into the bargain. He could do a lot worse!'

Sophie shook her head in laughing protest at his

indignation. 'Thank you, dear Uncle, for your championship, but we both know I am no beauty. I am too tall and I lack fashionable curves, to say nothing of my abominable hair!'

Thomas snorted. 'You judge yourself too harshly, m'dear. Not everyone dislikes red hair and you have omitted to mention that you have the loveliest eyes in Kendal! Not that it signifies; a man must consider more than looks when he weds.'

'Indeed.' Sophie acknowledged the truth of this statement with a little inclination of her head. 'But I must confess myself still puzzled. The baronet is wealthy. He has a fine house in London as well as estates in Cumberland. He does not need my dowry.'

'A gentleman always has more need of money.' An unusual note of cynicism entered Thomas Fleming's voice. 'Aristocrats never wed paupers, lass.'

'Nor do they usually marry into trade,' Sophie countered.

'True, but don't forget that Stanton's grandfather was nothing more than a blacksmith. He isn't one of your fancy noblemen with a pedigree as long as your arm. Perhaps he can see the sense in marrying a healthy lass rather than some over-bred ninny who won't be able to bear him sons for all her blue blood.'

Sophie coloured. Plain speaking did not offend her in the normal way, but the thought of sharing such intimacies with the baronet made her feel strangely uneasy.

'Now, Sophie, don't start being missish! It ain't like you.' Her uncle wagged a plump finger at her. 'You are a sensible puss and you've been brought up to understand the realities of life. I'll own that I've been glad to keep you here at home with me, but girls have to marry some time. You are twenty-one; it's high time you wed like all the rest of your friends. Or do you want to stay a spinster all your life?'

'Of course not!' Sophie shuddered at this dismal prospect.

'Well, then, Stanton can keep you in style and you'll be able to taste fashionable life in London too.'

'He's seventeen years older than me.'

'Is that what all this fuss is about? Are you wishing he was some romantic young fellow to sweep you off your feet?' Uncle Thomas shook his head in disbelief. 'I would have thought better of you, Sophie, than to let yourself get carried away by all that nonsense. Love belongs in those novels you read, m'dear, not the real world. Remember, marriage is a business affair.'

j At her suddenly downcast expression, his tone softened.

'Eeh, lass, he's had his pick in London, but it's you he wants to wed.'

'You think his regard for me may be genuine?' she asked hopefully.

'I'm certain of it. You are a good catch, but, if he's the man he seems, then that wouldn't have weighed with him unless he had a fancy to you.'

Sophie shrugged helplessly. It was hard to discern what the baronet was thinking, for his manner was always formally polite, but perhaps the world in which he moved regarded passion as vulgarly undignified.

To tell the truth, Sophie had never met anyone like Sir Pelham Stanton before, and she hardly knew what to make of him.

As she emerged from Holy Trinity Church after morning service one crisp Sunday last October a gust of wind had blown the frivolously beribboned hat from her head. Sir Pelham retrieved it and returned it to her with an elegant bow. Once introduced, he had become a frequent caller to the house in the Stramongate, showering Sophie with small, thoughtful gifts. His urbane charm and witty conversation brought a thrilling whiff of the great metropolis into their quiet life and

Sophie had never stopped to question his motives in singling her out.

Until now!

'Do you dislike him?' Doubt edged Thomas's tone.

'Oh, no, I find his company quite agreeable for the most part.'

'They say that love comes only after marriage and, although I can be no judge of that, I do know that this would be a good match.'

Sophie bit her lip. What her uncle said sounded reasonable, but a little voice murmured in her head that her feelings would not grow warmer in time and that she should trust her instincts and refuse this suitor now.

Desperately, she strove to ignore it and consider the many advantages of marrying such a man. Wealth and influence would indeed be hers, but, to her horror, she found she couldn't bring a single feature of the baronet's to mind. Another face, a devastatingly handsome face alight with a mocking pair of Viking eyes, kept intruding.

'I promise I won't push you into marrying him if that's what's worrying you, m'dear,' her uncle announced, seeing her hesitation. 'I think it is in your best interests and you'll never get a better opportunity to make a brilliant match, but I will leave the final decision up to you.'

Recovering her self-control, Sophie attempted to banish her foolish doubts. Her uncle was right. Marriage was about money, status and the need for children to carry on one's name. It was idiotic to confuse reality with her romantic hopes of falling in love with a man who would love her in return for just herself and not her dowry.

But most of my friends are married already and they are younger than I am; I might end up on the shelf waiting to find such a paragon, she thought ruefully. Perhaps it is better to settle for a man who seems fond of me and can offer me a life of security and comfort than to hang on to my foolish dreams and end up a lonely and embittered spinster.

Thomas heaved his bulk up from the armchair and came to pat her slender shoulder. 'I want only your happiness, lass,' he said gruffly. 'Agree to hear his suit and I swear that, if you should decide you can't stomach the fellow after all, then there'll be no more said.'

Sophie laid her own slender hand over his veined one and gave it a grateful little squeeze. 'Thank you, Uncle,' she murmured.

'Then you'll do as I ask?' he enquired hopefully.

Sophie nodded. She owed her uncle that much at least, and if she could not have love she would at least have the satisfaction of knowing that she had made an old man very proud and happy.

An hour later they encountered the baronet as they descended from the carriage at Abbott Hall.

'I have been waiting for you to arrive and, believe me, it was well worth the wait, Miss Fleming,' Sir Pelham cried. 'You look ravishing.'

'You are too kind, sir.' Sophie laughed coquettishly.

She did not altogether believe his compliments — she wasn't that vain — but it was pleasant to be admired, even when one's beauty belonged to artifice!

Their host, Sir Alan Chambre, greeted them warmly as they went inside.

'You know Sir Pelham, don't you, Alan?' Thomas Fleming enquired.

The eminent jurist nodded at his old friend. 'We have been introduced.' He smiled pleasantly at the baronet. 'Any friend of the Flemings is welcome in my house, sir.'

'Your servant, sir.' An elegant bow added distinction to Sir Pelham's greeting. 'It was kind of you to have invited me at such short notice.'

Sir Alan grinned at Sophie. 'Anything to oblige my favourite redhead.'

His teasing brought a militant sparkle to Sophie's eyes, but she knew him too well to rise to his bait.

In any event, it would have been foolish to protest. She was well aware of the ripples of interest her arrival on the baronet's arm had created in the crowded candlelit room. She could see the matrons already whispering behind their fans and knew they were busy speculating on how serious his courtship might be.

Wait until they hear the latest news, she thought, excitement bubbling up inside her as she began to realise what a stir such a betrothal would make. Plain Sophie Fleming, so sadly lacking in feminine accomplishments, had made a catch that would turn them all green with envy!

Stealing a look at her future betrothed from beneath her long lashes, Sophie experienced a flicker of pride.

Frequently described as handsome, a slight exaggeration pardonable in view of his fortune, Sir Pelham certainly cut an impressive figure. His height was only average and the trim proportions of his youth had thickened slightly, but he stood out in this provincial gathering by his fastidious elegance. Alone of all the men present, he wore neither wig nor powder, and his light brown hair had been cut short into the new, fashionable Brutus crop. It was a striking departure and one or two old-fashioned folk looked at him askance, but no one could fail to admire the deep blue satin coat he was wearing, Sophie reflected. It managed both to enhance the breadth of his shoulders and to proclaim him the most sumptuously dressed man in the room.

'You are looking a little flushed, Miss Fleming. May I procure you a glass of iced lemonade?'

Blushing faintly at her own thoughts, Sophie became aware that the baronet was gazing at her with an expression of concern.

She nodded hastily. 'That would be lovely. It is so hot in here!'

He led her over to a sofa near to the door, where it was cooler, and saw her seated. 'I shall only be a moment,' he promised with an ardent smile.

Sophie watched him thread his way through the crowd and sank back against the velvet cushions with a tiny sigh of relief. Since he hadn't asked her to marry him yet it was hardly modest to reveal the fact that she was thinking of saying yes! Nancy had always scolded her for her lack of discretion, but she hadn't a circumspect bone in her body. Worse, her face was much too expressive of her wayward thoughts!

The entrance of a latecomer in the doorway deflected Sophie from her musings.

Her dark brows rose in surprise as she took in the new arrival's outfit. Trust that woman to be the first in their circle to wear the new skimpy fashions that had left Uncle Thomas gasping when Sophie had shown them to him recently in a copy of the *Lady's Magazine*!

The high-waisted dress was made of a flimsy pale rose silk, which flattered Caroline Birkett's porcelain complexion and light blue eyes. Like Sophie, she was tall, but her figure was lushly curved and the low neckline revealed her magnificent bosom. A spray of ostrich feathers decorated her flaxen curls and she looked altogether so fashionable that Sophie's heart was quite wrung with envy.

I wonder if I could persuade Uncle Thomas to let me try something so daring? A tiny smile curved her lips. No doubt he would remind her that Caroline had the reputation of being fast, due to the fact that she appeared to spare no thought for her husband, often absent at sea, but gadded about accompanied by a variety of male escorts to every entertainment on offer.

For an instant, Caroline stood quite still, and Sophie suspected that she was deliberately holding her pose so

everyone could get a good look at her, but then she
turned her blonde head to address someone behind her,
apparently oblivious to the stir she had created.

An instant later her escort stepped forward into
Sophie's vision: a tall man clad in dark evening clothes;
his unpowdered head gleamed gold in the candlelight.

A tiny gasp escaped Sophie. It was her arrogant
stranger, but what was he doing here with Caroline
Birkett hanging with smug satisfaction on to his arm?

CHAPTER TWO

'WHY did I let you persuade me into coming here tonight?' Kirk Thorburn demanded quietly as Caroline laid a possessive hand upon his arm to draw him forward into the crowded room.

'Because it is time you stopped being a recluse, my dear friend,' she murmured in reply.

For an instant there was a flash of grief in his amazingly blue eyes, and Caroline sighed softly. 'Forgive me, I don't mean to criticise, but moping alone at Haraldsgarth will not bring Ingram back.'

'Nothing can bring my brother back,' he answered flatly.

Her fingers tightened sympathetically on his arm and she felt the tension in the rock-hard muscles beneath his plain black coat. 'Don't punish yourself, Kirk. There was nothing you could have done to prevent his death, even if you had been in England when it happened.'

'Perhaps not, but I intend to see that he is avenged.'

There was a quiet finality about his statement which curtailed further argument, and, dropping the subject, Caroline forced a lighter note into her voice.

'But for tonight, won't you try to enjoy yourself? Please? It will be good for you to meet some new faces and James will be furious with me if he discovers that I had failed to keep you entertained in his absence.'

The sombre expression on Kirk's face vanished. 'It is very sweet of you to persevere with me, Caroline. I don't deserve such kindness.'

'Nonsense, what are friends for?' she returned lightly, but she could not help the *frisson* of pleasure that shot through her at his smile. It is as well I am

25

happily married, no matter what the gossips might think to the contrary, she reflected silently. Kirk Thorburn was much too handsome for any woman's good. That smile of his could charm the devil himself!

'Look, here comes Sir Alan,' she exclaimed in some relief. 'He is a genial old busybody, but I'm sure you will like him.'

'Caroline, my dear, you look stunning.' Sir Alan bowed over her hand. 'I'll wager that pretty outfit cost James a goodly part of his fortune. He will need to make several more voyages to recoup it, eh?'

There was nothing malicious in his chuckles, and Caroline took it in good part.

'I knew I should be teased for introducing the latest fashions to Kendal,' she lamented, but her eyes twinkled.

'Damme, but I'll rejoice if all the lasses start wearing such gowns,' retorted Sir Alan with jovial honesty. Then, deciding that perhaps it was not quite *comme il faut* to harp on about such a delicate topic, he continued hastily, 'But where is James? Don't tell me he has set sail again.'

'I'm afraid so. A cargo came up that he could not resist.' Caroline made a small moue of resignation. 'However, as you see, I am well provided for tonight. Please allow me to introduce my escort, an old friend of ours recently returned from the Bahama Islands.'

The two men exchanged civilities for a moment or two and then the inquisitive jurist said, 'Did you meet Captain Birkett on New Providence, Mr Thorburn?'

'We became acquainted when he purchased a cargo of cotton from the plantation I helped my godfather to found. In spite of my finding him a hard man to beat down when it came to negotiating the contract, we became good friends,' Kirk explained. He smiled at Caroline. 'I met Mrs Birkett when she accompanied her husband on his next voyage.'

'My one and only trip to sea.' Caroline shuddered delicately. 'I am no sailor, I fear.'

The two men smiled and Caroline continued in the same light vein until she could let it slip that Kirk, having become the sole owner on his godfather's death three years ago, was in the process of selling the plantation.

'It should fetch a very handsome profit to add to the fortune Kirk inherited from his father,' she continued artlessly.

Sir Alan looked impressed. 'Do you intend to settle in England, sir?'

Kirk nodded, but did not elaborate.

Fortunately for Sir Alan's curiosity, this taciturn reply was ameliorated by Caroline swiftly interrupting with the information that Kirk intended to return to farming family property in Cumberland.

'Why on earth did you try to impress him by pretending I was some nabob?' Kirk demanded wrathfully when Sir Alan drifted away to converse with his other guests.

'Because it was the quickest way to establish your credibility, dear friend.' Caroline grinned at him unrepentantly. 'Don't worry, no one will question my claims.'

He frowned at her. 'I dislike deceit.'

'Oh, pooh, merely a little harmless exaggeration!' she exclaimed with a giggle. 'Alan was fascinated and I'll wager he won't waste any time in relating your excellent status to everyone who counts in Kendal.'

Kirk snorted, and she shook her head reprovingly at him.

'You may not care a toss for such things, but, believe me, it matters if you wish to be taken seriously. In a small place like this, appearances are very important, Kirk.'

'You think my present wealth might offset any

rumours about my wicked youth?' he enquired
ironically.

'Hush, don't talk about that, you provoking man!'
Caroline tried to sound stern. 'I doubt if anyone here
knows that you fled to join your godfather to avoid
scandal. Watendlath is remote enough, heaven knows,
and it was ten years ago.'

Kirk's grin faded. 'Perhaps you are right. It will not
help my cause if I set people's backs up. I need them to
talk to me freely if I am to discover the real truth about
that cheating bastard.'

'I know you suspect the baronet, Kirk, but tread
carefully.' Caroline's smooth brow furrowed at his
strong words. 'He is very well thought of and you will
achieve nothing if you lose your temper and accuse him
without proof. For your own sake, don't quarrel with
him if he is here tonight.'

Aware of the sense in what she said, Kirk did not
dispute this advice. 'I shall endeavour to control myself
if we meet,' he promised with a touch of irony, knowing
that his hasty temper would make it a difficult task.

'Good. Now come, let me introduce you to a few
people.' Caroline threaded her arm through his.

They began to circulate slowly around the elegantly
furnished room, exchanging greetings and polite civilities as they went.

'Heavens, what a shocking squeeze,' Caroline
remarked, but, receiving no reply, she glanced up at
her companion and saw that his gaze was riveted on the
other side of the room, where a log fire blazed in the
handsome marble fireplace.

'That girl, the one over there in blue, standing next
to the old gentleman, who is she?'

Caroline's brows rose. 'That is Miss Sophie Fleming.
She is the niece of Thomas Fleming, the snuff-merchant. Do you really desire an introduction?'

At his abrupt nod, she shrugged her shapely white

shoulders. What an odd choice he had made when there were several pretty girls discreetly ogling him behind their fans!

'Very well, but I must warn you that she is something of a hoyden. Her uncle dotes on her and popular opinion has it that his lack of discipline has encouraged her independence. She quite jumped down poor James's throat once when he was trying to explain how a new life as a slave in America might actually benefit some of the poor benighted heathens he has seen on his travels round Africa.'

'Is that why you dislike her, Caroline?'

'Oh, dear, I suppose I did sound rather spiteful!' Caroline pulled an apologetic little grimace. 'Admittedly, I do not care for her, but there is another reason why you would do better to set your sights elsewhere.'

He quirked an eyebrow at her hesitant tone.

'She is on the point of becoming betrothed, or so rumour has it, to Sir Pelham Stanton.'

'To Stanton?' Kirk echoed incredulously.

'Of course there has been no official announcement,' Caroline added quickly. 'The old gentleman would have trumpeted it from the rooftops if there had, but Stanton has been very persistent.'

'I suppose she is an heiress?'

A little startled by his shrewdness, Caroline nodded. 'She is an orphan. Both her parents were drowned one night in the Kent when their coach was swept from the town's main bridge during a storm. Sophie will inherit the old man's entire fortune.' She shrugged. 'And he is not in the best of health.'

'How convenient for Stanton,' Kirk murmured.

His gaze returned to the ill-matched pair across the room. It was definitely the same girl. Next to her portly little uncle, she looked taller than ever, but far more attractive than he remembered, thanks to the sparkling smile which animated her irregular features.

'You know, when we met this morning my impression was that she was deuced plain,' he said absently and then, seeing his companion's puzzlement, quickly outlined what had happened.

'I told you she was an oddity.' Caroline was relieved that there was such a simple explanation for his interest.

'Perhaps.' He paused and then continued thoughtfully, 'But I think it might repay me to strike up an acquaintance with Miss Fleming.'

'Kirk, what are you planning?' Caroline exclaimed uneasily, her relief turning to apprehension at the devilish expression on his handsome face. 'Stanton won't take it kindly, if you start flirting with her!'

'I know.' He smiled.

Dear heavens, they are coming over here!

Sophie had been watching them for the last half-hour.

To her chagrin, the man she had not been able to get out of her mind had not even noticed her. He had been much too busy talking to that shameless hussy!

Sophie suspected that she wasn't the only one to be aware of the stranger in their midst. His distinctive height and broad shoulders were causing several maiden hearts to flutter. He was clad in a simple set of evening clothes, consisting of a black coat superbly cut in broadcloth, a pale lemon waistcoat and white silk knee breeches, and somehow their very plainness was more eye-catching than the most sumptuous of satins. When allied to his deeply tanned skin and his short, unpowdered hair, gleaming like new-minted gold in the candlelight, they gave him an intriguing appeal no female was likely to ignore.

Disappointed he had not sought her out, Sophie had tried to follow his progress while attempting to respond to Sir Pelham. Fortunately the baronet, who was in full conversational flow, had not appeared to notice the newcomers and at length had returned her to her uncle before seeking entertainment in the card-room.

How offended he would be if he knew I'd scarcely heard a word he'd said, Sophie mused, free at last to think her own thoughts. A twinge of guilt assailed her, yet she could not prevent her gaze from seeking out that tall, distinctive figure once more. It was as if she were bewitched!

A momentary panic swept over Sophie as she watched the couple draw nearer. She was about to get her wish, but suddenly she felt nervous, as if this were her very first party!

He reminds me of nothing so much as some great lazy jungle cat, effortlessly graceful and somehow just as lethal, she thought, gulping hard.

Quelling a crazy desire to flee, she forced her gaze back to her uncle, but every other sense tingled. She was acutely aware of the way her heart was thumping and her palms had gone damp, but she didn't know what to do about it. She had never felt so unsure of herself in her life!

The introductions were being performed and Sophie strove to smile politely.

'Miss Fleming.'

In a daze she felt him take her hand in a cool, firm clasp, and then to her utter consternation he raised it to his lips. It was the briefest of polite salutes, but Sophie jumped as if she had been stung.

Blushing furiously at her own folly, she sought to cover her gaucheness by saying brightly, 'So we meet again, Mr Thorburn. I trust you enjoyed the snuff.'

'Eeh, what's this? Do you two know each other, then?' Thomas Fleming spoke up, eyeing his niece's unexpected blushes with anxious surprise before turning warily to survey the tall young man who appeared to be their cause.

About thirty, I reckon, and a handsome, well-built

lad, for all his skimpy coat and short hair. He must be respectable, I suppose, if he is a friend of James Birkett, but my Sophie is all but spoken for and I don't want her head turned. Damn it, Stanton should be here to pay court to her, not playing cards!

Kirk gave a discreetly edited version of how they had met. 'Your niece was kind enough to admire my snuff-box,' he added wickedly.

Sophie's cheeks vied to match her hair.

Wretched man, he was deliberately teasing her! Sophie fluttered her fan, trying to conceal her agitation. 'It was a very beautiful piece. You would have liked it, Uncle,' she murmured hastily.

Her remark distracted Thomas Fleming's attention as she had hoped it would and he beamed on Kirk, who obliged with a description of the snuff-box, though Sophie noted that he was careful to leave out any mention of the curiously wrought initial on the inner lid.

'*Quatre-couleur* gold, eh?' Thomas remarked and launched into an animated monologue on the techniques employed by the great French smiths to achieve varying shades of gold by alloying it with other metals.

Freed from the necessity of conversation, Kirk was able to study Sophie more closely. Her quick-witted response to deflect her uncle's curiosity and her determination to ignore his provocation aroused his admiration. Whatever else the wench was, she possessed both brains and courage!

Until this moment Kirk had been too preoccupied to take much notice of Sophie as a person in her own right. This morning she had first annoyed and then amused him, and just now Caroline had unwittingly given him an idea how he could use her as an instrument for forwarding his plans, but suddenly he was ashamed of his selfish attitude.

She had done nothing to deserve his enmity! What

was more, he would lay odds that her air of sophistication was a mere front. That elaborate gown and those
fancy jewels could not conceal her nervousness. Was
she as shy as this with all men? Kirk wondered if the old
man knew what he was doing, throwing such an
innocent at a wolf like Stanton.

From what he remembered of the baronet and from
all he'd heard since, Stanton was not the type to find
Sophie Fleming's slim, boyish figure appealing. Nor did
her irregular features make for beauty. Only her long-
lashed dark eyes could claim to be anything out of the
ordinary. They gave her thin face a piquant charm, but
he'd turn Turk if it was anything other than the girl's
dowry that Stanton was after.

'Let me tell you how Mr Thorburn and I first came to
be acquainted, Mr Fleming. I'm sure you'll find it a
most interesting story.' Caroline, who had seen
Thomas's wary glance, seized the opportunity to establish Kirk's worthy antecedents the instant the old man's
discourse on French goldsmiths rambled to an end.

She took a cushioned seat to one side of the fireplace
and patted the matching open-armed chair next to it.
'Come, we shall be very comfortable here,' she said
brightly with an inviting smile that left Thomas no
choice but to obey her summons.

'I fear we will have to entertain ourselves, Miss
Fleming,' Kirk remarked lightly. 'Would you care to sit
down?'

'I prefer to stand,' Sophie said stiffly.

'As you wish.' He smiled at her politely.

Sophie swallowed hard. He was close enough for her
to see the fine network of lines that crinkled the tanned
skin around his blue eyes. He must laugh often, she
thought dizzily.

His nearness seemed to be affecting her in the most
peculiar way. Her pulse was racing and her throat was
so tight that she could hardly breathe, let alone talk,

but, aware that her silence appeared ill bred, Sophie searched her mind for something to say.

'You're very brown. Are you a sailor too, like Captain Birkett, Mr Thorburn?' she blurted desperately.

He shook his gleaming head. 'No. I owe my tanned skin to the hot sun of New Providence.'

'That is an island in the Bahamas, is it not?' Sophie enquired. 'But you are a native of these parts, surely? Your name has a northern ring to it.' She frowned thoughtfully. 'And I can detect a faint trace of our local accent in your voice.'

Kirk hid a grin. Her artless conversation was far from the insipid remarks he expected from young ladies of her station. 'You are very shrewd, ma'am. I thought ten years away from Watendlath would have changed my speech beyond recognition.'

'What a very long time to be away from home!' Sophie exclaimed. 'How old were you when you left?'

'Almost nineteen,' he replied, amused by her shameless curiosity.

Sophie's expressive face revealed that she was doing mental arithmetic.

'I shall be thirty next August,' Kirk added helpfully.

'Oh, yes, indeed,' gasped Sophie, suddenly becoming aware that her curiosity had led her perilously close to discourtesy. She peeped up at him through her thick lashes and to her relief saw he was smiling. Thank heavens, she didn't seem to have offended him!

'I'm sorry, I didn't mean to cross-question you. You must think me very rude, especially after this morning. I should not have behaved the way I did, but you made me angry by glaring at me so impatiently.'

This frank apology disarmed Kirk. 'I must confess to being at fault there. I was in a hurry and patience is not one of my virtues. Dare I hope we can forget the incident and begin again?'

There was a sincerity in his deep voice that Sophie found compelling. 'I should like that.' She smiled at him, a dazzling warmth curling up the corners of her wide mouth. 'It would be nice if we could be friends,' she added shyly.

Kirk stared down into her heart-shaped face. It was amazing how that lovely smile transformed her plain features. She really was a most unusual girl!

His silence made Sophie hold her breath, hoping she had said the right thing. It was suddenly very important that he thought well of her.

I want him to like me! Sophie shivered at the intensity of her emotions. She barely knew him and yet somehow it didn't matter. He was the most attractive man she had ever met. Of course, he was very handsome, but there was more to it than that. Perhaps it was his air of casual confidence that drew her. He had all the assurance of a man accustomed to command, with none of the formal stiffness that marked Sir Pelham's behaviour. Whatever it was, Sophie sensed that he was a man of determination, whose steely strength could be relied upon.

'I should be honoured by your friendship, Miss Fleming,' Kirk murmured at last and, taking her hand to his, he bent his head to press an impulsive kiss against the soft skin of her inner wrist.

A wild excitement raced through Sophie's veins, making the pulse at the base of her throat beat rapidly. He lifted his golden head, but did not release her, and she made no move to withdraw her hand from his clasp.

To Kirk's astonishment, he could not drag his eyes away from the pulse he could see fluttering in the white column of her throat. A fierce desire to lay his lips against it possessed him, along with the certain knowledge that she would feel deliciously fragile in his arms!

Firmly he mastered the impulse and released the slender fingers which still lay imprisoned within his. He must be mad! The unfinished business of his brother's death was his priority. He had to find Ingram's murderer. It was a debt of honour and there could be no foolish involvements to distract him.

Disappointment flooded over Sophie. For one breathless instant she had imagined that he wanted to kiss her! Oh, she knew it was impossible that he should actually do such a shocking thing — the scandal would have raised the roof — but it alarmed her to discover how much she wanted him to throw convention to the winds!

'May I call upon you tomorrow afternoon? There is something I have to tell your uncle that I think you have the right to hear.'

It was a deliberate change of subject, and as his quiet request broke in on her turbulent thoughts Sophie played with the ivory sticks of her fan for an instant while she tried to regain her composure.

'I have an engagement with friends,' she murmured regretfully. 'We plan to take advantage of this weather to go skating. One of the meadows down by the river was flooded in the last thaw and now it has completely frozen over.'

He grinned. 'I had forgotten how cold winters here can be. You don't see much ice in New Providence. Imagine a palm-tree covered in snow!'

Sophie giggled at the incongruity he painted and somehow their shared laughter dissolved the lingering tension, and Kirk knew his decision was right. He had not planned to show his hand so soon, but if his suspicions about Stanton were right then the Flemings deserved to know the truth.

If I wait to gather enough evidence it might be too late to save her from that rogue, he thought, suddenly appalled by the idea that Sophie might become entangled in Stanton's web.

'Tell me more about the Bahamas,' Sophie begged, and, suppressing his anxiety, Kirk obliged.

His tales of blue skies, coral reefs and strange plants and birds of every hue made her eyes widen. 'How wonderful it sounds,' she murmured, enchanted by his description of a beach close to his plantation where the silver sand was lapped by clear turquoise water.

'May I ask you why you chose to settle there?'

'It was my godfather's idea. He had emigrated to Virginia to grow tobacco when I was very young. When the trouble out there began he supported the King's cause. Eventually, the rebels confiscated his property and he sought asylum in East Florida, which had not joined the other colonies in revolt, and he hoped to make a fresh start there.'

'But didn't the Treaty of Versailles give Florida to the Spanish when the war ended?'

'Indeed it did, Miss Fleming.'

His voice revealed his surprise and Sophie added shyly, 'My uncle often discusses politics with me. We have no other close family and in some ways he is in the habit of treating me as if I were a son.'

'Then perhaps you know that the same treaty restored the Bahamas to British rule. Many thousands of American loyalists decided to try their luck in the Bahamas. At the time I was keen to travel, and when my godfather wrote asking if I would like to join him in his new endeavour I accepted.'

For an instant there was a bleak expression in his eyes, but it vanished so swiftly that Sophie was sure she must have imagined it.

'Did you grow tobacco in New Providence?' Sophie asked with interest. 'It sounds a suitable climate for that crop.'

'We grew a little, but cotton was the main crop my godfather decided upon. It was very profitable and enabled us to make a success of the plantation, although in the last few years I began planting pineapples as an alternative. Cotton is subject to too many pests to be relied upon.'

'Pineapples! How exotic that sounds,' Sophie exclaimed with a grin. 'England must seem strangely grey and dull after living in such a bountiful place.'

'It wasn't all paradise, I assure you.' Kirk laughed. 'We had to contend with many difficulties, including hurricanes.'

Sophie's eyes widened. 'I have read about those winds. Are they as terrible as they sound?'

He smiled down into her interested little face. Her questions had revealed a keen intelligence, and it suddenly occurred to him that he had rarely enjoyed a conversation with a woman more. Most of them, even the clever ones like Caroline, were simply not interested in anything beyond their narrow domestic sphere.

A few moments later a loud cough from Thomas Fleming signalled the end of their tête-à-tête.

'It's almost suppertime,' he announced as he and Caroline rejoined them. 'Come, m'dear, Sir Pelham will be waiting for us.'

In the midst of her disappointment at the interruption, Sophie was aware that Kirk had stiffened.

Looking up at him, she saw that his smile had vanished, and she had the sudden conviction that even if her uncle invited him to join them, as she felt sure he was about to do, Kirk Thorburn would refuse.

And she knows there is something wrong too, Sophie concluded, catching a glimpse of the anxiety in Caroline's eyes.

'Kirk, would you be awfully disappointed if we missed supper? I'm afraid I've developed the most devastating headache and I'd like to go home.' Caroline laid an urgent hand on his arm.

'Pon 'rep, I'm sorry to hear you are indisposed,

ma'am. I should have enjoyed talking to you and Mr Thorburn over supper,' Thomas exclaimed regretfully as Kirk nodded acquiescence.

Thomas's earlier doubts had been allayed. Caroline had taken care to make her escort's position as a family friend very clear; he was no cicisbeo. Nor was there any danger of his turning out to be a fortune-hunter after Sophie's money. Although she had been discreet, Caroline had given him to understand that the lad was wealthy and his background eminently respectable.

'Indeed, sir, it is a pity. I am loath to leave, but. . .' Caroline managed a convincing sigh. 'Will you convey our apologies to Sir Alan?'

While her uncle, whose opinion of the flighty Mrs Birkett had risen considerably in the last half-hour, reassured her, Sophie stared thoughtfully at Caroline, whose rosy, flushed cheeks seemed to belie her headache.

I don't believe she is ill; she just wants to take Kirk away and have him to herself! Sophie's mouth compressed into a thin line. It isn't fair, she thought angrily; she is a married woman!

And what about you? Are you any better than she is to moon over a pair of Viking eyes when you are on the point of becoming betrothed to another man?

The annoyingly honest voice of her conscience delivered a swift warning blow, dissipating Sophie's anger in a rush of guilt.

'I hope we meet again soon, Miss Fleming.' Kirk bowed low over her hand.

Sophie dipped a polite curtsy, but said nothing. She was feeling too confused by the riot of conflicting emotions fighting for supremacy within her breast. What was the matter with her tonight?

Kirk controlled his swift stab of disappointment at her lack of response and was immediately rewarded by an invitation from the snuff-merchant to call upon them in the Stramongate if ever he should be passing that way.

'He seems a nice lad. I hope he calls; I should enjoy discussing the merits of Bahamian tobacco with him,' Mr Fleming said a moment later as he led his niece towards the dining-room, where an informal supper was being served.

Sophie managed to find a reply, but before she'd had time to recover her composure the baronet materialised at her side. His flowery apologies for the length of his absence increased her guilty sense of unease.

How could I have felt jealous of that woman? she thought in silent dismay. Good God, I had better sense than that when I was only just out! Now she did not even have the excuse of being a green seventeen-year-old for letting a handsome face turn her head!

'We have just been talking to a neighbour of yours,' Thomas announced jovially, interrupting the baronet, much to Sophie's relief. She was too angrily out of patience with her own folly to respond to Sir Pelham's elegant flirtation in the manner he expected.

'I was not aware that any fellow Cumbrians were present tonight,' the baronet replied, smiling, transferring his gaze to the elderly merchant.

'Aye, his family hail from Watendlath,' Mr Fleming said.

In the bustle of taking their places only Sophie noticed how the baronet paled at this information. Curiosity roused her from dismal thoughts about her foolish behaviour. Staring at him closely, she saw how a muscle twitched by the corner of his thin mouth as her uncle related their meeting with Kirk Thorburn.

'Really? What a coincidence,' drawled Sir Pelham, but his hand was shaking slightly as he reached for his glass of wine.

He took a gulp of the fine burgundy and then said,

'Fancy that fellow having the gall to turn up again in decent society. Still, he always was an impudent rogue.'

'What do you mean? Are you acquainted with Mr Thorburn?' The words came out more sharply than Sophie had intended, and she flushed when Sir Pelham raised his eyebrows.

'Unfortunately I do know him, my dear Miss Fleming, but nothing to his good, I'm afraid.' The baronet appeared to have recovered his habitual calm.

'The area around Derwent Water is not well populated with good families, but since the Thorburns have owned land there for generations and we were neighbours of a sort, I was allowed to visit Haraldsgarth during the school vacations,' he said. 'Although he was several years our junior, Kirk sometimes joined his elder brother Ingram and me on our youthful expeditions.'

A small shrug disturbed the perfection of Sir Pelham's coat. 'Naturally, as I grew older, my association with them ceased. My father was old-fashioned and had — er — rather traditional views on the subject of mingling with one's social inferiors.'

A charming, rueful smile accompanied this remark, as if to take away the sting of his words, but Sophie sensed that beneath his careful consideration not to offend their feelings the baronet shared his sire's haughty view. Glancing at her uncle, she saw from his slight frown that he too had noticed the unconscious disdain in Sir Pelham's tone.

True, her family were merchants and not aristocrats, but they had been wealthy and important citizens in Kendal for several generations, and Sophie had been brought up to be a lady. Until this moment it hadn't occurred to her that the baronet, who could boast no distinguished ancestors, might be snobbish enough genuinely to consider her beneath him.

It was a disturbing revelation, but she was too curious

to feel angry. 'Why do you describe Mr Thorburn as a rogue?'

Sir Pelham idly fingered the gold lace decorating his cuff. 'Really, it is not a story for your delicate ears, my dear young lady.'

Sophie's brows drew together in determination.

'You cannot be so cruel as to fob me off thus shabbily, sir,' she exclaimed forcefully.

Sir Pelham glanced towards Mr Fleming.

'My niece is not a child. I do not think you need to shelter her from the truth. And I must own you have whetted my curiosity,' the elderly merchant admitted. 'Furthermore, since I have issued an open invitation to visit us to that young man, I think it is as well if you enlighten our ignorance before any harm is done.'

'I bow to your wish, sir.' The baronet shrugged lightly and embarked upon his story. 'Kirk Thorburn may have done well for himself in the Bahamas, but some ten years ago he quit these shores under a cloud of disgrace. He had to leave because he had seduced a girl of gentle birth and good character. She was the daughter of the local parson and only sixteen, but when it was discovered she was with child he refused to marry her.'

'He denied that he was responsible?' Sophie asked faintly.

'Indeed he did, but he was not believed. He was known to be courting the girl, and although only eighteen himself, he already had the reputation of being a womaniser and a bad lot. She was a pretty young thing if my memory serves me correctly, but he preferred to run away, leaving her to bear the shame alone.'

'You know this story for a fact?' Thomas asked shrewdly.

'A lot of my information is based on hearsay—I was in London, you understand, when the scandal broke— but I believe the essentials to be accurate. There was the most dreadful gossip, of course, not helped by the

subsequent disappearance of the girl.' The baronet
heaved a dramatic sigh. 'No one ever learnt what had
become of her, and her distracted parents were convinced that she might have been driven to commit
suicide.'

Sophie shuddered.

'I'm sorry, m'dear, I had no wish to cause you
distress.' Sir Pelham's voice was gentle, but for an
instant Sophie was certain she detected a puzzling
satisfaction in his tone.

'Humph, I don't hold with gossip in general,' snorted
Mr Fleming. 'But in this case it sounds as if you have
every right to dislike the fellow, Sir Pelham. I wouldn't
trust a man who could behave in such a callous fashion.'

Sir Alan's servants, hovering discreetly to offer
tempting dishes, put an end to their conversation for a
while, but when they moved away, the baronet murmured piously, 'It was a long time ago. Perhaps Kirk
has changed for the better. We must hope so, I suppose,
if he intends to sojourn among us for any length of
time.'

It was a remark uttered with a damning lack of
conviction.

'Once a rogue, always a rogue!'

Her uncle's testy answer was so unlike his usual self
that Sophie knew that Sir Pelham's revelations had put
him out of sorts.

He liked Kirk and now he's disappointed, she
thought sadly.

Generous to a fault, her uncle was often inclined to
give the benefit of the doubt in his dealings with other
people. A firm friend, he hated to be proved wrong in
his estimation of anyone, but he could be implacable if
he discovered his trust had been abused. Sophie knew
she shared the same traits. Once her love or loyalty had
been given, it was given for life.

Which was why she simply could not understand how

Kirk could have so heartlessly betrayed his young woman. He must have cared something for her if he was courting her, she thought wildly, ignoring the plate of delicacies placed before her.

'You are not eating, Miss Fleming. Do try the game pie. It is very good.'

'I'm not hungry, sir.'

She glared at the baronet with something akin to loathing. How dare he sit there consuming his meal with every appearance of enjoyment when his sordid story had sickened her to the soul?

Sophie's flicker of rage died as she realised how unreasonable she was being. It wasn't Sir Pelham's fault that she felt so unhappy, but her own for being such a silly fool.

I ought to have known better, she scolded herself roundly. Just because I found him physically attractive, it was no reason to suppose his character was sound!

Sophie shivered. She had been in grave danger of throwing her cap over the windmill for a caressing voice and warm smile! Perhaps it was a good thing her fanciful daydreams had come crashing down around her ears before she'd had time to make an utter idiot of herself.

Her uncle was right. Falling in love was no way to go about choosing a partner to share one's life with. Such volatile emotions made one blind! Kirk Thorburn was a heartless womaniser, and from this moment on she would not let herself forget it.

CHAPTER THREE

OUTSIDE the town the River Kent had spilled over its banks to form a small, frozen lake. The shining swath of ice glittered temptingly in the pale afternoon sunshine, beckoning to the laughing party of young girls and their escorts.

'Come on, Sophie, I'll race you to that willow tree,' shouted a pretty brunette optimistically.

Pausing only to check that her new expensive iron skates were securely fastened to her boots, Sophie followed Charlotte Fletcher on to the ice.

It took both girls some time to recover their skill, half forgotten since last winter. After a lot of giggling and staggering tumbles they found their feet at last and soon were swooping about the ice, giving excited cries.

Sophie's spirits rose. Sir Pelhams's revelations last night had left her depressed, but now she spun and twirled with enthusiasm, glad to stop thinking for a while and let herself be caught up in the sheer magic of moving at such speed.

'Heavens, but I'm exhausted!' Charlotte giggled. 'I need someone to lean on.' Raising her voice, she shouted to the few remaining members of their party who stood chatting at the edge of the lake. 'William, come and join us!'

Her husband shook his head and gestured his reluctance.

'Oh, what a lazy-bones!'

Sophie laughed. 'He knows you too well.'

Charlotte's eyes sparkled as she dashed off to drag her reluctant spouse on to the ice.

Sophie watched their laughing antics with wistful

amusement. Charlotte and William had been married last summer. They didn't have much money and lived in a poky little house, but it didn't seem to matter; their happiness was obvious to everyone.

Deliberately, Sophie turned and looked in the opposite direction. Her mood was too fragile today to bear comparisons with her friend. Self-pity was even more abhorrent than envy and she would not let it spoil her sport!

The scene that met her eyes was colourful enough to ensure her resolve. The lake was thronged with people intent on enjoying themselves, many clad in a peculiar assortment of clothes to combat the freezing cold weather. Shawls, hats, coats and scarves in all the colours of the rainbow muffled bodies already swollen by extra layers of garments until all that could be seen were red-tipped noses and laughing eyes.

Frequent bursts of laughter as someone took a tumble or loud applause for a skilful turn of speed shattered the crystalline silence. One of the spectators had brought along his fiddle, and the cheerful music floated out over the ice, causing several couples to swing into an impromptu jig.

Suddenly Sophie found her hands clasped by a young boy she recognised as an apprentice to the town's foremost tailor.

'Come and dance, Miss Fleming,' he begged with an impudent grin, and laughingly she consented, much to his delight.

Sophie was soon as breathless as Charlotte had been and she was glad when the musician finally stopped playing to refresh himself from a hip-flask. Thanking her partner, she began skating back to the spot where her friends were gathered.

'Have a drink, my dear,' invited Maria Strickland as she reached the edge of the shallow lake and stepped off on to the frozen grass.

Accepting the welcome hot coffee, Sophie thanked the dark-haired woman who held it out to her.

'Would you like something to eat? I brought along a hamper of food, knowing how you young people would work up an appetite,' Maria said.

Her smile was warm, and Sophie reflected how much she liked this kind middle-aged woman, who was wife to one of her uncle's closest friends. Twenty years younger than Josiah Strickland, Maria, with her easy informality, was very popular. Having no children of her own, she took a particular interest in her stepson and his circle of friends.

Frederick Strickland, the only child of Josiah's first marriage, had been one of Sophie's earliest playmates. At one time the two merchants had hoped to make a match of it between their offspring, but they regarded each other like brother and sister. Then Frederick, who worked alongside his father in their wine-importing business, had fallen madly in love with a French girl he had met on his travels abroad and married her.

'I had a letter from Frederick yesterday,' Maria announced as Sophie bit into a crisp home-baked pasty. 'He is very well, but says that the weather in Bordeaux is atrocious. It has done nothing but rain, apparently.'

Frederick and Genevieve were paying an extended visit to her parents, and Sophie listened with interest to Maria's recital of their doings.

'Frederick sends you his regards.' Mrs Strickland paused, a twinkle in her fine grey eyes. 'But he wants to know the truth of these rumours he has been hearing about Sir Pelham Stanton.'

Sophie choked over the last morsel of her pasty.

'I'd. . . I'd rather not talk about it if you don't mind,' she murmured in a distracted manner.

Maria regarded her with surprise, having confidently expected her to laugh. It was not like Sophie to be so reticent! Over the years a close relationship had developed between them, and Maria had become accustomed to hearing her girlish confidences.

'Of course, my dear, but, if you do decide to change your mind, remember that I am always here,' she replied sympathetically, wondering what was troubling her young friend. It would be an excellent match, but those lovely dark eyes were filled with something suspiciously close to reluctance.

Sophie smiled mechanically. 'Thank you.'

'Would you like something else to eat?'

The red curls shook in answer, setting aquiver the small plume adorning Sophie's jade velvet bonnet. It was a colour that admirably matched her deeper green coat.

'I think I will have another turn about the ice before it is time to go,' Sophie explained. 'It gets dark so early that I expect we will be leaving shortly.'

Maria nodded and watched Sophie depart with a vague feeling of unease she couldn't put a name to.

Immediately Sophie was hailed by Charlotte and William, who were forming a long chain of skaters with the intention of travelling around the ice as quickly as they could. On the end of this line, Sophie was glad she had recovered her skill, for the tempo soon became hectic. The front leaders snaked into loops and wild turns with whoops of glee and she was swung from side to side with increasing rapidity.

She was on the point of dizziness when her gloved hands slipped from the coat of the person in front of her as the chain swung into a particularly frenzied arc, and she felt herself go spinning as she was flung outwards across the ice. Her balance couldn't sustain the momentum, and just as she felt herself beginning to fall a strong pair of hands grasped her firmly about the waist and hauled her upright.

Raising her gaze to thank her rescuer, Sophie met an amused pair of vivid blue eyes.

'You!'

Her gasp of alarm and the way in which she paled forestalled Kirk Thorburn's greeting. Instead he transferred one arm to support her around the waist before asking tersely, 'Can you skate towards the bank? Don't worry, I won't let you fall.'

For one weak moment Sophie allowed herself the luxury of permitting him to guide her across the ice. It was surprisingly reassuring to lean back against the broad bulk of his chest. One strong arm still supported her around the waist and she could feel the comforting warmth of his body penetrating her chilled frame. Like a child, she felt safe and protected, with no need to concern herself with what might happen next.

This strange lassitude lasted until they reached the shelter of the far bank and Sophie realised that she was at the opposite end of the ice from all her friends. Worse, there was hardly anyone about by this stretch of lake. The sun was already beginning to sink in a fiery ball, and as she gazed around she saw that the crowds had thinned.

Sophie's giddiness flared into new life as Kirk smiled at her. 'Are you feeling better now?'

He was still holding her close, and his nearness was beginning to arouse sensations in her treacherous body that owed nothing to gratitude. She could smell the clean, fresh scent of his skin and feel the warmth from his hands penetrating her garments.

Her pulse racing, she nodded and said abruptly, 'Thank you. You may release me.'

'Are you sure you won't faint?'

'I am not in the habit of fainting, sir.'

The annoyance in her voice seemed to convince him and he let her go, remarking, 'I'd hoped you might be here. I wanted a chance to talk to you, but I didn't expect our meeting to be quite so dramatic.'

Sophie hesitated. He might be an unprincipled womaniser, but she could hardly depart without hearing what he had to say when he had just saved her from a nasty fall. That would merely give him the opportunity to criticise her manners again. And yet she didn't want to stay. Listening to his deep, attractive voice sent peculiar quivers down her spine!

'What is it that you wish to say to me, sir? It is growing late and I must rejoin my friends.'

Her bald statement surprised Kirk. He stared down at her and realised that she had meant her answer to sound as unfriendly as her expression. There was no trace of last night's smile in her eyes.

He shrugged his puzzlement aside. He could deal with it later. This chance for a private conversation seemed heaven-sent.

'You'll find it's worth a few moments of your time, I fancy,' Kirk announced wryly. 'It concerns Stanton.'

'Sir Pelham?' Sophie's brows climbed in astonishment.

'Aye. Is it true you are about to become betrothed to him?'

'That is none of your business!' Angry colour flooded Sophie's cheeks.

'Probably not, but if you are thinking of marrying him I feel compelled to warn you that you are making a mistake.'

Sophie's fingers clenched together. 'Putting aside your impertinence, you are still talking in riddles. What could anyone have against a gentleman like Sir Pelham?'

'I'll grant he appears every inch the rich and elegant aristocrat, but I've known him too long to be deceived.' Kirk's mouth twisted savagely. 'He's a liar and a cheat, if not worse!'

A gasp escaped Sophie. 'However, he is not malicious, which is more than can be said for you, Mr

Thorburn. How dare you try and blacken his reputation when it is you who are the one with a wicked past?'

Kirk's expression darkened. 'I see he has been spreading his lies already. How very clever of him! No doubt he warned you to beware of anything I might say.'

Sophie bit her lip. It was true. On leaving them last night after the soirée, Sir Pelham had whispered in her ear that Kirk might attempt to malign him.

'Eighteen months ago I became involved in a minor dispute with his brother. I will not bore you with the details, my dear, but Ingram Thorburn had the audacity to claim I had not honoured a debt. It would not surprise me if Kirk has inherited his brother's grudge and tries to continue the quarrel.' The baronet's lip had curled scornfully. 'Men of his stamp rarely have scruples. However, I have no intention of giving in to blackmail.'

The heavy silence gave Kirk his answer. It hung uncomfortably between them for an instant, and then Kirk shrugged. Her lack of trust was only to be expected, he supposed, but somehow it was strangely hurtful, and his voice was rough as he continued. 'Believe what you wish of me, but don't let it blind you to the truth. Stanton is no fit husband for an innocent like you!'

'I think my uncle is the best judge of that,' Sophie snapped.

'Really?' Kirk glared at her. 'Has Mr Fleming actually investigated Stanton's claim to affluence?' His mouth twisted. 'Don't let him fool you. He cheated my brother out of a considerable sum of money and when Ingram tried to remonstrate he arranged for——'

'Enough! I will hear no more of your accusations, sir. I did not believe it when Sir Pelham said you would stoop to underhand tactics, but you have condemned yourself out of your own mouth!'

Sophie didn't know whether she was more furious
with herself for imagining that Kirk Thorburn was a
man whose integrity could be trusted or with him for
proving her wrong and shattering the illusions her
stubborn heart had clung to. Anguish gripped her as
she realised that Sir Pelham had not been mistaken in
his low estimation of Kirk Thorburn's character. He
was nothing more than a handsome-faced adventurer!

'You silly little fool. . .' Kirk struggled to maintain
his own temper. He longed to shake some sense into
her.

Sophie stiffened indignantly. She would not stay here
to be insulted! 'Good day, Mr Thorburn.' Her tone was
as arctic as the weather.

She turned to go, but Kirk's hand shot out to prevent
her. 'Wait. I haven't finished. There is more you must
know.'

'You have no right to detain me, sir. Pray release me
at once!'

In spite of her outrage, Sophie felt a warm glow
where he held her by the arm. It spread rapidly
outwards, as if he had lit a fire in her veins. Horrified,
she realised she liked him holding her. Worse, she
actually wanted to fling her arms around his strong neck
and melt into his embrace!

In the past, mild flirtations of the sort conducted by
her friends, which were all that a properly brought-up
young lady might enjoy, of course, had never interested
Sophie. None of the young men with whom she was
acquainted had stirred her senses, but Kirk Thorburn
was different. She had been attracted to him the instant
they'd met and now at last her instincts warned her that
this disturbing emotion she experienced in his presence
was desire.

A surge of wild panic set her heart slamming against
her breastbone. How was she to deal with these
unknown, frightening sensations? Until this moment it

had never even occurred to her that it was possible to yearn so very desperately for a man's mouth on her own!

Their eyes met. To her utter consternation, she recognised the same hungry expression in Kirk's vivid gaze.

The sudden surge of fierce desire which had shot through him when he touched her astounded Kirk. 'Sophie?' He murmured her name softly. He wanted to take her into his arms, but did not wish to frighten her.

Blushing furiously, Sophie wanted to reject his unspoken question, but her voice would not obey her. She could not even look away!

Kirk felt a blaze of satisfaction. He had not been mistaken. She felt the spark of attraction too. He began to draw her gently towards him.

'No!' Panic gave Sophie the strength to break desire's thrall and shake off his restraining hold. 'Leave me alone! I want nothing to do with you!'

Her cry was shrill. Heads turned in their direction.

'Listen to me. . . Wait!'

The green plume shook denial and she whirled away across the ice.

Kirk started after her and then halted abruptly.

People were already staring and he did not wish to cause any gossip that might hurt her reputation. Not that it would do him any good to chase after her; a group of skaters were hurrying to meet her and he knew he would get no further chance to be private with her today.

Damn it, he still hadn't told her the full story! She might declare that she wanted nothing further to do with him, but he would not give up so easily. A grim frown marred his brow. Tomorrow morning I shall try again, he vowed.

* * *

To Kirk's irritation he discovered it was impossible to carry out his vow. He presented himself at the Flemings' residence only to discover that neither Sophie nor her uncle were at home. When questioned, the maidservant, susceptible to his warm smile, told him that Miss Sophie was spending the morning with Mrs Strickland, helping her write out invitations for her forthcoming birthday celebrations.

Kirk frowned. He had met the Stricklands last night, but was not upon such terms with them that he dared invade their home and demand to see Sophie in private. Such an outrageous act would occasion the kind of gossip he was trying to avoid.

'Please give this to Miss Fleming on her return and tell her that I shall call on her this afternoon.' He handed over his card, glad he had followed Caroline's advice after all. When she had first suggested he might have calling cards printed he had laughed and told her he was a plain farmer and not some fashionable fop, until her insistence that they might prove useful during his quest had finally persuaded him.

The maid bobbed an acquiescent curtsy and Kirk strode off.

He was doomed to spend the rest of the morning uselessly trying to discover if any of the smaller snuff-merchants knew the origins of the snuff-box found clutched in Ingram's dead hand, but his thoughts kept constantly returning to the flame-haired little termagant who had spurned his offer of help.

On the other side of town, Sophie's red head was spinning. It had proved impossible to push Kirk Thorburn's dark hints aside. She could scarcely credit that his allegations might be true, but somehow she could not dismiss them. He had seemed too passionately sincere!

'Sophie, would you like to have a rest from this?'

Maria's amused voice broke into her preoccupied thoughts.

'Oh, I'm sorry,' she exclaimed guiltily, seeing the mess of blots her careless pen had made. 'I wasn't concentrating.'

'Never mind, we are almost finished in any case,' Maria replied cheerfully. She ripped up the spoiled invitation and tossed it aside. 'Let's have some tea.'

She rose from her task and went to pull the bell to summon one of the maids to the drawing-room in which they were sitting. It was a pretty room, recently refurbished in the latest style, copied by a local cabinet-maker from Master Sheraton's *Drawing-Book*. The delicate colours and naturalistic floral decorations were to Maria's taste, and her husband, trusting her superior judgement in such matters, was happy to indulge her whims.

'I was wondering whether we should also open up the conservatory for my party,' she said, turning back to Sophie. 'It would offer our guests somewhere pleasant to stroll if they tired of cards and dancing. What do you think?'

Sophie flexed her ink-stained fingers. 'Won't it be difficult to maintain the correct temperature for your rare plants if people are wandering in and out all the evening?'

'I'm not sure. I shall have to consult John. I'm sure he will know a way. He is a marvel!' Maria beamed happily. Her gardener's enthusiasm for the conservatory almost equalled her own.

Sophie grinned. Maria revelled in the amazement and envy her large, glass-walled hothouse created among her visitors! 'You love those plants as if they were children,' she teased, wiping her pen and setting it aside.

Maria's eyes twinkled. 'That was Josh's intention, I suspect!'

The conservatory had been erected to run the full length of the south side of the house soon after Frederick's wedding. Master Strickland's unusual surprise gift had delighted his bereft wife and channelled her considerable energies in a new fulfilling direction. It was an extravagance that had caused tongues to wag, but both the Stricklands thought it money well spent.

The maid arrived, and as Maria unlocked the tea caddy and carefully mixed the leaves to her requirements Sophie joined her on the pale straw-coloured sofa.

When the silver kettle had boiled Maria poured the fragrant beverage and handed her a delicate porcelain cup. 'And now that we have settled most of the arrangements for my birthday party, are you going to tell me what has been bothering you all morning?'

Sophie choked on the hot liquid. 'What do you mean? There is nothing troubling me,' she answered as lightly as she could.

'Oh, Sophie, when will you learn that you are a terrible liar?' Maria laughed. 'Your face always betrays you, my dear. I dare say you heard not one word in twenty of my plans to open up the doors between the drawing-rooms and clear them of furniture so that we could have a little dancing.'

A faint guilty colour rose in Sophie's cheeks. 'I haven't been much help, have I?' she murmured ruefully.

'That wasn't my meaning.' Maria quickly shook her dark head. 'I was merely wondering if you were worried about your uncle's health.'

'He did seem tired at breakfast,' Sophie admitted. 'But that is probably nothing more than a result of all our junketing since Christmas. No, I wasn't thinking of Uncle Thomas.'

She fell silent and Maria hesitated to press her. Casting about for a fresh topic of conversation, she said at random, 'I never got a chance to ask you yesterday, but what did you think of Caroline Birkett's outfit at Sir Alan's soirée?'

A fierce frown answered her. 'It was positively indecent.'

'Well, I thought it a trifle bold myself, but it is the coming fashion.' Maria smiled pacifically. 'Actually, that style would suit you, you know, Sophie. You have the height and slenderness to wear it, unlike me. I am much too short and dumpy to carry off such simple lines.'

Sophie snorted, but in her heart she knew Maria was right. She did envy Caroline's daring and wished she had thought of wearing such a striking gown first, but she wasn't going to admit it.

'It's not just her clothes; I dislike her attitude. James Birkett is a lovely man and yet she flaunts herself all over town in the company of the most undesirable types, like. . .like that Kirk Thorburn!'

'Didn't you like Mr Thorburn?' Maria questioned in surprise. 'I thought him charming, and he is so very handsome!' She laughed naughtily. 'One can quite see Caroline's point in his case. Why languish alone at home when one could be escorted by such a virile-looking man?'

Sophie's teeth ground together in an effort to hold in an angry reply. Oh, it was mortifying to feel so jealous of that. . .that hussy!

'Do you think she will ask him to be her escort to my party? I doubt if James will be home in time.'

'I didn't know you had invited her!'

'The Birketts' card must have been one in my pile.' Maria stared at her, puzzled by the vehemence in her tone. 'After all, I could hardly withhold an invitation. It would be an insult. We have known them for years and James often carries wine for us.'

'I suppose so,' Sophie muttered begrudgingly, but

she couldn't control the hot words that sprang to her lips. 'All the same, I detest the woman! It wouldn't surprise me if she was Kirk Thorburn's mistress.'

'Sophie!' Maria's eyes widened in shock. 'You really mustn't say such things. It is most unbecoming in a girl your age.'

'Even if it is true?'

'We do not know that.' Maria was distressed by the unsuitable turn their conversation had taken, but her sense of fair play drove her on to defend the absent Mrs Birkett. 'Caroline is a shocking flirt, but I doubt if she lacks all moral sense. She is not someone I regard as a close friend — she is too frivolous — but there is no harm in her. I do not think she would actually go so far as to betray James.'

Sophie sniffed, not in the least convinced. Maria always thought the best of everyone! She had seen the way Caroline looked at Kirk when she thought no one was watching!

Noting the stubborn set of her friend's mouth, Maria sighed. 'Really, Sophie, it is none of our business anyway. Caroline's reputation is James's affair, not ours. If he sees no harm in his wife associating with a man like Mr Thorburn, then neither should we.'

'Are you implying that there is something shady about Kirk Thorburn?' Sophie pounced.

Maria blinked. Heavens, what an odd mood the child was in! 'To be frank, my dear, I have heard rumours to that effect in the latest letter from my sister. Emma mentioned an old scandal which is circulating once again in Cockermouth, revived by Mr Thorburn's recent reappearance and the mysterious death of his brother.'

'Mysterious?' Sophie was momentarily diverted.

'Ingram Thorburn died in a fire at his farm last April. No one else was hurt, but there was a great deal of damage done, so much so that some people believed it

must have been started as a deliberate act of malice.'
Maria sighed. 'No one knows, of course, exactly what
happened, but talk that it was not an accident persists.
According to rumour, Kirk Thorburn believes his
brother had an unknown enemy and is searching for
proof.'

The mention of Kirk's name goaded Sophie's attention back to the main issue at stake. 'But Emma wrote
that it was Kirk Thorburn himself who was involved in
scandal?'

Maria agreed. 'However, it happened years ago and
it is an unsavoury tale. Can't we discuss something
more pleasant, my dear?' she pleaded, hoping that
Sophie's fierce curiosity wasn't aroused.

When she found that her young friend would not be
put off she reluctantly repeated Emma's story, which,
to Sophie's dismay, echoed Sir Pelham's version only
too accurately.

'However, Emma added that she thought Mr
Thorburn seemed changed by his time spent abroad.
She thinks he may well have reformed, which is why I
must ask you not to repeat the story to anyone else,
since it would be most unfair to spread such idle gossip,'
Maria concluded firmly.

Sophie nodded dully, hardly listening. In spite of the
fact that he had not bothered to deny it, she realised
that she had still been desperately hoping that the tale
wasn't true. Now she knew she had been deliberately
deceiving herself.

Ten years ago Kirk Thorburn had been a heartless
womaniser. Maria's sister thought him a reformed
character, but Sir Pelham Stanton believed he had not
changed at all.

Oh, I don't know what to think!

Sophie wanted to cry the words out aloud in bewilderment. Logic told her that Kirk was the kind of
determined man who if he bore a grudge might well act

upon it, but instinct denied that his motives might be underhand or cruel.

Despite all the evidence to the contrary, her foolish heart insisted that he was a man of honour, but Sophie was too afraid of her own feelings to listen.

'Why, uncle, I did not expect you home so early!' Sophie exclaimed in surprise as Thomas Fleming entered the cosy parlour. She had only just returned herself, having declined to dine with her friend. Maria's searching glances had made her feel uncomfortable, but all thoughts of the enigma that was Kirk Thorburn flew out of her head when she saw how grey her uncle looked.

Leaping from her seat, she ushered him towards his favourite armchair by the fire. 'Are you warm enough?' she chafed his cold hand. 'Have you eaten? Shall I tell Jennie to lay another place?'

'Nay, lass, don't fuss. I'm not hungry, only a little tired.'

Sophie bit her lips anxiously. Her uncle possessed a hearty appetite. It was a sure sign that he was feeling ill if he declined his dinner.

Thomas began to ask her how she had spent her morning, but it was obvious that he wasn't really listening to her answers.

Eventually, abandoning this pretence at normality, Sophie declared he must go to bed and rest.

'You are a bully, my lass,' Thomas protested, but so half-heartedly that she knew he wanted her to insist.

'If you have a nap now, I'll make you your favourite egg-custard tart for when you wake up,' she cajoled.

'What a wicked wench you are to bribe an old man so,' her uncle chuckled, but broke off laughing as a spasm of pain made him gasp.

'Shall I send for Dr Wilson?'

Thomas waved her anxious suggestion aside. 'Nay,

I'll be as right as rain once I've had a nap,' he said and asked her to ring for Ben, his manservant, to assist him to bed.

All through the solitary meal which followed Sophie pondered on whether she ought to ignore her uncle's instruction and send for the doctor. Leaving her dessert unfinished, she went upstairs to seek Nancy's advice.

'Reckon you'd best wait a while, Miss Sophie,' Nancy said. 'You know how it frets him to be fussed. Happen he will be feeling better when he wakes up.'

'Then in that case I will go and make him that tart I promised him,' Sophie decided, relieved to have something to do to take her mind off her worries.

'Change your gown first,' Nancy shrieked as she headed for the door. 'No sense in spoiling that pretty taffeta messing about in the kitchen.'

Sophie grinned, but did as she was bid. Nancy did not approve of her penchant for cooking and frequently scolded that it wasn't a ladylike occupation, but it was a hobby Sophie enjoyed.

'I don't know why you can't practice on your pianoforte or sit quietly with some embroidery,' Nancy muttered, helping Sophie into the faded blue gown she had chosen. 'And this old thing makes you look a fright. It is only fit for the rag-bag!'

A peal of laughter answered her complaints. 'But it is comfortable and it doesn't matter if I get stains on it.'

Nancy snorted.

Sophie ruthlessly dragged her curls back into a tight knot and confined them. 'Now don't scold, Nancy, darling,' she said quickly, seeing her nurse's outraged expression. 'I know I look terrible, but there's no one to notice except Mrs Gilpin, and she won't mind.'

Nancy's frown eased. 'Oh, very well, I suppose you can't have your hair dangling in your face when you are in the kitchen. But for the life of me I can't understand why you enjoy getting all hot and bothered in there.'

'It is my one talent,' Sophie quipped.

Her answer wasn't strictly true. She had some skill at sketching, but none of the other usual occupations thought suitable for a young lady interested her.

'You could do better if you tried,' Nancy retorted darkly.

'But let's face it, I'll never learn to sing in tune.' Sophie grinned.

Nancy laughed reluctantly and gave up.

Descending to the kitchens, Sophie greeted their cook and explained what she wanted to do.

Mrs Gilpin assigned one of the kitchen maids to help her and Sophie donned an apron and became happily absorbed in making pastry.

'The oven is hot enough whenever you are ready, Miss Sophie,' Mrs Gilpin announced, checking on the Robinson patented range Mr Fleming had installed recently to make their work easier.

'Thank you,' Sophie replied absently, trimming the edges of her pie-dish.

Seeing her concentration, Mrs Gilpin smiled fondly. She had never expected the childish interest Miss Sophie had displayed to blossom into this competence. The little wench had haunted the kitchen, begging to be allowed to roll out scraps of dough. Those happy sessions making cakes for her dolls had developed over the years until Mrs Gilpin thought the lass could earn her living as a cook.

Not that it would ever come to such a thing, of course. It was easy to forget it in this informal atmosphere, but Miss Fleming was a considerable heiress. The old master had no other close relatives. All the money from the business and the snuff-mill itself would go to her.

The man who marries her will be a lucky fellow, thought the cook. Not only would he control her fortune, but she was an intelligent, sweet girl, not spoilt for all that the old master had indulged her. Oh, she liked getting her own way right enough, and she had a fierce temper, but underneath it she was a kind-hearted lass with a sense of fun and no snobbish airs.

Sophie was just mixing the eggs, milk and sugar for her custard when Jennie appeared with the message that someone wished to see her.

'What, now?' Sophie frowned in annoyance.

'The gentleman did call this morning,' the maid explained. 'He says it's urgent.'

'Damn. I suppose I shall have to come, then,' muttered Sophie under her breath.

'I'll see to this for you,' Mrs Gilpin promised, indicating the unfinished tart.

Sophie smiled her thanks and, stripping off her apron, reluctantly left the kitchen.

'You said he was a stranger. Didn't he give his name?' she asked as they hurried across the hall.

Blushing, Jennie confessed he had left his card earlier. 'I forgot to give it to you, Miss Sophie.'

Sophie shrugged. It was too late to worry now, but as she glanced down at her shabby dress she was glad her visitor was not Sir Pelham. He was always praising her flair for choosing tasteful, well-cut gowns that flattered her tall, thin figure, and she could imagine how his eyebrows would climb if faced with her present dishevelled appearance.

Jennie had shown the caller into the morning-room. It was the most modern room in the house and used almost exclusively for the formal entertainment of visitors. Thomas Fleming preferred to relax in the comfort of the parlour, with its oak panelling and massive old-fashioned furniture, but he had let Sophie have a free hand in re-decorating the morning-room when she was seventeen.

'You'll need somewhere to receive your guests now

you are out, lass,' he'd told her with a jovial smile. 'Pick what you like and hang the expense.'

The result of Sophie's efforts was charming. She had chosen a delicate classical-style suite of matching furniture in beech gilt upholstered in pale green satin. This colour was echoed in the window drapes and it combined well with the jonquil wash on the walls and the darker green carpet to give an airy, springtime effect, which was heightened by the clever use of several landscape paintings.

Unfortunately, the visitor standing gazing out of the window and drumming his long fingers impatiently upon the white-painted sill did not accord well with the graceful harmony of the room. His unusual height and broad shoulders stood out with shocking impact against the feminine delicacy all around him, and there was an air of almost palpable tension about his superbly muscled figure.

'What are you doing here?'

At Sophie's gasp of surprise Kirk whirled round.

'You are not welcome in this house, sir. Please go.' Sophie spoke quickly, but her starved senses greedily drank in every detail of his immaculate appearance. He was wearing a coat of navy corduroy with a double-breasted short waistcoat in a paler blue. Light cream pantaloons clung revealingly to his long legs, and Sophie had to drag her fascinated gaze away from the muscles in his strong thighs that this new fashion displayed.

'Not before I've said what I came to say.'

Kirk resisted the impulse to tug at the tight folds of his muslin cravat. He had gone to a great deal of trouble for this interview, abandoning his usual casual attire in the hope that his smart appearance would create a favourable impression. Old Mr Fleming was known to set great store upon respectability.

The thought that he might also wish to impress Miss Fleming was one he decided firmly to ignore.

'Mr Thorburn, I told you at our last meeting that I did not wish to listen to your accusations. If I had known you would have the audacity to pursue me in this shameless manner I would have given orders that you were not to be admitted. Please leave at once.' Sophie's tone was cold, but her fingers unconsciously pleated together in a manner that betrayed her nervousness.

Kirk laughed mockingly. 'How very prim and proper you sound, not in the least like the girl I know.'

Sophie reddened. He had the knack of throwing her off balance. 'You do not know me at all,' she retorted angrily, but even as she snapped the words at him she knew it wasn't true. In some strange way, it was as if they had known each other for years, as though instinct had taken over to reveal the hidden depths of feeling normally kept concealed.

Stepping to one side, she threw the door open still wider. 'Now please go, or I shall be forced to call for assistance!'

To her alarm, he strode across the room and banged the door shut. 'Will you stop this damned silly play-acting and listen?' he demanded, his patience wearing thin.

Sophie made a snatch for the handle, but he was too quick, and, planting his wide shoulders against the white-painted panels, he growled, 'I've had enough of this nonsense. Sit down!'

Sophie glared at him indignantly, but the angry look on his handsome face dictated prudence, so she decided to do as she was bid. 'Well?' she said curtly.

'I'm sorry. I realise that I'm behaving badly, but it is vital you hear what I have to say.' He gave her a rueful smile. 'If I promise not to shout at you again, may I continue?'

Kirk's quiet apology surprised Sophie. She gazed at him uncertainly and then gave a little confused nod of assent. 'Please sit down,' she murmured.

Kirk swiftly left his post to join her on the elegant sofa. 'I know you will find this painful, but please hear me out. The person to whom you are contemplating becoming betrothed is not what he seems. It would be a dreadful mistake. He is a dangerous man.'

About to contradict him, Sophie paused, trying to consider his statement fairly. 'It is true I have known the baronet for only a few months, but I cannot think him capable of dishonourable behaviour. He is too much of a gentleman.'

'Appearances are deceptive. My brother committed the same error of trusting Stanton, and it led to his death.'

Staring at Kirk's grim expression, Sophie suddenly understood his meaning. 'You cannot think the baronet killed your brother!'

Her dismayed exclamation made him start. 'You have heard about the fire?'

'A little,' Sophie admitted and reluctantly explained.

'Then you will see I must discover the truth. It is a debt of honour. I have to bring Ingram's murderer to justice, and I believe Stanton was responsible, because——'

'You must be mad!' Sophie interrupted. In other circumstances she would have been tempted to laugh. 'How can you imagine that Sir Pelham could lose his cool self-possession long enough to commit an act of such violence? The whole idea is ridiculous!'

'I do not think he was the one to actually strike Ingram down. He would not care to soil his hands,' Kirk replied roughly. 'But I'd stake my life he arranged it and the fire which almost destroyed Haraldsgarth.'

Sophie shook her head in bewilderment. He seemed

so convinced, so sincere! 'Do you have proof of what you say?' she asked.

'I have one clue I am following, but nothing that would convince a jury as yet. However, the circumstances fit damningly.'

He gave her a searching look, wondering how much he dared reveal. Could he trust her not to go running to Stanton?

'Please, if you expect me to believe you, I must know more.'

Her anxiety convinced him and he nodded curtly.

'It began almost a year ago when I received a letter from Ingram saying that he had been cheated out of a considerable sum of money. Stanton had tricked him into selling some shares our family had held for many years in a Borrowdale wad mine. My brother was not a worldly man; he didn't realise how their value had soared due to the recent increase in demand and he let Stanton have them for a pittance.'

Sophie digested this information. She knew that this pure form of graphite was highly prized. Uncle Thomas had told her that it was used for medicinal purposes and in the manufacture of cannon balls as well as being an important material for artists. A single pack-load could fetch up to eight hundred pounds, and blood-curdling stories abounded of how it was stolen and smuggled out to the coast at Whitehaven and Ravenglass.

'When Ingram discovered he had been gulled he tried to get Stanton to pay him the proper value of the shares, but Stanton refused,' Kirk continued in a grim tone. 'Ingram persisted, and I think it was in order to silence him that Stanton had him murdered.'

'I'm sorry, I still cannot believe you.' Sophie shook her head slowly. 'Even allowing that the baronet would ever behave in such a dreadful way, it simply doesn't make sense. Why on earth should he gull your brother? The scandal had he been found out would have been ruinous! Only someone who was desperate for money would take such a risk, but Sir Pelham is rich.'

'You misunderstand. Stanton has run through his fortune and is heavily in debt.'

'In debt?' Sophie ejaculated in lively astonishment.

'He is a gamester. He has been careful here in Kendal, but money flows through his hands like water. His creditors in London forced him into seeking refuge in the country last autumn, but time is growing short for him. Unless he finds a rich wife to rescue him, they will very soon catch up with him.'

Kirk paused. Her lovely eyes were dilated with shock, and he felt a brute, forcing her to hear such unpalatable facts. 'Without money his position is vulnerable. He knows I am on his trail and he dare not risk a scandal when he needs all the influence he can muster. He must marry soon or he will be disgraced.'

'Are you saying that he only wishes to wed me for my money?' Sophie felt the blood drain from her face.

There was a fleeting sympathy in his face which convinced her that she had hit the nail on the head. Was she so unattractive, then? So plain and unladylike that she couldn't catch a suitor except with her dowry?

'You insolent knave!' Sophie's hand flew up in swift, unthinking reaction. It hurt unbearably to hear her secret fears voiced by the one man whose admiration she craved.

The blow left a red mark on his cheek and for an instant an answering anger flared in the vivid blue eyes, making Sophie regret her impulsive slap. It took a considerable effort not to shrink away from him, but she managed to keep her composure and continued to glare at him, her chin proudly tilted. 'How dare you suggest such a thing?'

However, Kirk made no attempt to retaliate in kind, but merely shrugged.

'I meant no insult.' Surely she couldn't be so foolish

as to imagine *he* thought her unattractive? 'Stanton simply cannot afford a poor bride. He would not marry the Goddess Venus unless she came decked in garlands of gold!'

'Or, to put it more bluntly, I could be as plain as a pikestaff and he would still marry me; is that what you mean?' Sophie enquired with awful sarcasm.

'Damn it, woman, why must you harp on about your looks? It doesn't matter a whit whether you are a beauty or no. It is Stanton's perfidy which concerns me and should concern you.' Anxiety for her made Kirk's voice rough. 'If you haven't the sense to see that, then perhaps I'd best speak to your uncle without further ado.'

Humiliatingly conscious of her shabby appearance, Sophie felt her self-confidence ooze away. He sounded so indifferent! Why had she been so foolish as to imagine he might desire her?

A sickening sense of disappointment swept over her. Suddenly, even his wild accusations seemed irrelevant, set against the discovery that Kirk Thorburn was only interested in her because Sir Pelham sought to make her his bride.

'My uncle is unwell. You cannot see him.'

Abruptly, Sophie got to her feet to indicate the interview was over.

Kirk rose. 'You will pass on my message?'

Sophie raised her eyebrows. 'I shall think about what you have said.'

Kirk's mouth thinned at her dismissive tone. 'Take care that you do, Miss Fleming.'

She shrugged, and with a curt bow he strode from the room.

CHAPTER FOUR

'AND now let us kneel and give thanks for the many blessings the Lord has bestowed upon us. . .'

The sonorous voice of the parson echoed throughout the old church of Holy Trinity, but it barely penetrated the shell of Sophie's troubled thoughts as she sat in the Fleming family pew.

A light touch on her arm reminded her of her surroundings.

'Thank you, Sir Pelham,' she whispered hastily, glad that she had accepted his escort. He had been kindness itself the last few days and his discreet attentiveness was soothing to her stretched nerves.

Throughout the rest of the service she marshalled her wits to concentrate on what was being said, but as the congregation began to file out her anxiety returned.

They encountered the Stricklands outside the church in the usual Sunday morning press of people exchanging greetings with their neighbours.

'Please try not to worry; I'm sure your uncle's illness is just a temporary setback.' Maria smiled at her encouragingly. 'I'm convinced he will be better in time for you to attend my party on Wednesday.'

Sophie nodded, but her manner was strained.

Several other acquaintances drifted up to ask after her uncle's health, and Sophie tried her best to respond cheerfully, but she was relieved when the baronet smoothly intervened by announcing it was time he took her home.

Wearily, she let her head sink back against the velvet squabs of his comfortable carriage.

'Perhaps Dr Wilson could prescribe a sleeping

draught for you, my dear, to ensure you get a proper rest.'

Sophie's eyes snapped open. 'Forgive me,' she murmured in some embarrassment, realising that the rocking motion of the vehicle had almost lulled her to sleep. 'I never take such things; I dislike the idea of interfering with nature,' she added in a firmer tone.

'There are times when drugs may be useful.' The baronet looked amused by her disapproval.

Sophie shrugged. 'Perhaps.'

Accepting her dismissal of the subject, the baronet turned to lighter matters, but although she pretended to listen to him Sophie was thinking about her uncle, whose heart was not strong. The chill he had taken a week ago had turned feverish, and she sensed that Dr Wilson was more concerned than he admitted.

In the last few days she had scarcely left the sickroom, but this morning Nancy had insisted that she needed a breath of fresh air when Sir Pelham called to see if she wished to attend divine service. It wasn't until they were seated in the ancient church that Sophie had begun to worry in case Nancy had packed her off because the crisis in Uncle Thomas's illness was approaching.

I'll never forgive myself if anything happened to him while I wasn't there, she thought in anguish, realising afresh how much she loved the old man who had made her the pivot of his life.

Hurrying indoors, Sophie was alarmed to find Nancy awaiting them in the hall, but a quick glance at her smiling face told a different story from the one Sophie feared.

'His fever has broken at last, Miss Sophie,' Nancy announced joyfully. 'I sent for Dr Wilson and he says that it's just a matter of rest and good nursing now.'

Relief exploded in Sophie's chest, easing the tension

that had gripped her ever since her uncle had been confined to his bed.

'Nancy, ask Jennie to bring up a bottle of the best claret to toast his recovery,' she cried in jubilation. Turning to her escort, she added hastily, 'Pray excuse me; I must see how my uncle does.' And she rushed up the oaken staircase without a backward glance.

Ten minutes later she came dancing into the morning-room, her face aglow. 'He is sleeping peacefully.'

'So you are at last convinced that the good doctor spoke the truth,' the baronet remarked with a little burst of laughter that rang distinctly hollow.

'I'm sorry, I shouldn't have deserted you in such a rag-mannered way.' Sophie suddenly realised that he was offended.

A spurt of irritation clouded her happiness. Devil take the man; need he always be so touchy? Surely he didn't think she had intended any insult? Or was he such a dry stick that he couldn't see she had acted solely on impulse?

The baronet had already helped himself to the claret, so Sophie poured herself a glass and forced herself to sit down without giving vent to the irritation she felt. To be fair, in his eyes she supposed she had behaved discourteously, but it was her nature to act without thinking first.

Surely he must know that by now, she thought rebelliously. Impetuosity might not be considered lady-like, but if he was so hell-bent on marrying someone prim and proper why was he dancing attendance on her?

'To Master Fleming.' Sir Pelham raised his glass. 'It is good news about his health.'

'I'm glad you think so,' Sophie replied somewhat tartly, immediately forgetting her resolution to curb her unruly tongue.

'My dear, I hope you speak in jest! I would be

wounded to discover that you doubted my sincerity.'
The baronet's tone was earnest. 'Naturally, I esteem
your uncle most highly, but it has been even more
disturbing for me to see you so anxious on his account.'

Sophie avoided his gaze. She tried to cover her
confusion by smoothing the green and white striped
skirts of her Italian taffeta gown, but his words startled
her.

'You do not doubt I am most fond of you, I hope,
Miss Fleming?'

Sophie blushed. She couldn't help remembering his
frequent attempts to please her. 'Sir, you are too kind,'
she muttered, feeling miserably uncharitable, because
only a moment ago she had inwardly cavilled at his
punctiliousness.

The baronet's expression grew warmer. 'Indeed, I
am happier than you can imagine at Mr Fleming's
recovery, for it gives me the opportunity to speak at
last.'

Sophie stiffened warily.

'It did not seem appropriate to ask you in such
difficult circumstances, but now I do not think I can
contain my impatience any longer.' His reserved smile
flickered, but his manner remained so dignified that for
an instant Sophie wondered if her vivid imagination was
leading her astray, until he drew out a small velvet ring-
box from the pocket of his extravagantly tailed morning
coat.

Opening it, he held it out towards her.

'My dear Miss Fleming — or dare I call you Sophie? —
will you do me the honour of becoming my wife and
accepting this bauble as a token of our betrothal?'

The magnificent diamond glittered in the light, and
Sophie's eyes widened.

'Sir. . . I was not expecting a declaration,' she
faltered.

'Your modesty is most becoming, my dear. I quite

understand, but surely my proposal does not come as a complete shock? We have known each other for only a short time, but, unless I am mistaken, your uncle has spoken to you of my intentions.' The baronet's tone was indulgent, but Sophie sensed his eager impatience as he waited for an answer.

'My uncle did mention the matter before he became ill,' she admitted reluctantly. 'But to be frank with you, sir, there has been no time of late to think on how I must answer you.'

'Then can you give the matter some thought now?' Sir Pelham laughed with unaccustomed joviality.

Sophie responded with a strained smile and a little shrug. 'I shall do my best,' she murmured, knowing how much her uncle wanted the match.

Clearly the baronet had been expecting a different answer. For an instant a frown creased his brow, but it disappeared so swiftly that Sophie could not gauge if he was annoyed or not.

'You do not have anyone else in mind, I hope?'

The unexpected sharp question made Sophie jump. 'No, indeed.'

'Only I did hear a little rumour that you had been seen with Mr Kirk Thorburn.' The baronet's voice was once more smooth. He smiled at her deprecatingly. 'I am aware he has a great charm for unwary ladies, but I should not like to think of you becoming embroiled in his unsavoury net.'

Sophie's brows rose indignantly. 'I trust that remark was not meant to be taken seriously! I encountered Mr Thorburn while skating, and our meeting was as brief as it was accidental.' She glared at him. How dared he spy on her?

'That is reassuring news.' The baronet's smile became sympathetic. 'Believe me, my dear, I did not intend to question your conduct, but I must confess myself anxious. That man regards me as an enemy and he is unscrupulous enough to use any means to injure me. Everyone in Kendal must know how I feel about you. It is no secret.'

'You think he is spiteful enough to try and engage my affections merely to hit back at you?' Sophie gasped.

'Sadly, I would not put such a false, despicable trick beyond him,' the baronet sighed.

Sophie tasted blood as she bit her lip in a fierce effort to contain the instinctive denial that rose in Kirk's defence. He couldn't—wouldn't—behave in such a shabby way. . .could he? But what if the baronet was right? A flood of pain washed over her as she realised how little she knew of the real man behind that handsome Viking face.

'I can see I have inadvertently distressed you, my dear, so perhaps we should put aside such unpleasant speculations,' Sir Pelham continued smoothly.

Sophie nodded hastily. The whole idea was abhorrent!

'Then, to return to our original conversation, dare I hope for an answer today?'

Sophie shrugged helplessly. 'I think not, sir.' Her mind seemed bogged down and all her usual decisiveness was left floundering in confusion.

'Ah, well. I must bow to your wishes, but I cannot pretend I am not disappointed.' Stretching out his hand, Sir Pelham deposited the ring-box on a giltwood side-table. 'However, let this small token of the deep respect and affection I feel for you remain here to remind you of me in my absence.'

'Oh, please, take it home with you! It is too valuable! I should be in dread of something happening to it.'

'Nonsense,' the baronet chuckled. 'I'm sure you will take the greatest care of it, my dear.' He brushed an imaginary speck of dust from his breeches. 'Yet you are right, of course, in thinking that it cost a pretty penny. It actually belonged to a Queen!'

Her look of enquiry made him preen. 'Ah, I knew you would be impressed, my dear! What woman could resist such a gem, eh? Well, I shall not tease you any longer. It is one of the stones that made up Marie-Antoinette's celebrated necklace. I saw it in Jeffrey's—the famous jeweller's in Piccadilly, you know—on my last visit to town and decided to buy it for you. Nothing is too good for the next Lady Stanton!'

Sophie wondered at his lapse of taste. To be sure, it was a very beautiful ring, but it seemed vulgar to talk of money in the circumstances, and, what was more, its history struck her as decidedly unlucky. That infamous diamond necklace had helped contribute to the present imprisonment of the lovely, foolish Queen of France, hardly an omen to boast of!

This view had obviously not occurred to the baronet, for he was smiling, almost as if he considered matters satisfactorily settled.

'I must take my leave, my dear.' Sir Pelham rose to his feet and Sophie closed her mouth on the further protests which burned her lips. Plainly they would do no good, and she did not wish to provoke an argument. She owed him something in recompense for her dilatoriness!

'Due to the press of business affairs, I will not be able to wait upon you as usual, but I hope I will see you at Mrs Strickland's birthday celebrations.'

Sophie's red curls nodded in agreement. Maria had been insistent that she should take a respite from the sick-room, and now that her uncle was recovering there was no need to disappoint her friend.

'Excellent,' murmured the baronet, bending low over her hand. He straightened. 'I know it is the fashion for young ladies to tantalise, but I shall hope you will be kind enough to give me your answer then, my dear Sophie.'

Feeling trapped, Sophie forced herself to smile. 'Of course.'

'I'm sorry, sir, you cannot see the master. Them's Miss Sophie's orders, I durst not admit you.'

Kirk stared in frustration at the maid's apologetic face.

'Yet I've heard that Master Fleming is recovering.'

'Aye, sir.' Jennie's expression brightened. 'But Dr Wilson says he needs peace and quiet lest he has a relapse.'

Kirk nodded abruptly. He felt tempted to ignore convention and push his way into the house, but he had no desire to be the cause of any setback to the old man's health. Caroline had already mentioned that Thomas Fleming had suffered a heart attack the previous year, and Kirk did not doubt the wisdom of the doctor's advice.

'Then may I speak with Miss Fleming?'

Jennie coloured unhappily. She had taken a shine to this handsome, well-spoken gentleman who had called several times in the last few days, but Miss Sophie's orders had been very clear. 'I'm afraid not, sir. She's not at home.'

A frown darkened Kirk's eyes. He was convinced the girl was lying.

Taking his leave, he realised any optimistic hope that he might encounter Sophie Fleming by chance was also doomed to failure. The wench was avoiding him!

In desperation he decided to consult Caroline.

'I applaud your generosity in wanting to warn Mr Fleming, Kirk, but do you think it is wise to continue to involve yourself?'

Caroline had risen from partaking of her customary breakfast in bed to accommodate his precipitate arrival and sat facing him in her pretty little parlour. 'After all,

you have already informed Sophie of your suspicions,'
she continued.

'I suppose I should wait until I have firm proof about
Stanton's perfidy, but I hardly think that signifies in the
circumstances,' Kirk muttered irritably. 'Once she
becomes betrothed to him it will be too late to break
things off without a great deal of unpleasant gossip.'

Refusing the offer of refreshment, Kirk began to
pace about the room in a way that threatened to give
Caroline a headache.

'What a restless fellow you are,' she sighed, faintly
piqued that he had no eyes for the charming picture she
made reclining upon a scroll-backed *chaise-longue* in a
state of fashionable dishabille worn especially to
impress him.

'I'm sorry.' Kirk came to a halt. 'I'm behaving like a
fool, and at this hour too! It was good of you to agree to
see me, Caroline.' He smiled at her with a warmth that
melted her irritation. 'Particularly when all I do is
contradict your excellent advice.'

'Nonsense!' Caroline coloured a little and, making
the effort to control her wayward thoughts, she begged
him to sit down while she considered the matter further.

'Perhaps I could invite her here. I should be happy to
act as a chaperon.'

'I do not think she would accept,' he replied wryly.

'Whyever not?'

Kirk tugged at his neckcloth in a manner which
suggested it had suddenly grown too tight. 'We. . . we
parted with angry words and I think she has taken me in
dislike,' he muttered, unwilling to say more.

Caroline's eyes widened. He had said nothing earlier
of a quarrel! 'Hmm, that does make things difficult,'
she murmured.

There was another short silence.

'I have it!' Kirk exclaimed. 'You must go and see her,
Caroline. She might listen to you.'

Caroline's mouth formed a little circle of astonishment. 'But, Kirk, I hardly know the girl!'

'That hardly signifies.' He shrugged this objection aside impatiently. 'In fact, it might work to our advantage. You have no axe to grind; she is more likely to heed your warning than mine.'

Personally Caroline thought this hope was a trifle sanguine. 'But she knows that I am your friend and she might think my advice prejudiced.'

'It's a risk we will have to take.' He leant forward in his chair. 'Please, Caroline. I know it is a lot to ask of you, but I cannot bear the idea of sitting idly by and letting her commit the folly of marrying that brute.'

Caroline blinked. She knew him for a kind-hearted man in spite of his impatient temper, but this zeal for Sophie Fleming's welfare seemed a little excessive. He had only just met the girl, after all! 'That is very commendable of you, my dear,' she said rather tartly. 'Yet I could have sworn you had it in mind at Sir Alan Chambre's soirée to make use of her in some way to trap Stanton.'

'It did occur to me that I might be able to provoke him into a duel by arousing his jealousy,' he admitted, somewhat shamefaced.

'Well, I'm glad you changed your mind.' Caroline shuddered. 'I know you are an excellent shot, but I detest duels. They are nasty, dangerous affairs!'

He smiled at her in amusement. 'Men hold a different view of such things, my dear.'

'Oh, affairs of honour!' Caroline sniffed. It was never possible to talk to any man sensibly on the subject of honour, and Kirk was more stubborn than most. 'All the same, Kirk, although it might afford you great personal satisfaction to do so, I cannot see how blowing a hole in the baronet would solve the problem of showing him to blame for Ingram's death. Everyone would still continue to think the fire just a tragic accident.'

Kirk nodded. 'It was precisely for that reason that I changed my mind about using Miss Fleming. Leaving aside the impropriety of causing her distress, I cannot risk losing my temper with that man. If I do, I play straight into his hands.'

Caroline thoughtfully pleated a fold into her wrapper. 'Indeed, he would simply claim you were unhinged by grief and had a grudge against him because he had benefitted by Ingram's unwise sale.'

Waiting for proof was the advice she had already prescribed, but she knew how it galled his impetuous nature to bide his time when he longed to take direct action. 'Have you managed to learn anything further about the snuff-box?'

'Nothing.' He shook his fair head impatiently. 'No one here in Kendal recognises it.'

'He must have purchased it in London.'

'No doubt.' Kirk's large, well-kept hands clenched into tight fists. 'It is a poor lead, but it is the only proof I have, other than the letter which Ingram wrote to me last February. But Stanton was at Haraldsgarth the day of the fire, I know it!'

The baronet, of course, had denied it and no magistrate would doubt his word without convincing evidence to the contrary.

'I'll have to go to London to see if I can discover anything new there,' Kirk said.

'What if a betrothal takes place before your return?' Caroline enquired delicately.

A savage frown appeared on Kirk's handsome face.

'It must be prevented.' He fixed her with his vivid gaze. 'Sophie will not receive me, but you could see her as my emissary, Caroline. Please, there is no time to waste. Won't you try, as a personal favour to me?'

Unable to refuse this appeal, Caroline sighed in

resignation. 'Oh, very well, my friend, but I dare say I shall regret it!'

'Miss Fleming.'

Sophie turned at the sound of her name and saw a chaise drawing up. Her grip tightened on the selection of books she had just chosen from Manson's circulating library when she realised who had hailed her.

'May I give you a lift home?'

'No, thank you, Mrs Birkett. I do not wish to inconvenience you.'

'But I am going that way.' Caroline beamed. 'It is no trouble at all.'

Sophie smiled politely. 'You are very kind, but I enjoy walking.'

'Of course, but actually I wanted a word with you.'

Faced with such persistence, Sophie hesitated, and Caroline quickly added, 'Look, it is coming on to rain. Please get in, my dear, you don't want to get wet.'

Sophie was of the opinion that she would prefer a drenching to Caroline's company, but good manners forced her to climb into the carriage.

'What was it that you wished to say to me, Mrs Birkett?' she enquired after they had exchanged polite inanities for a moment or two.

Caroline forced a smile. 'Oh, heavens, it is rather delicate,' she murmured with pretty hesitation.

Sophie's dark brows lifted in supercilious silence.

'It has to do with Mr Thorburn,' Caroline began, feeling rather daunted by this lack of encouragement. 'I understand that he has made you privy to the circumstances of his brother's death.'

Sophie's mouth thinned. 'Yes, but I do not see that it is any of your business.'

Her bald statement made Caroline wince. What an uncouth, prickly girl she was!

'You may be right, my dear, but the fact remains that

Kirk is anxious on your behalf. He feels that you do not truly comprehend the dangers of allying yourself to a man like Stanton.'

Sophie could feel her temper beginning to bubble.

'My matrimonial plans are no concern of Mr Thorburn's!' she snapped. 'You may tell him to keep his anxiety to himself, since you appear to be his emissary. I do not believe he is correct in his suspicions concerning the baronet and I do not wish to hear another word on the whole ridiculous subject.'

'Have you mentioned the matter to your uncle?'

'Of course not! He is too frail to be worried with such nonsense.' Impatience made Sophie's tone sharp.

'He might not think it was nonsense,' Caroline countered. 'You might not like it, Miss Fleming, but the facts fit. In my opinion Stanton is guilty.'

'Really?' Sophie smiled scornfully. 'And your — er — close friendship with Mr Thorburn has nothing to do with how you came to this conclusion, I suppose?'

Caroline flushed angrily. 'You do not much care for me, Miss Fleming, and I admit that the feeling is mutual, but there is no need for us to descend to insults. Whatever you may think to the contrary, Kirk is merely a family friend. My relationship with him is perfectly proper.'

Sophie stared hard at her gloved fingertips. She was aware she had overstepped the bounds of propriety, but she couldn't force an apology from her tight throat. Every bone in her body was jealously screaming that Caroline was lying. If she wasn't Kirk's mistress, then she wanted to be. Her very tone betrayed her!

'This conversation was intended as a sincere warn-ing,' Caroline broke the tense silence. 'You think I am interfering, but you are young and inexperienced ——'

'But not in need of advice from you!' Sophie flashed back rudely.

Caroline sucked in her breath. 'Very well, have it

your own way, you stupid girl! I promised Kirk I would try and persuade you to see sense, but if you will not listen then let the results of your obstinacy be on your own head.'

'You are just jealous because I am marrying a man of rank and fortune,' Sophie declared, but for all her efforts her voice came out uncertainly.

Caroline laughed. 'You poor little fool, Stanton will make mincemeat of you! All that interests him is your dowry.'

The blood drained from Sophie's face, leaving her deathly white.

'Oh, damn, I should not have said that. . .' Caroline stretched out a repentant hand, but Sophie shrugged it off and in one swift movement banged hard on the roof to alert the coachman to stop and then wrenched open the door.

Before Caroline could stop her she had jumped down even as the chaise slowed and was hurrying away down the street.

Watching her go, Caroline sighed. She had probably made things worse. 'Not that I ever stood a chance of success,' she murmured ruefully. For whatever reasons of her own, that stubborn young madam was determined not to listen to anything Kirk Thorburn had to say!

Maria Strickland's birthday party was in full flow by the time Kirk arrived with Caroline on his arm. The news of Sophie's rejection of his advice had come as a blow and it had not improved his temper to be kept kicking his heels for over an hour waiting for Caroline to complete her toilette.

'What do you think of my new gown? Is it too daring for Kendal?' Caroline asked with a giggle of excitement as she swept into the parlour.

'You look stunning,' Kirk replied, concealing his

impatience. How the devil could it take so long to dress in so little? All she was wearing was a wisp of white silk gauze!

'I fear we shall be late,' he added, offering her his arm, and in the carriage he reflected, not for the first time, that his ideal woman wouldn't give a damn whether her curls were in place or her rouge perfect.

His thoughts made him suddenly smile cynically. He was asking for the moon!

Maria and her husband were still receiving guests in the entrance hall.

'Mr Thorburn, how nice of you to come!'

Maria's greeting was filled with warmth. She still felt rather guilty at having betrayed the story of his youthful peccadillo and was determined to do all she could to make him feel welcome in her home.

Kirk was pleasantly surprised by her friendliness and his devastating smile was still in place when he strolled into the salon a few moments later.

It was the first thing Sophie saw.

Automatically she noted that he looked incredibly handsome in formal evening dress. His dark blue coat was set admirably across his broad shoulders and there was scarcely a crease in his satin knee-breeches. A chaste white waistcoat and elegant neckcloth completed his distinguished appearance.

Her heart began to beat faster.

Fortunately, a few minutes earlier the baronet had quit her side to seek entertainment at the faro-table Mr Strickland had set up in the smaller salon and there was no one to observe the way her colour fluctuated at Kirk's approach.

'Miss Fleming.'

His bow was a model of propriety, but Sophie remained tense. 'Where is Mrs Birkett? I had expected to see her here with you,' she murmured after a hesitant pause.

'She is talking to a friend in the drawing-room,' he replied.

Some of Sophie's tension ebbed when he did not pursue the subject. She had been half expecting him to launch into a tirade berating her for refusing to listen to Caroline.

'Don't worry, I won't cause a scene,' he murmured, reading her thoughts.

Sophie cursed her expressive face. 'I should hope not,' she muttered. 'I'm not in the mood to hear a lecture, thank you.'

'Then dance with me instead.' He held out a hand towards her.

Sophie's card was full, but her partner for the next dance had not yet appeared. 'Very well.' Recklessly she nodded. Why not? She might never get another chance after tonight!

They were just in time to join a set forming for the quadrille, and as Kirk led her on to the floor Sophie experienced a rush of excited pleasure.

To her delight she discovered that he was an excellent dancer, moving with elegant precision through the complex steps of the *grande ronde* and the *pas de zephyr*.

She was enjoying herself so much that she was determined to ignore the constant ache in her left ankle, but to her chagrin a particularly sharpe twinge of pain made her footsteps falter as the dance drew to its conclusion.

'Take my arm,' Kirk urged, alarmed by her sudden pallor.

'I'm perfectly all right,' Sophie declared, but she was glad to obey him. 'It is only my wretched ankle playing up.' She smiled gamely. 'I sustained an injury in a fall from my pony when I was a child and suffer for it occasionally.'

She had also twisted it slightly jumping down from

Caroline's coach, a fact she did not wish to admit in case it reminded him of the disagreement between them she wanted to ignore. 'I shall be as fit as a fiddle again if only I can sit somewhere quiet for a moment or two.'

'You know this house much better than I do. Where do you suggest?'

'The conservatory might make a suitable spot for recuperation,' she answered and was thankful to lean discreetly on his arm as they made their way towards this quiet haven.

'Very impressive,' Kirk announced as he gazed admiringly about him.

'Maria would be delighted to hear you say so. She was very disappointed when her gardener advised that the present weather was too cold to leave all the doors open so that her guests could stroll in and out of here as freely as they wished. She said it was the penalty of having a birthday on the twenty-third of January!'

Kirk nodded. Her remarks explained the deserted silence of this enchanting green paradise.

'I'm sorry Mrs Strickland was disappointed. However, it would be a pity to spoil this peaceful oasis with a chattering throng.'

'Does it make you a little homesick for the Bahamas?' Sophie asked impulsively.

'How acute of you, Miss Fleming,' he drawled to cover his embarrassment at her unexpected perceptiveness, and then was sorry for his sarcasm when she blushed.

'Forgive me, you are right of course. It does remind me of my plantation,' he murmured, gently pressing her fingers, which still rested upon his coat sleeve.

Sophie's pulse quickened. She was suddenly very aware of the fact that, defying convention, they were completely alone.

The warm, perfumed silence wrapped itself around them and she had the craziest notion that they had stepped out of ordinary everyday reality into an enchanted world.

She took a deep breath to dispel this absurd fantasy, but the languid air did nothing to ease the tight knot of tension twisting in her stomach.

'Shall we sit down?' Kirk pointed to one of the charming little rustic benches Maria had scattered about the conservatory for the comfort of those who wished to sit and admire her plants.

Sophie agreed with a nervous smile, but she was in such a state that she forgot to favour her sore ankle. A yelp of pain escaped her as her full weight bore down her left foot.

'Allow me.' Kirk swung her up into his arms.

'Please, there is no need. Put me down,' Sophie implored as he carried her towards the bench.

'It is no hardship.' He grinned. 'You are as light as a feather.'

Sophie subsided into silence. Of their own volition her arms slid around his neck. I am only steadying myself, she told her uneasy conscience, but she knew she was lying.

Her cheek came to rest against his shoulder and she let out a sigh of voluptuous content. She could smell the clean, fresh scent of the cologne he had used and feel the warmth of his skin. Her eyelids drooped to a languorous close. His arms felt so strong, so safe. . .so desirable!

Sophie's eyes snapped open in horrified shock. What on earth was she thinking of? She had no right to let her wayward imagination wander off into such improper daydreams!

'Are you comfortable?'

Kirk settled her carefully upon the bench and Sophie hastily nodded her thanks, trying to hide her blushes in a flurry of arranging her amethyst satin skirts.

He sat down next to her. To her relief he did not

appear to notice her disordered breathing, but began
making remarks about the plants all around them, and
after a few moments she felt composed enough to lift
her gaze again.

'That's better,' Kirk murmured.

Sophie laughed nervously. 'Whatever do you mean,
sir?'

'Your eyes are much too beautiful to hide, my sweet.'

The gentle teasing note in his voice made Sophie's
heart skip a beat. 'I. . .I don't know what you mean,'
she whispered.

'Don't you, Sophie? You have the loveliest eyes in
Kendal — eyes any man must admire.'

She could only stare at him silently, her tongue
paralysed by shyness.

'What, no blistering retort to put me firmly in my
place? You surprise me, Miss Fleming.' Kirk smiled at
her with a faintly mocking amusement, but beneath his
banter lurked a note of passion. 'I wonder if I dare hope
your acquiescence will stretch a little further?'

Sophie's mouth began to tremble and his need to kiss
her grew intolerable.

'Silence gives consent, so they say,' he murmured
wickedly, drawing her into his arms with a skilful
dexterity that left her breathless. 'Do you consent,
sweetheart?'

'Yes. . .no! I mean, let me go! This is madness!' she
gasped.

'Is it?' he enquired. 'Then tell me you feel nothing
when I do this. . .and this. . .'

The touch of his lips was as gentle as the caress of a
butterfly, brushing against the exposed curve of her
white shoulder, exploring a path of exquisite sensation
into the secret hollow of her throat.

Sophie jumped as if she had been stung.

'Please. . .you mustn't,' she muttered feebly.

'Why not?' he demanded in a hoarse whisper. 'Are

you going to pretend that you don't feel the same way I do?'

'We hardly know one another,' she wailed.

'What has that got to do with it?' He laughed a little wildly, his arms tightening. 'Oh, Sophie!'

His golden head dipped and as he captured her mouth Sophie's feeble opposition dissolved completely. She couldn't control the wild excitement that flooded her suddenly shaking limbs, but clung to him as tightly as she could, eager for the wonderful sensations he was arousing in her untutored body to continue.

'Sweetheart!' Her uninhibited response brought a growl of surprised delight to Kirk's throat. He deepened the kiss, parting her lips until their breath mingled.

At the intimate touch of his tongue, all rational thought fled. Nothing mattered any more but the incredible pleasure pulsating through her entire body. Her eyes were tight shut, but for the first time in her life she felt she could see. At last she understood the emotion she had scorned in her friends!

Dazzling flashes of colour exploded behind her lids. It was like being engulfed in a hot, vibrant sunburst, she thought in a daze, a sunburst of desire, and she was no longer blind to its devastating power! This was the passion poets raved over, and it was sweeter than she had dreamt possible!

'God, but you are desirable!'

Kirk tore his mouth away from hers for an instant and looked down at her flushed face. 'I ought to return you to your chaperon,' he muttered feverishly.

Sophie moaned in protest. Wordlessly, she buried her fingers in the thick curls that clustered at the back of his neck and pulled his head down to hers.

Kirk groaned as her tongue teased his, darting into the warmth of his mouth with an instinctive wantonness. He hadn't bargained for this! In some dim corner of his mind, he was aware that she had no idea of the dangerously powerful urges she was releasing in him, but her passionate abandonment was rapidly making restraint impossible.

His hand slid across the amethyst bodice to cup her left breast. She quivered with shock, her eyes snapping open. He released her mouth, giving her the chance to withdraw, but instead she smiled at him slowly with an unconscious seductiveness.

'I like it when you hold me,' she whispered.

'I like it too,' he replied with a hoarse chuckle.

Very gently he began to caress her. Through the thin satin he felt her nipple harden, and the last vestiges of sanity were lost.

The waves of desire sweeping over her made Sophie's head spin. When she felt him push the low *décolletage* of her gown aside to stroke her naked flesh she had to bite down hard on her lower lip to prevent an exclamation of pleasure.

His long brown fingers were so skilful! Sensuously, she pressed herself against him. Their bodies were so close! She wanted to rip aside his waistcoat and immaculate linen shirt to feel the nakedness of his skin beneath her own hands. . .

'Oh!'

Still breathing hard, Kirk forced himself to let her go. Moving away, he grinned at her ruefully. 'I'm sorry, sweetheart, but that's what happens when you drive a man almost to distraction.'

Her cheek stained crimson, Sophie dropped her eyes in confusion. Cursing her lack of sophistication, she realised that she didn't have the faintest idea how to handle the embarrassing situation her folly had led them into.

Realising that she had been genuinely shocked by his body's arousal, Kirk forced aside his own frustration. She looked so ashamed as she fumbled to set her gown to rights that he couldn't be angry in spite of his aching loins.

'Let me help you,' he murmured.

With a kind of numb resignation Sophie abandoned her attempt, and within a few moments he had restored even her tumbled curls to order.

The uncomfortable silence continued.

'Sophie, you mustn't be upset. . .' Kirk began awkwardly, but a fiery glance from her dark eyes made him pause.

'My behaviour has been disgraceful.' Sophie forced her chin high, but her voice shook. 'Please accept my apologies, sir.'

'Your apologies. . .?' Kirk was dumbfounded.

'Yes! I had no business kissing you!'

Her anger puzzled him. 'Apologies be damned! I enjoyed it!'

'Oh, don't!' Sophie gazed at him beseechingly. 'Please don't say such a thing. We are little more than strangers; there can be no possibility of intimacy between us.'

'If you believe that nonsense you'll believe anything,' Kirk declared roundly, putting his arms around her again. 'Time and the conventions of society have got nothing to do with it. The kind of attraction we felt for one another just now obeys no polite rules.'

'It is wicked to give in to carnal impulses,' Sophie whispered.

'And yet God fashioned desire to bring men and women together.' His vivid gaze was lit by tender amusement when she shook her head violently. 'Sweetheart, you'd feel better if you admitted the truth; you wanted me as much as I wanted you!'

'I can't!' Despairingly Sophie struggled to pull free from his embrace. 'Oh, don't you see? I cannot, dare not feel anything for you, Kirk Thorburn. I am already promised to another man!'

CHAPTER FIVE

'STANTON?' Kirk snarled the name. 'Good God, you haven't consented to marry him, have you?'

Miserable, Sophie nodded.

'You little idiot!' Kirk was appalled. 'Of all the damned stupid things to do!'

'There is no need for you to be so rude,' Sophie retorted, her drooping spirits beginning to revive.

'I beg to differ there, my girl. I suppose you thought you owed it to your uncle, but ——'

'I do not need to justify my actions to you,' she interrupted angrily, his abrasive tone restoring her self-possession as if by magic.

Kirk bit back a savage answer and took a deep breath. 'Your uncle is old and ill and I dare say he is fretting to see you and his business suitably settled, but ——'

'And what is wrong with that, pray?' Sophie demanded.

'Nothing, but ——'

'My uncle has a right to be concerned for the future. He is my guardian,' Sophie interrupted once more. 'I owe him everything and it is my duty to repay his kindness.'

'Will you let me finish?' He glared at her. 'I don't doubt that your motives were honourable, but you must have taken leave of your senses. Do you really think sacrificing yourself in marriage to that murdering cheat will serve your uncle's interests?'

'It is merely your prejudice that paints Sir Pelham in such a villainous light. Everyone else thinks he is the best catch in Kendal!'

Her heated reply brought a look of scorn to his handsome face. 'So, now we come to the truth. You have a fancy to be my Lady Stanton and play the fine aristocrat. Flaunting a title is of more interest to you than the truth.'

'Oh, don't talk such fustian rubbish! You sound like one of those wretched sansculottes,' Sophie exploded. 'Of course I wish to see justice done. If your brother was murdered, then the person who did it deserves to be punished, but I am sure you are mistaken in assuming Sir Pelham to be the man responsible.'

She let out a sigh and impatiently pushed aside one of the curls that had fallen on to her hot forehead. 'Oh, Kirk, there is no point in going over this same ground again! I don't wish to quarrel with you. I want us to be friends.'

'Then tell Stanton you have changed your mind.'

'I cannot. I have given him my word.'

Restlessly, she twisted a fold of her gown in her fingers. 'You are right in thinking that I agreed to the match to please my uncle,' she continued in a low, rapid voice. 'He was delighted by the news. In fact, when Sir Pelham suggested it, he gave his permission for the betrothal to be announced immediately.'

Kirk grimaced. The baronet was wasting no time.

'When is this announcement to take place?'

'Tonight. At supper. The Stricklands already know.'

Sophie glanced down nervously at her shoes. 'It must be almost that time now. I had better go.' She did not have to add that she dreaded the baronet coming to look for her and finding her alone with Kirk, for her expressive face revealed her thoughts only too clearly.

'Sophie, I can't let you go ahead with it.' Kirk grasped her by the shoulders as she made to rise.

She lifted startled eyes to meet his intent gaze.

'Kirk?' Excitement made her voice emerge as a husky whisper. 'Oh, Kirk, what do you mean?'

Too late Kirk perceived the full enormity of his
behaviour. A gentleman did not seek his pleasure with
respectable young virgins! His only excuse was that he
had imagined she would respond in kind with a flirtatious
kiss or two, but her passionate abandonment had
aroused an answering flame in him which had consumed
all sense. In the circumstances he could hardly blame
her for thinking he intended marriage!

A searing guilt assailed him. He was in no position to
look for a bride. His duty was to avenge his brother's
death, and his own personal life had to take second
place to this debt of honour.

Sophie touched her dry lips with the tip of her
tongue. Could she have possibly misunderstood him?
Surely not! Unless all her senses were lying, she
couldn't believe he had merely been leading her on for
his own amusement. He must care something for her!
Oh, why didn't he speak? She would have preferred
one of his fearsome outbursts of rage to this dreadful
silence.

Kirk swallowed hard. Her great dark eyes were
watching him anxiously, and he angrily cursed his own
folly. How the devil was he to explain without hurting
her?

'It would be a great pity to waste yourself upon a
scoundrel like Stanton. If I were the marrying kind, I
could look no higher for my bride. I am not in that
fortunate position, but there must be a dozen more
worthy suitors you could choose from in Kendal alone,'
he said lightly, masking his true feelings.

The last remnant of joy was wiped instantly from
Sophie's expression. What a fool she was! He hadn't
been about to propose at all!

Kirk felt a complete blackguard. 'Believe me, you
are too good for Stanton. You deserve a better life than
he could give you,' he continued gruffly.

Her feelings were in such turmoil of humiliation that

Sophie scarcely heard him. How idiotic she'd been to think he was serious! His scandalous behaviour was nothing more than the automatic reaction of a confirmed womaniser who finds himself alone with any woman who wasn't a positive hag.

Her cheeks burned with embarrassment. Bitterly, she reflected that she ought to have learnt by now that her main attraction was her dowry. Men didn't admire her skinny body or her independent tongue.

'Thank you for your concern, sir,' she said coldly, getting to her feet in an angry rustle of skirts. 'But you must forgive me if I decline to take your advice. You see, somehow I have come to doubt the wisdom of listening to a single word you say!'

Kirk rose, pride warring with his innate honesty. 'Sophie, I know I have not behaved as I ought, but I swear to God I didn't mean to hurt you.' The words were wrenched from him.

'Hurt?' Sophie forced a light trill of laughter, ignoring the conciliatory hand he stretched out to her. 'Do not flatter yourself, Mr Thorburn. I must confess myself a little shocked at my own folly, but then I am not used to the society of gentlemen like yourself who find it amusing to occupy their idle moments by taking advantage of unwary girls. Or do you deny that you are a rake, sir?'

A muscle flickered at the corner of Kirk's well-cut mouth, but he did not attempt to defend himself. He deserved her scorn. He should never have succumbed to the temptation to kiss her. If anyone had walked in and seen them her reputation would have been hopelessly compromised and it would have been his fault.

Sophie waited for a second, silently praying that he would deny her accusation.

Still he remained silent.

'I hope we never meet again, Kirk Thorburn,' she said in accents of frozen despair and walked from the room, the ache in her ankle nothing compared to the pain he had inflicted on her heart.

'Ah, here comes Josh now. They must have hitched up the new team,' Maria Strickland announced. 'If you have finished your coffee, my dear, I think we should be leaving, or it will be dark before we reach Stanton Hall.'

'Of course.' Sophie obediently swallowed the last hot mouthful and reached for her gloves.

An errant beam of sunshine lancing in through the window of the coffee-room caught her left hand, bathing the ring she wore. Instantly, the huge diamond flashed with scintillating fire.

Like a beautiful rainbow, Sophie thought with a touch of bitterness.

She could take no pleasure in her betrothal ring. It acted as a constant reminder of a night she wanted to forget. Sir Pelham had placed it on her finger only moments after she had fled from Kirk Thorburn, and not all the congratulations of her friends had been able to wash away her feelings of despair.

Almost six weeks had passed since that night, but the memory of her humiliation had not lessened. She still writhed inwardly whenever she thought of her shameless behaviour.

In a way, she was glad of the whirlwind of activity that had followed on the announcement of her betrothal. They were fêted everywhere as everyone vied to entertain the happy couple, and having to present a joyful face to the world had kept her from dwelling on her stupidity, except in the privacy of her bedroom.

Her deception had been aided by the shocking news from France. The execution of King Louis was the talk of the town, and whenever she felt unable to respond in the manner befitting a bride Sophie rapidly turned the conversation into a discussion about the dreadful events going on across the Channel.

Nancy, of course, guessed something was wrong, but Sophie was able to brush her anxious questions aside, and, fortunately, her uncle entertained no such suspicions. His delight was only marred by the fact that his ill health made it impossible for him to accept Sir Pelham's invitation to visit Stanton Hall.

'I should have liked to meet this aunt of his and see where you will be living once you are wed,' he had said rather wistfully one chilly afternoon towards the end of February when Sophie sat by his bedside, busy penning a list of things she wanted to take with her.

Sophie immediately abandoned her task and announced that she would not go if it displeased him.

'Nay, lass, it ain't fair to disappoint the man,' Thomas protested. 'We've already agreed to the scheme and you know he's mighty keen to show off his home. I'm just being selfish. You'll have Nancy to take care of you and I know that Josh and Maria will make sure you don't come to any harm on the journey.'

Sophie nodded, agreeing that it was providential that the Stricklands intended to visit Maria's sister in Cockermouth at the end of the month and were therefore able to offer her their protection. A journey north so early in the year was beset with hazards, and Thomas felt easier in his mind entrusting Sophie to his old friends rather than to any hired bodyguards. The baronet himself would not be accompanying his fiancée but going on ahead to attend to urgent business matters and make sure all was in readiness for his guests.

'I mustn't begrudge him your company, lass. You'll soon be home again, and then once you are back from your honeymoon I'll be able to visit you at Stanton Hall,' Thomas continued in a voice of determined cheer.

Sophie nodded. They were to be married in the first

week of May, and Pelham had suggested a bridal trip to
Portugal.

'Normally I would have taken you to Italy, my dear,'
the baronet had informed her with one of his gracious
smiles. 'But travelling across France, the way things are
at the present. . .!' He had shuddered delicately.

'No.' He had bobbed his head decisively. 'Portugal
shall do us very well. I have friends in Oporto. It will be
pleasant to visit them and no doubt you will enjoy the
sea voyage.'

Sophie had agreed. She had never been abroad
before and she had always longed to travel.

It was the only thing she was looking forward to.

Sophie stifled a sigh. She had made her decision and
it was the right one, but the prospect of being Lady
Stanton did not enthrall her. Her future was assured,
but her feelings for the baronet had not altered one
whit, in spite of all the pretty speeches he had made her
since she had agreed to marry him.

Thank God he did not deem it necessary to show his
devotion in a more physical way!

Apart from an occasional dry salute pressed upon her
cheek he had not sought to kiss her. His restraint came
as a relief, since she was already dreading the intimacy
which would follow upon the wedding ceremony. The
thought of permitting him the kind of embrace she had
offered so freely to Kirk Thorburn kept her awake at
nights. Her only consolation was the conviction that he
would not expect her to enjoy the sexual act.

His fashionable world did not consider such behaviour necessary in a wife, she reflected, but decreed that
aristocrats took mistresses instead for their pleasure.

Pelham would not think it odd if she did not respond
to him, but deep in her heart Sophie knew that she was
not cold. Her response to Kirk's touch had taught her
that there could be a wild delight in the joining of a man

and woman, but her instincts warned that such pleasure only came with love.

And I do not love Pelham and I doubt I ever will!

'Sophie, don't forget your muff, my dear. It is so cold out here.'

Maria's voice broke in on Sophie's troubled thoughts, and, picking up the sealskin muff, she followed her friend out into the innyard, where Nancy had already resumed her place in the Stricklands' travelling berlin.

It was a well-sprung conveyance and Maria had taken care to furnish plenty of rugs and foot-warmers to combat the severe weather, but they had been travelling since first light, and they were all weary of the gruelling journey by the time Derwent Water came into sight an hour later.

'Thank heavens we are nearly there!' Maria exclaimed. 'I declare I am shaken almost to pieces. These roads are nothing but pot-holes!'

'It's the recent icy spell that has made them worse than usual,' Josh said with a placatory smile. 'We should be grateful that they are at least clear of snowdrifts, my love.'

Maria laughed. 'I might have known you would take the most optimistic view, dearest husband.' She glanced at Sophie, who was sitting next to her, expecting to see an answering gleam of amusement on her friend's face at this male perversity, but the younger woman was lost in the brown study that seemed to envelop her whenever she thought no one was looking.

Looking away again, Maria encountered Nancy's gaze, and recognised the same anxiety that troubled her. There was definitely something wrong!

As the berlin laboured over the last few miles along the lakeside Maria had no eyes for the view, but sat racking her brains. Absurd though it seemed, she was beginning to wonder if Sophie's depression could have some connection with Kirk Thorburn. That handsome young man had disappeared the day after her birthday party and Maria had heard that he had gone haring off to London.

Thinking back, she remembered how he had abruptly quit her party. He hadn't even taken his leave of them, and, unless she was mistaken, his departure had come as a surprise to Caroline Birkett too, which also indicated it was a snap decision.

But what could have compelled him to behave in such an unconventional way? The only unusual event that evening was the announcement of Sophie's betrothal, but why should that have affected Kirk Thorburn? Even if Kirk disliked the baronet, and from Caroline's conversation she had gathered that there was no love lost between them, it seemed very uncivil to walk out just for that reason alone.

Unless. . . Maria bit her lip. No, she was being foolish! There was no reason to suspect he cared a straw for Sophie or she for him!

And yet. . .why was Sophie so lacking her usual sparkle? Where was the joyful anticipation of a prospective bride on a visit to view her future home? About to be reunited with her betrothed after a week's absence, she looked more like one of those unfortunate French *aristos* condemned to the scaffold!

Suddenly Sophie's reticence on the subject of her betrothal assumed a disturbing aspect. Could it be that she never spoke of the baronet because her heart had been engaged by another man? If so, it did not bode well for this marriage!

Maria sighed. Probably she was being over-imaginative, but all the same she decided that she must have a long talk with Sophie before they left for Cockermouth. Sir Pelham's aunt was to assume the task of chaperonage, but their departure would leave Sophie without an equal to confide in.

'Here's the gatehouse,' her husband's voice cut into

her musings, and Maria joined the others in craning her neck to see more of their surroundings.

'Why, 'tis a palace!'

Nancy's exclamation was full of awe and, in spite of her determination to appear cool, Sophie also found herself goggling at the magnificent house which came into view as they swept round the final curve of the long drive.

Sir Pelham had told her that it was a modern house, having been designed for his father by the well-known architect John Plaw only fifteen years ago. Set in a formally landscaped park, it was a Palladian master-piece, framed by views of snow-topped mountains.

'What a marvellous situation,' Maria remarked, flut-tering her fan to conceal her surprise.

Sophie hadn't been expecting anything so grand and she glanced uneasily at Master Strickland when he pithily observed that such an enormous place must devour money.

'It's as well Sir Pelham is a rich man, eh, Sophie lass,' he laughed. 'Otherwise all your dowry would be spent in a twinkling.'

Fortunately the slowing of the coach saved Sophie from having to find a suitable reply.

The baronet appeared at the top of the imposing flight of entrance steps as they emerged, stretching their cramped limbs and breathing deeply of the cold fresh air after being so long confined in the stuffy interior of the berlin.

A haughty-looking butler accompanied his master and Nancy effaced herself, ready to follow in this dignitary's footsteps. He would show her the way to the servants' quarters, where hopefully she would be able to thaw out with a hot drink before starting to unpack her mistress's belongings.

'Welcome to Stanton Hall,' Sir Pelham greeted his guests, and ushered them inside.

The vast entrance hall was decorated with Italian marble columns and scantily draped statues set into recessed niches around the walls. An enormous fire roared from a hearth big enough to roast an ox in, but her first glimpse of her new home struck a chill of dismay into Sophie. She stared down at what seemed an acre of black and white marble lozenges stretching out before her and tried to imagine herself mistress of all this imposing grandeur.

'Come, you must be frozen to the bone. I have ordered tea to be served in the gold drawing-room,' the baronet announced, so plainly cock-a-hoop that Sophie knew he was enjoying their stunned amazement.

A wide marble staircase, heavily embellished with ornate carving, curved up to the first floor, where the baronet led them into an apartment as grand as its name implied. The heavy velvet curtains, the luxuriously thick carpet and every stick of furniture in the massive room, all were coloured gold or decorated in gold-leaf. Even the walls had been hung in a rich yellow silk, and Sophie blinked as her dazzled eyes tried to take in such overwhelming opulence.

'What a delightful room,' Maria said weakly, breaking the silence. 'And such a glorious fire, so inviting on a day like this one!'

Sir Pelham ushered both ladies towards it, making a fuss of finding them the most comfortable chairs.

Sophie smiled at him stiffly. She knew she ought to speak, but the expected compliments would not come to her lips. Her new surroundings appalled her!

Luckily the baronet mistook her silence for awe and, over tea, served in a magnificent set of Sèvres porcelain, he expounded lengthily upon the precious *objets d'art* that littered every available surface of the room.

'I hope you will share my love of collecting beautiful things, my dear Sophie,' he concluded at last.

'I'm afraid I know little of art,' Sophie admitted.

'It will be my pleasure to teach you.' He smiled at her with such patronising smugness that Sophie almost ground her teeth.

He would do better to learn a little restraint himself first, she thought rebelliously. The pieces he treasured were undoubtedly handsome, taken on an individual basis, but they were so tightly crammed together that the beholder had difficulty in distinguishing between them. The whole effect reminded her of nothing so much as a gaudy painting she had once seen of an Arab bazaar!

She would never had dreamt that the baronet could be capable of such vulgarity. In personal dress he showed good taste, his obvious liking for expensive fabrics balanced by a certain modesty in style, but now she began to wonder if that restraint was due to the influence of his tailor.

'My housekeeper shall show you to your rooms.' Sir Pelham rang the bell after they had finished their refreshments. 'We dine at seven. I prefer to keep town hours, you understand, even in the depths of this wilderness.'

He spread his hands in a gesture of apology. 'Unfortunately my aunt will not be joining us. She has a nasty head cold and has asked me to present her apologies.'

He chuckled. 'However, my chef has been instructed to produce something special in honour of your arrival.'

Sophie stifled a groan. She felt so weary that all she really wanted was an early, light supper, preferably served on a tray in her room.

A hot bath eased her aching muscles and revived her a little. Nancy had laid out her clothes, and she was almost finished dressing when a light tap at her door announced Maria's arrival.

'I've come to see if you are ready, my love.'

'Very nearly. You look extremely grand.' Sophie

said, half turning from the dressing-table, where Nancy was arranging her hair.

'I thought I had better make an effort, since the baronet seems to set such store by fine appearances.' Maria laughed. Her formal gown was of purple shot-silk and she gave the matching beplumed turban she wore a little pat to ensure it was in place.

Sophie grinned. 'Well, I cannot hope to hold a candle to such elegance. The most I can wish for is that the dining-room is warm. This outfit was not designed for icy draughts.'

'What nonsense you do talk, Sophie! You look enchanting. I knew that the new fashions would become you,' Maria scolded.

Sophie had indulged in several new dresses for this trip, all of them in the latest high waisted style. Tonight was the first time she had worn any of them and it felt very strange to wear something so flimsy after the stiff, embroidered dresses she was used to.

'You'll catch your death,' sniffed Nancy, twisting the last bright red curl into place. 'Immodest, that's what these new gowns are.'

Sophie chuckled. Nancy was cross because she'd had her waist-long hair cut to a new, fashionable shorter length and, even worse, had abandoned her stays. They were no longer practical, and all she wore beneath the delicate, semi-transparent ivory muslin was a single petticoat and a pair of white silk tights. For the first time in her life there was an advantage to being slender!

Nancy brought her the matching pair of heel-less ivory silk slippers, and Sophie was thrilled to see what an improvement they wrought. She didn't tower over Maria, who was wearing a pair of ordinary high-heeled shoes, half as much as usual!

'Where is Josh? Has he gone down already?' Sophie asked, accepting the silk shawl Nancy handed her and draping it prettily over her arms.

'I left him sleeping,' Maria confessed.

Sophie nodded. It was easy to forget that Josh was almost her uncle's age. He had the upright figure of a much younger man, but she wasn't surprised that he was tired after their early start and bone-shaking journey.

'I shall wake him before we go downstairs.' Maria yawned and hastily tried to cover it.

'It would have been more considerate of Pelham to postpone his elaborate plans until we had all recovered,' Sophie muttered irritably, picking up her fan.

'Perhaps, but I am sure he meant well,' Maria soothed.

'Like giving me this room?'

Sophie's wry enquiry forced a reluctant chuckle from the older woman. 'But it is pretty,' she murmured.

'Only if you like pink,' Sophie retorted. It was a colour she never wore, since it clashed with her hair. 'What's more, I'm scared to sit down. I feel like an elephant trespassing in a rose garden.'

Maria hid a grin. She could see exactly what Sophie meant. All the furnishings were frivolously gilded rococo, so flamboyantly carved and spindly-legged that they lacked any comfort. Worse, after a while the pink and white décor felt distinctly stifling. Its cloying sweetness was more suited to a porcelain figurine, a dainty Dresden shepherdess perhaps, rather than the needs of a real woman like her tall, red-headed friend.

When they entered the dining-room a short while later Sophie's growing conviction that the baronet had let pride get the better of his common sense was finally sealed.

This is worse than all the rest, she thought, subduing a desire to giggle.

Everything was in shades of red: glowing scarlet, deep crimson and a vibrant poppy that assaulted the senses. Even the massive table, groaning under a plethora of silverware and crystal, was a rich mahogany. How could anyone eat in such overpowering surroundings? Sophie was sure it would defeat a heartier appetite than hers.

'Never mind, my dear,' Maria whispered under the cover of seeking their places. 'Josh was just the same. No eye for colour at all! You will be able to reform Pelham's taste once you are wed.'

The meal was as elaborate as Sophie feared.

'Are you not hungry, my dear?'

'I'm afraid the journey destroyed my appetite, Pelham,' Sophie said quickly. 'This is delicious, but. . .' With a polite smile she laid down her fork, abandoning her struggle with the rich chicken *à l'Orleans*. 'I simply cannot manage another mouthful.'

'No matter.' The baronet smiled back at her, but Sophie sensed that he was annoyed.

They repaired to the drawing-room, where the baronet insisted that they play cards until the tea-tray was brought in.

Guilt warred with resentment in Sophie's breast as the long evening dragged on. She felt exhausted by the time they were finally able to escape to bed, where she tossed and turned in the soft embrace of her goose-down mattress.

Perhaps it is unfair of me to be so critical when Pelham went to such efforts to entertain us, Sophie thought, but she couldn't prevent a suspicion forming that pride and vanity lay behind his welcome, rather than any real desire for their comfort. Either that or he was completely lacking in sensitivity!

Could he really be so self-centred, so careless of the feelings of others?

Sophie bit her lip, her uneasiness deepening. How little she knew of the real Pelham! Today had revealed

completely unexpected facets to his character, unwelcome traits she had never suspected he possessed.

I scorned Kirk when he told me that there was a
hidden side to Pelham's nature, she mused unhappily,
and then pulled herself up sharply as she realised where
her thoughts were leading.

She was not going to think of that man! She had shed
her last tears over Kirk Thorburn. No matter how vain
Pelham was, at least he had always behaved honourably
towards her. No, she had made her decision and now
she must abide by it. It was too late for foolish regrets!

That first evening set a pattern for the next few days. Sir
Pelham entertained them lavishly, but his attitude was
patronising. He seems to expect us to fall in with his
every whim, Sophie thought indignantly, when her mild
protest that she did not wish to play cards every evening
was brushed aside with the dismissive comment that
everyone of quality indulged in gaming.

Maria and Josh were too polite to complain of his
condescension, but Sophie hated being treated like a
half-witted child. Her resentment bubbled over on the
evening that the baronet invited the neighbouring
gentry to the Hall to meet his future bride.

'I cannot understand it! When he was courting me in
Kendal he professed to admire my independence, so
why does he now dislike me saying what I think?' she
demanded angrily of Maria after the dinner party was
over. 'It seems he wants me to be nothing more than his
echo. I am beginning to believe all he requires is a
passive doll!'

'Many men hold such narrow views concerning their
wives, I'm afraid, my dear,' Maria murmured in a
placatory tone, hiding her own misgivings. She
wouldn't have dreamt of saying so to Sophie, but to her
it had seemed almost as if the baronet was ashamed of
his betrothed.

It was understandable perhaps that he had made no mention of Sophie's connections with the tobacco trade, but why had he deliberately fostered a false impression that she was of aristocratic birth? It was all very worrying, and Maria wished that tomorrow was not their last day at Stanton Hall.

They had been kept so busy that she hadn't found the right opportunity to speak privately to Sophie about Kirk Thorburn, but she could see that this was not the moment to do so. Her young friend was in no mood to share confidences.

'I think it wisest to try to get some sleep, my dear,' she advised. 'It is very late and you are tired. Things will seem better in the morning.'

Sophie snorted disbelievingly, but when she awoke the next day to bright sunshine she began to feel more optimistic. The air was noticeably warmer and the thought that spring was on its way at last was cheering. Perhaps Pelham, who professed to dislike winters in the country, would also be in a better mood.

It was a Sunday and they were to accompany the baronet to the morning service at the little sixteenth-century church of Saint Kentigern in the parish of Crosthwaite, a tiny hamlet close to Keswick. The servants' humbler waggon followed the baronet's opulent carriage, and Sophie enjoyed the drive.

'How charming,' she remarked, enchanted by her first glimpse of the tiny church.

Sir Pelham raised his brows. 'I find it cramped and inconvenient. If it were not for the fact that I come here to exchange greetings with my acquaintance I would open up the chapel at Stanton Hall.'

Sophie bit back a rejoinder. So much for her hopes that his difficult mood might have improved!

I wonder if his ill temper has anything to do with Conrad, she mused as they slowed to a halt.

Sir Pelham's private secretary, a tall, fleshy young

man in his late twenties named Simon Conrad, had arrived at the Hall last night. Sophie had been introduced to him at breakfast, but he had soon excused himself, disappearing into Sir Pelham's study, where he had remained closeted with his employer until it was time for the baronet to leave for church.

There had been little time for Sophie to form an opinion of Conrad — he had not accompanied them — but his arrival certainly seemed to have brought Pelham no pleasure.

'Is something wrong, sir? Did your secretary bring bad news?' she enquired in a low voice as the baronet handed her down from the carriage.

'What? No, no, my dear. Pray don't trouble your pretty head with such gloomy thoughts!'

His joviality seemed forced to Sophie, but she obediently fell silent, curbing a sigh of regret.

The service was excellent, but Sophie found her mind wandering. How she wished Pelham would treat her as an adult! She had always hoped to marry someone who believed marriage was an equal partnership, but it was going to be very difficult if Pelham persisted in acting as if she were an irresponsible idiot, incapable of offering him friendship or support.

On the way home Maria remarked, 'That was an excellent sermon. It is a pity your aunt had to miss the service.'

'Indeed, Mrs Strickland, she was very disappointed,' the baronet answered smoothly, not missing the edge to Maria's tone. 'Her illness has been most unfortunate. I know she regrets not having made your acquaintance sooner, but she has expressed the desire that you will take tea with her this afternoon so that she can at least meet you before you leave. You intend to make a very early start tomorrow, do you not?'

Maria nodded, mollified by this promise. It would have been a dereliction of the duty she owed to Thomas

Fleming to leave Sophie in the care of a woman she hadn't laid eyes on, although Sophie herself had met the old lady.

The baronet had accompanied Sophie to Mrs Stanton's overheated boudoir the previous day. Sophie's first impression was of a tiny, stooped figure bundled in shawls, huddling over an enormous fire.

Reporting back to the anxious Maria, Sophie had played down the extent of Mrs Stanton's obvious ill health, not wishing to alarm her friend, but she had been shocked by the old lady's air of fragility. She had barely said a word during the brief meeting, and Sophie knew that her uncle Thomas would be furious if he found out how the baronet had misled him.

Thank God Pelham's behaviour is not ardent enough to make it necessary to require a real chaperon, she thought with a silent giggle as the carriage swept up the long drive to the Hall. Otherwise Maria might insist on staying, and I know she is looking forward to seeing her sister.

Sophie had wondered if Pelham would become more lover-like in the privacy of his own home, but his manner had remained coolly dignified, even on the rare occasions Maria had tactfully left them alone for a few moments. Although she was relieved by his restraint, a tiny part of Sophie felt rather insulted. Was she so unattractive?

Perhaps I would feel better if he did show some signs of desiring me. Sophie tried to picture the baronet sweeping her into a wild embrace and almost burst out laughing at the incongruous image. He was much too distant and self-contained ever to behave as Kirk Thorburn had done. . .

For an instant she was back in Maria's conservatory. . . She could feel Kirk's strong hands at her waist, smell the intoxicating scent of his skin, taste his lips on hers. . .

The longing to be back in his arms was as sharp as a knife!

Sophie abruptly shook her head to clear it. She was a fool to remember that kiss, just as Kirk was a fool to imagine that the baronet could ever lose his icy self-possession long enough to commit murder!

Such self-delusion was dangerous. Too much thinking led only to useless regret. It was best to concentrate on the reality of here and now!

There are plenty of good things in my life, she thought determinedly. I will never go hungry or bare-foot and soon I shall have the rank and status my friends envied.

And love, what about love?

I shall love my children, she told herself defiantly, ignoring the scream of protest that rang in her head.

Determined to look on the bright side, Sophie pinned a smile to her lips as she bade her friends farewell early the next morning.

'If you need me, send a message at once,' Maria whispered, leaning out of the carriage window. 'I'm not sure I trust Mrs Stanton to look after you as I would wish.'

Sophie shook her glowing curls in laughing protest, but Maria's expression remained anxious.

Pelham's aunt had been much livelier when they had taken tea with her yesterday, but it was plain that Maria wasn't entirely convinced that someone so frail was a suitable chaperon.

'Perhaps I should stay.'

'You haven't seen Emma in months,' Sophie said in a coaxing tone. 'I wouldn't dream of spoiling your visit.'

She giggled and added naughtily, 'Anyway, Pelham isn't likely to try and ravish me, you know!'

'Sophie!' Maria couldn't help laughing, and the awkward moment passed.

When the berlin could no longer be seen Sophie

stopped waving and turned to her betrothed. Sir Pelham, who had courteously stood back to allow her a few moments of privacy, came to claim her arm to escort her inside.

'Dare I ask you to excuse me this morning, my dear? I'm afraid Conrad brought a mountain of papers for me to examine.'

Sophie shrugged lightly. 'I'm sure I can entertain myself, Pelham. I'm not entirely helpless.'

'Of course not.'

His jovial smile did not reach his eyes, she noticed.

The morning dragged slowly. Annoyed that she should miss Maria so much, Sophie tried to settle to some embroidery in the drawing-room, but found she couldn't concentrate.

What am I doing here? she thought, in a sudden panic.

Her luxurious surroundings seemed to close in on her and Sophie felt like a bird in a cage. The claustrophobic sensation was suddenly so intense that she cast aside her tambour-frame and fled outside to the wide marble terrace which overlooked the gardens.

The cold, crisp air was like wine to her gasping throat. Gradually her heart ceased to thud and her flushed cheeks cooled, but it took several moments before her panic had ebbed sufficiently for Sophie to take any notice of the magnificent landscape laid out before her.

It was marvellously executed, but somehow the very formality of the French *allées* radiating between the *bosquets* of evergreen trees, cool green lawns, fountains and marble statues suddenly struck her as unbearably false in contrast to the wild natural scenery beyond the gates.

Sophie's head was whirling. Was her betrothed like this elegant sham? Would his gentlemanly façade crumble and revert to rough nature once the wedding was over?

Stop it! Stop letting your vivid imagination run away with you because you are feeling lonely and homesick, she scolded herself silently.

She drew a deep breath. Very well, she *was* disappointed with the way things had turned out, but dissatisfaction with her betrothed was no reason to think him a monster!

'What you need, my girl, is some exercise to blow away these cobwebs from your brain,' she muttered, moving indoors again and going swiftly up to her room.

Knowing Nancy was bound to exclaim over her pallor, Sophie did not ring for her. She did not need assistance to exchange her delicate morning gown for a warmer walking dress in blue merino. A thick pelisse, her stoutest boots, a neat little bonnet, and she was ready.

At the door she checked.

Her enormous betrothal diamond winked back at her as she stared down at the hand holding the doorknob, and after the briefest of hesitations she stripped the ring from her finger and laid it away in her jewellery box.

It feels a little loose in this cold weather, she told herself, but even as she tried to rationalise her decision Sophie knew she was prevaricating. It wasn't fear of losing the diamond that prompted her, but a growing dislike for all that it symbolised!

'Should the baronet request my presence, please inform him that I have gone for a walk and may not return in time for luncheon,' Sophie instructed the footman who opened the front door for her.

Once beyond the elaborately wrought gates an indescribable feeling of freedom lightened her steps. Not caring where she went, she turned southwards, following a path alongside the lake.

An hour passed and Sophie paused to rest, perching

upon a handy boulder. She hadn't been hurrying, but the going was rough and muddy and now her weak ankle was aching. She was also beginning to feel hungry.

'I should have brought some provisions with me,' she told an inquisitive sparrow watching her from a nearby bush.

She grinned at the notion of demanding bread and cheese from Sir Pelham's haughty butler.

'Perhaps I could scoop up some water in my hands,' she added, eyeing the pebbly shoreline doubtfully. Thirsty as she was, she didn't relish the idea of accidentally slipping and falling into the lake. 'It looks shallow here, so I dare say I wouldn't drown, but I'll warrant it's cold.'

'As cold as Pelham Stanton's heart,' a deep voice behind her affirmed.

CHAPTER SIX

SOPHIE's head jerked round so abruptly at the familiar sound of his voice that she felt the muscles in her neck protest.

'What are you doing here?' she demanded, scrambling from her perch with more haste than dignity.

'I live in the next valley.'

This answer was so unexpected that Sophie could think of no reply.

Kirk Thorburn gazed at her with a hunger he could not conceal. God, how he had missed her!

Sophie's cheeks flamed.

'I. . .I must be going,' she murmured, quelling the longing to cross the narrow stretch of earth that separated them.

'Wait!' Kirk moved a step nearer. 'Our meeting like this isn't entirely coincidental. I'd heard you had arrived at the Hall and I've been keeping a watch in the hope that I might get the chance to speak to you.' He paused significantly. 'In private.'

'Then I must regret that I did not bring along my maid,' Sophie retorted, cursing her independence. 'For I have nothing to say to you, sir.'

'Sophie, surely you have realised by now what a mistake this betrothal is ——'

'Please!' Sophie flung up her hand to cut him off, scared he might give voice to her own doubts. 'Pray do not seek to interfere, I beg of you!'

Pride dictated that she defend her decision. Tilting her chin at him defiantly, she added haughtily, 'I am perfectly content with my betrothal.'

The sharpness of her answer was belied by the shadows in her eyes, and Kirk frowned.

'I don't believe you,' he stated flatly.

Sophie bristled. 'You have no manners, Kirk Thorburn!' She glared at him. 'Why don't you just go away and leave me alone?'

'I can't.'

The intensity of his gaze pierced the defences Sophie had striven to raise against her own unruly emotions. She shivered helplessly as he continued in the same gruff tone, 'I have tried, God knows, but I cannot bear the thought of you in that scoundrel's clutches. He will make you dreadfully unhappy, sweetheart.'

'Don't call me that!' Sophie's voice quivered.

This would never do! In another moment she would be in tears and he would guess she still cared for him, no matter how hard she tried not to.

'You must think me a fool to believe you have any real interest in my happiness after what happened last time we met,' she snapped.

Kirk's tanned skin assumed an unaccustomed tinge of colour. 'I know I behaved badly,' he muttered. He cleared his throat. 'But that doesn't alter matters.'

Sophie shrugged pettishly and Kirk's beautifully shaped mouth twisted. Was she rejecting his advice from mere pique?

'Are you so spoilt that you would cut off your nose to be revenged on your face?'

Sophie gasped. How dared he say she was spoilt? 'You have no right to criticise me, sir. Why should I believe your wild accusations? For all I know, your motive might be envy.'

Kirk let out a bitter laugh. Envy? Well, perhaps, but how could he admit he would give anything to stand in Stanton's wedding shoes? She would never believe him; he could hardly credit it himself!

In the past Kirk had been careful not to let any

woman come too close. He enjoyed their company, when he could spare time from his exacting duties on the plantation, but that disastrous business with Rebecca Hurst when he was only eighteen had taught him to be wary of giving his heart.

The blow Becky's treachery had dealt him had destroyed his youthful faith in women. It might have turned him bitter if his nature had been less resilient. Fortunately a passionate affair with a French widow on New Providence soon afterwards had restored his confidence and helped him to see things in perspective.

Several pretty girls had succeeded Louise as his mistress, but he had never felt anything more than a mild affection for any of them. His heart had remained untouched. . .until now.

'I find nothing amusing in this situation, sir.' Sophie glowered at him. Why was he looking at her with that rueful smile? She did not understand him!

Deeply disturbed, she knew she had to get away. 'Pelham says you are nothing but a trouble maker. I will not listen to you.'

'Then, by God, I shall make you listen, you stubborn minx!' Kirk exploded, seizing her as she turned to go.

'Put me down!' Sophie shrieked in alarm as he swung her up over his shoulder.

Ignoring her, Kirk strode over to where his horse stood waiting with well-trained patience and, before Sophie had time to grasp his intention, flung her over the bow of his saddle.

Leaping up behind her, he spurred the bay into motion, and they wheeled off at a speed that drove the little remaining breath from Sophie's lungs.

Bounced against the stallion's side, Sophie could do nothing but try to shield her face from being bruised. The ground seemed terrifyingly close and she was petrified by the thought of falling beneath those flashing hoofs.

She had no idea of where they were going. Her field of vision was limited to the shiny, sweat-stained coat of the great beast beneath her and the strong smell of hot horseflesh filled her nostrils.

The journey seemed to last forever, but at last the stallion slowed and came to a halt.

'Down you come.'

Strong hands plucked her from her uncomfortable perch, but as her feet touched the ground Sophie's knees buckled.

Kirk expected her to hurl a torrent of abuse at his head, but she surprised him.

'I think I am going to be sick,' she gasped weakly as he hauled her upright.

'Oh, no, you're not, my girl.' Kirk crushed a pang of remorse as he observed her greenish pallor. 'All you need is to get your breath back.' Propelling her towards a fallen tree trunk, he pushed her down on to it. 'Sit here quietly for a moment while I stable Sultan. I won't be long.'

Glowering after his departing back, Sophie subsided on to her rough seat. After a few moments her stomach stopped performing somersaults, and as her head cleared she was able to take in her surroundings.

'What on earth. . .?'

Mystified, she stared at the ruin before her. Once upon a time it must have been a handsome dwelling, for enough remained to show that it had been a substantial building.

Sophie's indignation gave way to curiosity. To judge by its construction, it had probably been a farmhouse. Indeed, there were outbuildings scattered close by, but, unlike the house, they were in good repair. Kirk had presumably disappeared into one of them, but there was no sound of any animals. . .nor any other sign of life!

The silence was faintly eerie and Sophie could not

repress a little quiver of relief when she spotted Kirk emerging from the stables. Getting to her feet as he approached, she said without preamble, 'Why have you brought me here?'

'To view your betrothed's handiwork.'

This sardonic reply made Sophie gasp. Her shocked gaze flew back to the ruined farmhouse. '*This* was your brother's property?'

'Aye. Those smoke-blackened walls are all that is left of Haraldsgarth,' he said grimly.

Sophie touched her dry lips with her tongue. Such wholesale destruction made her own problems seem insignificant. No wonder Kirk was so angry! 'Perhaps it can be repaired,' she murmured rather helplessly.

'Oh, I shall restore it! My family have farmed in this valley since Viking times and I have no intention of letting Stanton's miserable conniving force us out.'

There was a fierce ruthlessness in his words that made Sophie shiver. He would let nothing stand in his way.

'I hope you do manage to restore your home, Kirk,' she said with quiet sincerity.

He raised his brows at her and then nodded in curt acknowledgement.

'But now I have seen it, I would like to go home,' Sophie continued with all the firmness she could muster.

'No.'

This bald reply infuriated Sophie. 'Oh, for heaven's sake!' she snapped. 'I am prepared to overlook your disgraceful behaviour in dragging me up here, but you go too far, Kirk Thorburn! I insist on returning to Stanton Hall at once!'

'Very well, then, off you go,' Kirk replied with a grim dark humour.

Sophie flinched involuntarily. 'You expect me to ride down there unescorted?'

'Oh, no,' he said sweetly. 'I'm not loaning you my

horse. You will have to walk. It isn't far. Not much more than five miles.'

To her annoyance Sophie heard her voice emerge as a squeak as she protested, 'Five miles? But I don't even know the way!'

'Then you'll have to wait until I'm ready to take you, won't you?' he remarked, smiling at her pleasantly.

Sophie glared at him. 'And when will that be?'

'When I'm convinced you finally understand what I have been trying to tell you,' he said, dropping his flippant manner.

'You have no right to detain me!'

'Maybe not, but you are staying here until you see sense.'

'If by that you mean until I agree to give up my betrothal, then hell will freeze over first!'

Kirk laughed harshly. 'I wonder, Miss Fleming. Perhaps you will see things differently after spending the night in the barn.'

Sophie blanched. Surely he couldn't intend to keep her here overnight?

'You cannot. . .you simply cannot treat me this way!' she spluttered indignantly. 'It's barbaric. I *must* return to the Hall before they start to worry.'

'The solution is in your own hands.' Kirk shrugged. 'When you are ready to listen, I'll be in the barn.' And he strode off, leaving Sophie to glare after him in furious frustration.

Three hours later the sun had been obscured by thick cloud. Sophie looked up at the ominous black sky with resentment. Rain was all she needed to complete her misery! She hadn't had anything to eat or drink since breakfast and she was chilled to the bone.

After Kirk had disappeared she had made an attempt to find her way out of this God-forsaken valley, only to discover that she had no idea which way to turn once

she finally came in sight of the lake. The wide expanse
of Derwent Water had shimmered before her anxious
gaze. If only she had managed at least to catch a
glimpse of the direction Kirk Thorburn had taken!

To add to her frustration, there wasn't a dwelling in
sight nor a soul to ask. Hating to admit defeat, Sophie
hesitated, but after several long moments common
sense prevailed. If she took the wrong track she would
soon be hopelessly lost, and already the brief day was
dwindling. In a few hours it would be dark and the
temperature would drop even lower.

Much as she was loath to admit it, her only chance of
safety lay back at the derelict farm. Surely Kirk would
stop playing this silly game once he realised that she did
not intend to give in to his bullying?

This hope had buoyed Sophie's weary footsteps as
she trudged back up the narrow track to Haraldsgarth,
but to her disappointment Kirk had not emerged when
she resumed her seat on the fallen log.

Now an icy wind sprung up and with each passing
minute the sky was growing darker. No matter how
often she swung her arms and legs in a brisk circling
movement, she couldn't get warm.

I shall have to ask him for shelter soon before I turn
into a frozen statue, she decided bitterly, but even as
the thought occurred to her her pride rebelled.

Damn it, I won't beg! It isn't fair! I won't meekly
humble myself like some penitent when I have done
nothing to deserve such Turkish treatment, she raged
silently.

How long this wave of fresh fury would have lasted
Sophie was never afterwards sure, for just at that
instant the heavens opened and a deluge of rain
descended upon her unprotected head.

In a few moments she was soaked until, gasping and
spluttering, she rose slowly to her feet. Fighting her
reluctance, she began to move towards the barn. . .

'You stubborn little fool!'

Blinking the rain out of her eyes, Sophie saw Kirk appear, looming up out of the dense curtain of water like some avenging Norse god.

He swept her up into his arms.

'Let me go!'

Kirk ignored her shriek of protest and ran for the barn, where once safely inside he set her down.

'Thank you!'

Sophie's tone was heavy with sarcasm, but Kirk didn't seem to notice as he busied himself with closing the heavy wooden doors, cutting off the noise of the lashing rain and icy wind.

'Come over here to the fire.'

Her eyes growing accustomed to the gloom, Sophie saw that an iron brazier glowed in the centre of the barn, shedding light and heat. Further illumination was provided by a lantern hanging up on a post, and the first thing she noticed was an artist's easel placed beneath it to catch the light.

This oddity puzzled her, but she didn't stop to wonder at it once she spotted the only other contents of the barn: a straw pallet and a few items more usually found in a kitchen.

Her dark brows rose.

Kirk stretched out an encouraging hand. 'Don't worry. There are no rats and the floor is clean. I swept it myself only yesterday.'

So it was true. He was *living* here!

Her nose wrinkled disdainfully. 'How cosy,' she murmured, and had the satisfaction of seeing a muscle twitch by his well-cut mouth.

Kirk let his hand fall back to his side. He should have expected it, but her scorn was painful.

'I am here because it is the best place for me to concentrate on drawing up plans for a new Haraldsgarth,' he said curtly.

Sophie's cheeks vied with her hair. 'How was I to know you were an architect?' she muttered sulkily.

Kirk shrugged. 'I learnt the rudiments of the trade when I helped raise several houses on New Providence. Once the weather improves, the builders I've hired can begin.' He paused and added sweetly, 'I will supervise their work, but I won't join in their labours, you understand.'

A quiver of annoyance ran through Sophie, but she stayed silent, unhappily aware that she deserved his sarcasm, having behaved with a snobbishness almost equal to Pelham's.

'Occasionally, when I tire of my own company, I stay with some friends who live further up the valley,' Kirk continued in a more conciliatory tone. 'But they are farmers who work hard for their living, and I don't like to impose on their kindness too often.'

Sophie stamped her foot. 'I don't care if they are Emperors of China,' she shouted, losing her precarious hold on her patience. 'All I am interested in is going home!'

To her mortification, Sophie felt angry tears prick at her eyelids, and she tried to blink them away.

Kirk saw them, and the blistering retort died on his lips.

'You are cold and wet and no doubt hungry too. Why don't we postpone this discussion until you feel more comfortable?'

Sniffing hard to combat the tears which still threatened, Sophie wondered if he was trying to apologise.

Kirk crossed to the straw pallet and snatched up a blanket.

'Here, get out of that wet dress and wrap yourself in this. You'll soon warm up if you sit by the fire.'

Sophie stared at him in consternation.

'Don't worry. I'll make myself scarce while you

change. It's time I checked on Sultan anyway. He doesn't like rain-storms.'

He smiled at her. 'Will five minutes suffice? Then I'll make you some hot soup.'

Sophie nodded, trying to tell herself it was the promise of food that suddenly made her feel more cheerful and not the effect of his engaging smile.

Once he had gone she stripped off her sodden clothes down to her lace-trimmed chemise. Modesty demanded she cover her bare arms and shoulders, but, having done so, she quickly discovered that the least movement dislodged the blanket from its place.

'I'll never be able to eat huddled up like this,' she muttered impatiently.

Yanking it off, she tried again, this time twisting the rectangle of grey wool around her so that it came taut across her breasts, where she secured it by tucking in the loose end. It probably looked inelegant, Sophie reflected, wishing she had a mirror, but it was no more revealing than a ball-gown, and at least she now had her hands free.

Next she removed the pins from her hair and shook it loose to dry off. Thank goodness she'd had it cut! Bestowing the hair-pins in the pocket of her pelisse, she caught sight of her boots peeping out from beneath the uneven hem. Deciding they looked ridiculous, she pulled them off, exposing her pretty silk stockings, before draping her wet garments over a large cart-wheel propped up against one wall.

Sophie moved towards the brazier. She couldn't see any chairs or even a stool, and she was wondering if Kirk's claim that the floor was clean was true when the door swung open to admit him.

'Let me pull the pallet up for you,' he offered, striding forward to arrange it.

His manner was so briskly impersonal that Sophie's faint shyness concerning her costume faded.

'Come, won't you sit down?'

Sophie considered refusing. It seemed most improper to sit on his bed, such as it was, but then this whole situation was unconventional, she decided, watching him strip off his wet coat.

His waistcoat and neckcloth followed, and Sophie swallowed hard when she caught a glimpse of his sun-bronzed throat.

Don't be such a ninny, she told herself sternly. You have seen men in their shirt-sleeves before now!

'Why are you smiling?' Kirk asked, throwing another blanket over the pallet to make it more comfortable.

'I was just wondering what Nancy would say if she could see me now,' Sophie admitted with a chuckle, amusement vanquishing her embarrassment.

'Your Mrs Nelson strikes me as a practical soul who would tell you to make the best of things.'

Sophie nodded. It seemed silly to refuse the only comfortable seat available, so she sat down on the pallet, keeping a careful hold on her improvised costume.

Kirk began to prepare their meal. Swiftly extracting bread from a knapsack, he laid it on a pewter platter before carefully tipping the contents of a stone jar into a saucepan.

Placing this on top of the glowing coals, he said, 'It won't take long to heat up.'

After a few moments a savoury aroma arose from the pan, blotting out the faint lingering smell of hay that still permeated the barn.

Sophie's mouth began to water. She hadn't realised how hungry she was until now!

A well bred young lady, Sophie reflected, ought to be more concerned with the indelicacy of her predicament, but all she was aware of was a delicious contentment stealing over her. She was warm and dry at last, and when Kirk handed her an earthenware bowl filled to the brim with thick, hot soup a little sigh of pleasure escaped her.

'This is really good,' she murmured, after a few eager spoonfuls.

Kirk grinned. 'I'll convey your compliments to the cook when I next see her.'

Sophie stiffened involuntarily. 'You didn't make it yourself?'

His laughter rang out. 'I wish I could cook. It would be useful, but luckily Rose often provides me with supplies.'

So her name was Rose. But who was she and why did Kirk speak of her so warmly?

Sophie continued to eat, but her pleasure in the meal was diminished, and when Kirk offered her more of the flat, coarse bread she refused.

'Clap bread is an acquired taste, I suppose.'

Sophie's curiosity overcame the pang of jealousy that had assailed her. 'Is that what it is called? It doesn't taste like the bread we have at home. Do you know what it is made from?'

'From oatmeal, I believe,' Kirk replied absently, watching how her dark eyes sparkled in the mellow light.

She looked a different girl from the fashionably sophisticated creature he had encountered in Kendal. Her hair was drying into a riot of soft curls that fell to her shoulders, framing her piquant little face, and the rain had washed away the powder and paint she usually wore.

Sophie put aside her empty bowl and raised a self-conscious hand to her nose. Was he staring at her loathsome freckles?

'Is my face dirty?' she demanded.

'On the contrary, you look lovely,' Kirk said slowly, meaning it. Oh, she would never be a conventional beauty — her features were too irregular for that — but she glowed with vibrant life in a way that was utterly enchanting.

'You are making a mock of me,' Sophie declared once she had recovered her breath.

'Well, I must admit your costume wouldn't find its way into the fashion-plates,' he agreed so solemnly that Sophie almost giggled. 'But otherwise you look charming, Miss Fleming.'

Sophie stared at him, a small flame of excitement igniting in her veins.

Something in her expression made Kirk catch his breath. He started to stretch out his hand to her and then came to his senses.

'I'd better clear these away, unless you want some more? I think there is a drop of soup left.'

His gruff manner restored Sophie to reality. Sternly she told herself to stop being so foolish. He was a womaniser. He couldn't help flirting with her, but it meant nothing!

When he had removed the debris of their impromptu meal Kirk returned to sit on the end of the pallet, being careful to leave the maximum space possible between them.

'Are you feeling better now?'

Sophie nodded.

'Then may I ask you a question? Are you sure you haven't had any second thoughts about this betrothal?'

'Oh, Kirk, must we talk about it?' A little sigh escaped her, but she knew from his expression that he wouldn't be put off so easily.

'Stanton Hall is not as I expected,' she confessed, her fingers playing with a fold of grey wool. 'I find it rather overpowering, but I suppose I shall grow used to it in time. Unfortunately Pelham's behaviour has changed to suit his surroundings.'

'And that disturbs you? Good. I'm glad you are beginning to see sense.'

'I'll admit I'm disappointed,' she agreed, 'but that doesn't mean I believe he is a murderer.' She met his gaze with more calmness than she felt. 'Did you find the proof you were looking for? Have you discovered the owner of that snuff-box?'

'Not yet, but I've hired an agent to continue the search.' Sophie heard the frustration in his tone as he continued gruffly. 'London is too big a place to comb in such a short time.'

'Then why did you return so soon?'

Kirk merely shrugged, unwilling to answer.

Everything had gone wrong in London. Bad news about the sale of his plantation had reached him. He hadn't expected it to fetch so little and he wished he had taken more care to refute Caroline's extravagant claims.

Even worse, he hadn't been able to stop thinking about Sophie. His instincts warned him that she was in danger from the baronet, distracting him from what he knew should be his real purpose. Troubled by the thought that he was neglecting his duty, he had redoubled his efforts, but in the end had been unable to resist hiring an ex-Bow Street Runner and returning north.

'Have you met Stanton's aunt yet?' Kirk asked abruptly, trying to ignore his uneasy conscience.

Sophie nodded. 'I suppose you were acquainted with her when you were a boy.' Something in his expression told her that he knew how frail the old lady was.

'Aye, a kindly woman, but blindly devoted to Pelham,' Kirk said, his tone grim. 'She used to shield him from any trouble even then.'

He took Sophie's hands in his own and pressed them urgently. 'Can't you see what a devilish situation you are in, Sophie? Old Mrs Stanton cannot protect you. She rarely leaves her room, and I doubt if she would gainsay her nephew's wishes, whatever they might be.'

Sophie stared at him in troubled silence. In Kendal she would have pooh-poohed the idea that she might have anything to fear from the baronet, but somehow after his incredibly arrogant behaviour it didn't seem so far-fetched any longer.

'But there is no reason for Pelham to harm me,' she said at last. 'Not that he cares a straw for me,' she added, with a little grimace. 'I've learnt that much at least. He was merely pretending to admire me in Kendal, but he thinks me beneath him.'

'He was always a fool.' There was a warmth Kirk could not conceal in his voice.

Sophie was intensely aware of the fact that he was still holding her hands. 'Kirk, I cannot break off my betrothal just because I've realised that Pelham is overbearing,' she said a little breathlessly. 'Many men behave arrogantly and most husbands expect their wives to be meek and obedient. How can I disappoint my uncle for such a trivial reason?'

'Trivial?' He raised his brows at her.

She blushed. 'Everyone will condemn me if I jilt Pelham.'

'I didn't think you'd care if people gossiped.'

Sophie shook her head, setting her curls dancing in exasperation. 'Of course I would care! No girl wishes to be left a spinster, you know. It's different for men, but scandal can ruin a woman's reputation.'

She halted abruptly, giving him a troubled look, and Kirk guessed what she was thinking.

'In spite of what Stanton may have told you, I was *not* responsible for getting Becky Hurst with child,' he said emphatically. 'Oh, I don't deny I was in love with her at the time, but we were a pair of young innocents. Nothing more than the exchange of a few kisses passed between us.'

Sophie believed him. A weight seemed to drop away

from her heart, but she knew that her situation had not changed and she returned to the attack.

'Kirk, I cannot stay here overnight without a chaperon. Surely you can see what a furore it would cause?'

Kirk hadn't given this aspect of the matter a thought. He had been much too concerned with trying to knock some sense into her stubborn head. She had made him so angry that he had acted on impulse, but now his temper had cooled.

'Perhaps I should not have been so hasty,' he murmured.

'No, you should not,' Sophie said darkly, remembering the indignity of being thrown over his horse like a sack of potatoes. 'I shall have bruises for a week!'

'Did you hurt yourself when we rode up here?' Kirk was appalled. 'I'm sorry, I never dreamt you might do so.'

The shocked dismay on his face touched Sophie's heart.

'It doesn't matter,' she said swiftly.

'But it does! I hoped I might persuade you to listen to me, perhaps even induce you into returning to your uncle, but I didn't stop to think things through.'

A little smile flickered over Sophie's face for an instant. 'I am impetuous myself,' she consoled him.

Kirk wasn't listening. 'Your poor arms,' he murmured, staring at the ominous patches already darkening the soft skin.

He lifted his guinea-gold head. 'Forgive me, I wouldn't have had this happen for the world!'

'Oh, Kirk,' Sophie breathed, her right hand gliding up to bestow a gentle benediction upon his cheek.

Kirk stiffened at her touch and for an instant they remained frozen in the same position, the silence so tense that it was almost palpable.

Then in the same instant that she swayed towards

him he caught her in his arms so fiercely that the breath was almost crushed from her lungs.

'Sophie! Sophie!'

His sun-bronzed face swam before her vision and giddily she closed her eyes. With a long, shivering sigh, she yielded to his kiss.

With exquisite slowness his mouth took possession of hers. Gently, his lips brushed hers in a delicate caress, which gradually deepened as the moments ticked by, until their tongues were entwined in a passionately exciting duel.

The blood drummed wildly in Sophie's veins. Her body was awakening to feelings which made her long for more than just kisses. She clung to Kirk, forgetting her betrothal, Pelham, Uncle Thomas, everything, as the fire his skilful caresses were kindling blazed into a passion beyond reason.

'Kiss me, Kirk, kiss me hard!'

Casting aside all reservation, Sophie sank back into the enveloping softness of his bed, her urgent hands reaching up to pull Kirk down with her. For one brief moment he resisted, and impatiently she transferred her slim fingers to tug at the wrapping of grey wool which covered her, flinging it aside.

Kirk swallowed hard as the blanket fell open, revealing her slender body, clad only in her lace-trimmed chemise. It was made of a lawn so fine that it was semi-transparent. He stared hypnotised at her firm young breasts rising from the low neckline, the rosy nipples clearly visible through the thin material.

'Don't you like me, Kirk?' Sophie asked in a provocative voice she hardly recognised as her own.

'You little witch, you make it impossible for a man to resist,' he replied hoarsely, his control snapping as she held out her arms to him.

He lowered himself to the pallet and Sophie felt her body suffuse with heat as their lips met in another passionate kiss. Her heart was beating so frantically that she felt giddy, but she wanted the moment to go on forever and was desolate when he lifted his mouth away.

'You are utterly intoxicating,' Kirk said, his breath rasping in his throat.

His gaze roamed over her body and elation fizzed through Sophie's veins at the desire in his eyes. Knowing she wasn't pretty, she had never thought she would have the confidence to try and tempt a man. Instinct alone had given her the confidence to behave so boldly, but now for the first time in her life she felt truly beautiful!

They kissed again and the desperate desire for him to touch her breasts as he had done once before grew intolerable. She pressed herself even more closely to him and Kirk divined her wish.

'Oh, yes!' A sigh of exquisite relief escaped her as he pushed the flimsy barrier of her chemise aside, his long, skilful fingers moving to cup the softly swelling flesh, stroking and caressing both breasts in turn until Sophie moaned with pleasure.

At his touch her nipples hardened, exciting them both, until Kirk swiftly dipped his head to capture one rosy crest.

His mouth was hot and thrillingly moist against her sensitive skin and Sophie gasped as his tongue circled her nipple, teasing and sucking with an expertise that made her clutch at his shoulders, her senses reeling.

Through the mists of passion wreathing his brain, Kirk was dimly aware that he ought to draw back, but when he reluctantly raised his head to tell her so Sophie let out a little wail of despair.

'Oh, don't stop, don't ever stop!' she implored, eagerly guiding his mouth back to her breast.

A few delicious moments later the urgent desire to feel his naked skin against her own made Sophie tug imperiously at his shirt. 'Take it off,' she whispered. 'I want to touch you too.'

Infected by her madness, Kirk's resolve melted. He sat up and pulled the shirt over his head with an unsteady laugh, throwing it aside into the darkness that lapped their small, warm island of enchantment.

Sophie shivered with delight as his virile chest rubbed against her bare breasts. She ran her fingers experimentally over the bronzed skin, feeling the muscles beneath. The light glinted off the short golden hairs as she ruffled them between her exploring fingers. They felt surprisingly soft to the touch, and Sophie was fascinated.

'What are you thinking?' Kirk asked, intrigued by her silent attentions.

She chuckled throatily. 'Just how delightfully different your body is from mine. So strong, so brown, so hard. . .Oh!'

Kirk could not help grinning as a crimson blush climbed from her neck to her hairline as she realised what she had said. . .and how entirely appropriate her comment was!

'Darling Sophie, that's the effect you always have on me, I'm afraid,' he murmured wickedly.

Sophie's embarrassment faded when she saw the tender warmth in his eyes. 'You aren't laughing at me at all, are you?' she exclaimed in relief.

'Not in the least, sweetheart.'

'Well, it was an idiotic thing to say!' Sophie coloured faintly even as she giggled.

'You are adorable!' Kirk couldn't restrain his need to kiss her again.

Laughter died as their lips met, and their mutual passion was reborn in a frenzy of caresses, each one a little bolder than the last, until Kirk's hand slid lightly over the silk of Sophie's stocking to discover the equally smooth skin of her inner thigh.

His long brown fingers explored delicately, slowly climbing higher and higher. . .

Sophie clung to him with her eyes fast shut, her breath coming in short little pants. The feelings he was arousing in her were excitingly new and so vividly intense that she could barely keep still. . .

'Oh!' She gasped aloud in a sudden flare of ecstasy as his skilful fingers found the core of her being and he began to gently caress her tenderest flesh until she trembled with pleasure.

A liquid heat suffused her, and of their own accord her hips began to writhe against him. . .

'God help me, but I want you so!'

Kirk's voice was a harsh thread of sound, shattering the silence.

'Sophie, do you understand what I'm saying?' Kirk transferred his hands to her shoulders, gripping them tightly. 'If you want me to stop, my darling, it must be *now*, for I don't think I shall be able to if we carry on even for another second!'

Sophie's eyes fluttered open. 'What. . .what did you say?' she asked reluctantly, as his urgency penetrated the pleasure-drugged haze of rapture that enfolded her.

'This is madness!'

Releasing her, he sat up abruptly.

Every fibre of her being screamed in protest. 'Kirk?' She tried to put her arms around him, but he shrugged her off.

'Sweetheart, I'm no saint!' he growled.

All at once Sophie was catapulted back into harsh reality. For the first time, she could feel the straw prickling against her back and hear the rain drumming on the roof. An icy draught swirled across her naked bosom and she shivered.

'I'm sorry,' she whispered, flushing painfully. 'I hope you don't think. . . I mean. . .I wasn't deliberately. . .' She stumbled to a piteous halt.

Kirk took a deep breath, forcing down his frustration. 'No, I know,' he said tightly. 'And, believe me, I am sorry too. More sorry than you'll ever know,' he concluded ruefully.

He stood up quickly and retrieved his shirt. 'I'll bring your clothes. They ought to be reasonably dry by now.'

Totally tongue-tied with embarrassment, Sophie kept her gaze on the floor and nodded silently.

She had hastily adjusted her chemise by the time he returned with her dress.

'It's still damp, I'm afraid.'

'It doesn't matter.' Sophie took it thankfully.

By the time she had finished dressing she felt a little more composed and was able to tidy her hair with hands that no longer shook.

Kirk had already donned his coat and was inspecting the weather from the door of the barn. When Sophie joined him she saw that it was dark and the rain was still lashing down.

'Heavens, do you know what time it is?'

Kirk shook his head. 'I left my watch behind at the Hyndes',' he said. 'But I reckon it is about six — maybe seven — o'clock.'

Sophie gazed at him in dismay. 'I had no idea that it was so late!'

He grinned at her suddenly. 'Well, no. We were a trifle preoccupied.'

Sophie blushed, but then began to laugh, unable to resist the wicked twinkle in his eyes.

Laughter was a useful antidote to embarrassment, she decided. Her incredible foolishness had led to the brink of disaster. If Kirk had not acted so selflessly she would have thrown away her virginity and counted it well lost!

'I was to blame, Sophie,' Kirk said. 'If I had not been so stupid and kidnapped you there would have been no opportunity for me to behave so badly.'

His uncanny ability to guess her thoughts no longer astonished Sophie. 'Thank you,' she murmured, accepting the apology, even though the stubbornly honest voice of her conscience knew it was not deserved. *She* had wanted him to make love to her, and they both knew it! Even now she still yearned to put her arms around him and feel his lips on hers.

Stifling this dangerous longing, she said, 'Kirk, will you take me back to the Hall now? Nancy will be frantic——'

The rest of her request was drowned out by a clap of thunder.

Kirk glanced at the sky. 'I suppose I could borrow a mount for you from the Hyndes'. . .' He paused, seeing a look of dismay cloud her expressive face. 'You *can* ride?'

Sophie swallowed nervously. 'Not very well,' she admitted.

Kirk shook his head. 'Then I don't think I can take you back tonight,' he said. 'Sultan hates storms. He won't suffer a stranger on his back all the way to Stanton Hall.'

'But we can't stay here!' Panic made Sophie's voice rise sharply.

'I agree.' Kirk's tone was wry. He was unwilling to trust his self-control a second time. Another moment and he would have taken the gift she offered so freely, plunging into the yielding softness of her delectable body and satisfying the aching need that held them both in thrall.

A cold sweat broke out along his spine. God, what a mull he had made of things!

'There's no help for it; you'll have to come up to the farm with me and spend the night there.'

Sophie opened her mouth to protest at this abrupt pronouncement, but closed it again as she realised he was right. But how on earth was she going to explain to

Pelham? He was bound to ask what she had been doing, wandering so far away from the Hall.

'The Hyndes are perfectly respectable. No one will question your reputation once they know you stayed with them, and I'll arrange your return first thing in the morning,' Kirk reassured her.

She nodded and tried to smile.

'Good girl.' Kirk touched her shoulder briefly and moved to unhook the lantern. 'Come, we had best be leaving.'

They ran for the stable and were drenched before they reached its shelter.

'Here, take this and tie it over your head.' Kirk finished saddling up his horse and offered her a piece of ragged sacking. 'It's fairly clean.'

Sophie gazed at it, her lip curling. 'No, thank you!' she shuddered.

'You'll lose your bonnet,' he warned.

'Oh, very well!' Sophie took it with a grimace and fastened it around her head and shoulders like a muffler.

Kirk opened the stable door and the fierce wind swirled around them, making Sultan snort and back, his burnished hoofs dancing.

'Up with you.'

Sophie stared at the great stallion and her mouth dried with fear. 'Kirk, I. . .'

She swallowed hard, sensing his impatience. Somehow it didn't seem the right moment to confess she was frightened of horses! So with a silent prayer she allowed him to toss her up into the saddle, where she sat rigid with tension while he led Sultan outside.

'Hold him while I shut the door.'

Sophie obeyed, her stomach churning. She had never sat on such a big horse before and the ground seemed very far away.

The wind howled, snatching at Sophie's hair and

tugging loose several strands as it drove the rain into her face like an icy lash. Sultan neighed shrilly and began to prance.

'Steady, boy, steady.' Kirk's voice was soothing. Quickly completing his task, he vaulted lightly up behind Sophie. 'You did splendidly.'

Thankfully Sophie relinquished the reins into his care. She could feel the warmth emanating from his tall, strong body and began to relax.

Recognising his master, Sultan settled, and they trotted sedately out of the yard.

'Lean against me if you wish.'

Sophie was glad to avail herself of this invitation, but away from the farm Sultan's stride lengthened. Seized by panic, she jerked bolt upright, burying her fingers deeply into the dark mane.

'Don't worry, I've got you.' Kirk adjusted his grip on the reins to hold her securely within the circle of his arms, but even his deep voice did not carry easily above the shrieking wind.

The narrow track became rougher still as the valley contracted. Her vision blurred by rain, Sophie could hardly make out the dark looming shapes that surrounded them, but she knew that they must be the mountains, so close that they seemed about to fall on them.

From somewhere near by a crashing noise that must surely be a waterfall thundered above the storm, and she had to fight the impulse to clap her hands over her stunned ears.

'Not far now.'

Sophie nodded to show she had heard. It was impossible to attempt conversation, but she could see that they were close to a river. The rushing waters tumbled past, an occasional flash of white spray shining eerily in the dark as they began to climb once more.

Sultan was nervous. If Kirk wasn't such a superb

rider he would throw us both, Sophie thought, as the
stallion bucked and reared. Every tooth in her head felt
as if it was being loosened, and she had almost begun to
think that her ordeal would never end when she beheld
a light ahead.

Kirk swung himself down with an ease she could only
envy as she allowed herself to tumble stiffly into his
waiting arms.

'Oh, thank God,' she groaned with relief.

Kirk chuckled. 'Never mind, sweetheart. You'll feel
better once we are inside.'

Sophie hadn't the energy to contradict him. The short
but hellish ride had left her exhausted and caked in
mud; even her face was bespattered with it. A hot bath,
a soothing tisane and the tender ministrations of Nancy
might restore her, but she doubted it!

Stop wishing for the moon, Sophie Fleming, she told
herself sternly.

Squaring her shoulders, she followed Kirk down a
muddy path, which led to the long, low farmhouse. It
was pitch-black inside the low porch, but Kirk's hand
did not falter. He turned an iron handle and the heavy
wooden door swung smoothly open.

'Watch out ——'

Kirk's warning came too late and Sophie let out a
squeak of surprise as her shin came into painful contact
with an iron horseshoe fastened to the centre of a broad
oak beam let into the floor of the doorway.

'A charm against witches,' Kirk informed her
apologetically.

Sophie gritted her teeth, resisting the impulse to
make sarcastic comments about the foolishness of his
friends' primitive beliefs.

It was almost as dark inside the house as it had been
outside. Sophie peered around her, trying to judge her
surroundings by the faint crack of light showing from
under a door at the other end of the rough-walled

passage they were standing in. It was quite long and about four feet wide, she decided, and she could just make out a shelf at shoulder-height running along its length.

'Keep to the middle and follow me,' said Kirk.

Sophie moved cautiously after him. Beneath her feet was a pebble floor, and her skirts brushed against lumpy shapes, which she imagined must be sacks lining the walls.

Kirk opened the far door with a shout of greeting and then they were in what Sophie at first took to be another, narrower, passage, but it turned out to be just a short corridor which opened out abruptly into what she guessed was the main living-room. It was a small, squarish chamber, dimly lit and dominated by a massive hearth, which took up most of one wall and was slightly raised above the slate-flagged floor.

But the room was empty.

CHAPTER SEVEN

'Where the devil can they be?'

Sophie scarcely heard the anxiety in Kirk's exclamation. An enormous funnel-shaped plaster chimney canopy rose above the hearth. It jutted out into the room at a height higher than Kirk's head before it narrowed and disappeared into the smoky darkness of the rafters, and her attention was riveted to the blazing fire it sheltered.

'Do you think your friends will mind if I warm myself?' she asked, her teeth chattering.

Kirk recovered his composure. 'Of course they won't,' he said briskly.

They both moved forward under the canopy and Sophie let out a sigh. 'Oh, that's better!' She closed her eyes blissfully. 'I could toast myself all night!'

Kirk grinned involuntarily. She looked a complete urchin, but he suspected that for once she was oblivious to her appearance.

The area in which they were standing was brighter than the rest of the room, thanks to the firelight and a pair of candles glowing in their tin candlesticks. Noticing them, Kirk experienced profound relief. His will power was not about to be tested to breaking-point, thank God!

'Will cannot have gone far,' he announced. 'He is too thrifty to waste good candles. He would have snuffed them out if he intended to stay away for more than a few minutes.'

Such notions of economy had never played any part in Sophie's life, and she blinked in surprise. 'I thought your friends would be rich,' she blurted without thinking.

Kirk laughed somewhat harshly. 'No one who farms for their living hereabouts is rich, sweetheart. It is the fancy landlords like your betrothed who wring the easy money out of these dales.'

Sophie's cheeks coloured. She wished he had not brought Pelham's name up! 'I did not mean to imply your friends were not gentlemen,' she said stiffly, trying to suppress the wish that he had brought her to less stark surroundings.

'Gentlemen? I doubt if Will or his son Ned would care to describe themselves as such.' Kirk's tone warned her that he knew what she was thinking. 'I'm sorry if you are disappointed, but my friends are simple statesmen. . .'

He checked at her puzzled look. 'You would describe them as small freeholders, but, don't worry, you needn't fear for the sheets. We dalesmen are quite civilised, you know.'

Sophie gasped indignantly. She was too exhausted to realise that the strain of the last few hours was also beginning to tell on Kirk, and heard only the sharpness in his tone.

'You are being very unfair, Kirk Thorburn,' she said angrily. 'If it weren't for you, I would not be in the awkward position of having to ask strangers for help. Or have you forgotten why we have to seek shelter? It is your fault —— '

The sound of the front door banging made her pause. Footsteps followed, and she hastily composed her expression to serenity.

An elderly little gnome of a man dressed in brown fustian advanced into the room, followed by another man, similarly dressed, but much younger and broadly built.

The older man's weather-beaten face broke into a

smile as he caught sight of them. 'Why, Kirk. Welcome, lad. I'm sorry we weren't here to greet ye, but we were checking on the flock.'

'Will.' Kirk shook the older man's hand. 'I've come to ask you a favour. Do you think you could shelter a friend of mine tonight?' He drew Sophie forward. 'We were caught out by the storm.'

Suppressing her annoyance, Sophie exerted herself to exchange polite greetings with her host and his son.

'Aye, both of ye must stay the night.' Will nodded his balding head vigorously. 'Ye can have my chamber, Miss Fleming. I'll sleep up in the loft with the others.'

Sophie flushed. 'I have no wish to inconvenience you, sir,' she murmured.

It hadn't occurred to her that there would only be one bedchamber.

'Ain't no bother, lass.' He turned to his son. 'Ned, go and see to Sultan,' he ordered.

With a silent nod the tall young man left the room.

'Now, will ye take a bite of supper?'

Sophie was so tired that her appetite had deserted her, but she sensed that the old man would be disappointed if she refused, so she accepted his hospitality with a pretty show of thanks that won her a smile of approval from Kirk.

Pointedly Sophie ignored him. The impudence of the man! Did he think she had no manners?

'Mebbe ye would like to wash your hands first?' Will asked her hesitantly.

'Please!' Sophie suddenly realised what a fright she must look.

'Come with me, lass.'

Sophie followed her host to a door at the opposite end of the room. It opened on to a small bedchamber, and when Will had lit the solitary candle that stood on the plain wooden wash-stand he said, 'I'll fetch ye some hot water and a clean towel.'

It was too dark to see much of her surroundings, but Sophie noticed a rocking-chair under the window and a carved kist at the foot of the half-tester bed, which took up most of the remaining space. Although uncurtained, it had a handsomely carved bedhead of fruit and flowers entwined in an intricate design.

Experimentally, she pressed the mattress with the flat of her hand. It felt hard, but mercifully free of lumps.

Sophie longed to stretch out her weary limbs, but she resisted the temptation. Her gown was muddy and she didn't want to spoil the coverlet.

A knock at the door heralded her host's arrival. 'Here ye are.' He set down a jug and sliver of soap on the wash-stand. 'I wish I could offer ye some dry clothes, but perhaps this will do ye later as a nightgown. Kirk thought ye might like it; it's one of his. He keeps a change of clothes here, ye see. It'll be too big, of course, but it's good linen and clean.'

'Thank you.' Sophie took the shirt he held out to her. The material was fine and soft and she could smell a hint of lavender lingering in its folds.

I wonder who took such trouble to launder it so nicely? Was it the mysterious Rose?

The thought popped unbidden into her mind, but she dismissed it firmly. She had enough to worry about without indulging in such useless speculations.

The bedchamber was unheated, and Sophie shivered as she completed her hasty ablutions. Once she was comparatively clean she turned her attention to her hair. Most of the pins had fallen out and her ringlets were in painful confusion. Lacking a comb, she could only attempt to smooth them with her fingers.

There was no dressing-table, but a glance in the little mirror hung up on the white-washed wall revealed what a dismal failure her efforts had been.

'You look terrible,' she told her reflection.

Her re-entry into the living-room brought the three

men seated at the massive oak dining-table to their feet.
Feeling somewhat self-conscious, Sophie allowed Will
to usher her to a chair next to Kirk's, and a plate loaded
with a generous helping of rabbit pie was placed before
her.

'Will ye try some ale, Miss Fleming?'

'Do you have any tea?' Sophie responded without
thinking.

'Nay, we don't drink tea, 'cepting on rare occasions.
'Tis too dear,' Will informed her rather apologetically.

'Oh, I see.' Sophie coloured, cursing her tactlessness.
'Then I'll take some ale, if I may,' she said, avoiding
Kirk's gaze as she accepted the pewter tankard he
handed her.

He had changed out of his muddy clothes and was
wearing a suit of dark green corduroy. It was plainly
cut, but, watching him covertly under the pretence of
eating her meal, she decided that no one would ever
mistake him for a simple farmer. He had the unmistak-
able air of a man accustomed to authority, his manner a
blend of assurance and self-confidence that had no need
to resort to arrogance.

He is the true gentleman, not Pelham, Sophie
thought in a sudden blinding flash of understanding. He
is easy in his own skin; he doesn't need to shore himself
up with fancy clothes and possessions to prove his
worth.

If Pelham were here now he would be trying to lord it
over everyone. Annoyed though she was with him,
Sophie knew that Kirk would never stoop to such
tactics.

He is different. He has no need to impress anyone.
That's why Will and Ned like him. They sense his
friendship is genuine.

And it is one of the reasons why you love him, the
same little voice in her head said so matter-of-factly
that it took Sophie a moment to register its import.

She sat very still.

Could it be true? Had she really fallen for a man everyone else believed to be a womaniser? Oh, she knew she was attracted to him in a physical way! That had never been in any doubt, but love was more than just desire. There had to be liking too, and respect. She had never been in love before, but she was sure of that. Just as she was sure that she enjoyed Kirk's company more than anyone else's. He might drive her distracted at times, but she was never bored when he was around.

I care about him, she thought dreamily; that's why I can't stop thinking about him. I wasn't really sure of my feelings until today, but as soon as I met him again I knew it wasn't infatuation. He is very good-looking, but there is more to it than that. I admire him. He has more determination and energy than any other man I've met, and I want to spend the rest of my life making him happy.

Sophie took a deep breath. She had answered her own question.

Sophie awoke to a hard grey light pouring in from the uncurtained window. Momentarily disorientated, she lay quite still, her brain whirling.

Of course! She was at the Hyndes' farm in Watendlath. Kirk had brought her here last night after they had been trapped by a rain-storm.

Kirk. A rosy glow of warmth enveloped her as she thought of him and the tender way he had bidden her goodnight.

When supper had ended Will Hynde was all for a sociable discussion of what had brought Sophie to the shores of Derwent Water, but Kirk had intervened.

'I think Miss Fleming is tired, Will,' he had said gently, curbing the old man's chatter.

'Aye, mebbe it would be best if ye retired, lass. Ye look right pale.' Will had smiled sympathetically. 'I'll

lay fresh sheets on the bed and put in a hot brick to help
warm ye.'

He had bustled off, firmly refusing Sophie's tentative
offer of assistance with a chuckling comment that he'd
been a widower for many years and was well able to
manage domestic chores.

'I'll away and fix Dad up a pallet in the loft,' Ned had
said, getting to his feet. 'There's one ready for ye, Kirk,
if ye've a mind to stay.'

'I think I must.' Kirk had smiled ruefully. 'From the
sound of it, that rain hasn't abated yet.'

Even the thick stone walls of the farmhouse could not
disguise the noise of the storm, and Ned nodded.

'Shall I check on Sultan for ye afore I go up?'

'No, thank you, Ned. I'll see to him myself in a
minute.'

The room seemed very quiet when Ned had gone,
and Sophie desperately wanted to say something to
break the silence, but it was as if the knowledge of her
true feelings lay like a lead weight on her tongue.

'Sophie. . .' Kirk started to speak and then stopped.

She stared at him as he abruptly pushed back his
chair and began pacing the flagstones.

'I. . . I. . . Blister it, but I don't know how to say this
to you!' Kirk ran a hand through his thick hair in a
distracted gesture.

Sophie rose to her feet in alarm. 'Kirk?'

He turned back to face her, his expression rueful.

'I'd be a liar if I pretended remorse for what happened earlier at Haraldsgarth, but I don't want you to
go to bed thinking I am a complete boor. You are a
well-bred young lady; I shouldn't have treated you that
way and I'm sorry if my lack of control upset you.'

Sophie echoed blankly. 'Upset me?'

A tinge of red showed in his sun-bronzed face and
realisation dawned. 'Oh, I see,' she murmured.

He looked so uncomfortable that she was tempted to

tease him, but she shook her head and said firmly, 'There's no need to apologise for treating me as a flesh-and-blood woman! I'm not some mindless porcelain figurine, Kirk; I was as much to blame as you.' She lifted her chin defiantly. 'It was very wrong of me, but I wanted you to kiss me.'

Kirk stared at her with dawning respect. 'By God, but you are honest, Sophie Fleming!' he exclaimed.

Every other woman he had ever known would have pretended a simpering coyness, happy to enjoy the pleasure of their misdemeanours while laying the blame upon his shoulders.

Sophie shrugged. 'I know. It is very inconvenient!' She grinned at him suddenly. 'I wish I were not so outspoken. You can have no notion of the trouble my unruly tongue gets me into.'

He crossed to her side in a couple of swift strides and, clasping her hands in his, smiled down at her.

'Don't ever change, Sophie,' he said softly. 'You are unique.' And he raised her hands to his lips and kissed them both in turn before releasing her.

'Sleep well and try not to worry. You will be back with Nancy in the morning.'

Sophie had drifted off to bed on a cloud of happiness, where, contrary to her expectations, she had fallen asleep as soon as her head touched the pillow.

Her dreams had been sweet.

Sophie smiled. Not even the uncomfortable thought that she still had to face Sir Pelham could disturb her this morning.

She stretched luxuriously, inhaling the faint smell of lavender that arose from her unconventional night-gown. She snuggled its generous folds around her. It had given her a secret pleasure to wear something that belonged to Kirk.

I wonder if he is awake yet, she thought, wishing she knew what time it was.

Then, just as she was debating on whether or not it was too early to rise, she heard voices.

The sound was surprisingly loud, and as she glanced up she saw to her astonishment that the inner wall of the bedchamber did not reach the ceiling. Last night it had been too dark to notice, but it wasn't a solid wall at all, but merely a wooden partition, dividing the chamber from the living-room.

'Damn it, are you sure, Will?'

Sophie detected Kirk's deep tones.

'I hope I'm wrong, lad, but Ned seemed certain, and ye know how good he is with nags.'

'Yes, of course. Well, I'd better go and see for myself.'

Kirk's voice sounded fainter, as if he was moving away.

On the point of leaping out of bed to go and find out what was wrong, Sophie was startled by a brisk knock at the door.

'Come in.'

A brown-haired young woman in her late twenties entered. She had a pretty face, but Sophie saw how her figure was heavily swollen by pregnancy.

'Good morning to ye. I'm Rose, Will's daughter,' she announced with a cheerful smile.

'*You* are Rose!'

The girl nodded, plainly puzzled. 'Aye. I'm married to Sam Braithewaite. We live close by. Did Dad not mention it?'

'Er — no.' Sophie fell back against her pillows, stifling the urge to giggle. So much for her wild imaginings! Let that be a lesson to you, Sophie Fleming, she admonished herself, not to be so hasty in future.

Rose smiled at her placidly. 'I'm glad to see you have recovered, miss. Dad came over early to tell us how you had got caught in the storm, and I've brung ye something to wear.'

'How very kind of you!' Sophie sat up and beamed at her. 'I'll get up.'

'Nay. 'Tis a bitter morning. Bide where ye are 'til I've fetched you some washing water and then I'll help you get dressed.'

Amused by Rose's brisk manner, Sophie nodded meekly and stayed under the covers until the older girl returned.

'You were right. It is a lot colder today,' Sophie observed with a shiver when she emerged from her warm nest.

The chill in the air encouraged her to wash quickly, in spite of feeling rather stiff and sore from yesterday. Her undergarments had dried overnight, and she put them on as Rose unwrapped the gown she had brought.

'I hope it will fit you,' Rose said doubtfully. 'Dad never said you were so tall.'

Correctly guessing that the plainly styled brown kerseymere was probably Rose's best, Sophie smiled polite thanks, but her heart sank. Those wide skirts were years behind the fashion and brown was not her colour; it drained her pale skin of life.

As she had feared, the gown did nothing to enhance her looks. The bodice, cut for Rose's ample curves, hung loose on her in an unflattering manner and the skirt was several inches too short, revealing a scandalous amount of slim leg.

'Eeh, it won't do! I am sorry!' Rose shook her dark head. 'Mebbe you'd best wear your own dress after all.'

Sophie picked up the stained merino. She had hung it over the back of the rocking-chair to dry, but it was still very damp.

'Perhaps I could try sponging it clean for ye. 'Tis still windy. It ought to dry quite quick,' Rose suggested doubtfully.

'I think it is beyond help,' Sophie replied with a faint grin, dropping it carelessly on to the floor. 'And anyway, there isn't time. So I think I shall have to wear your gown if you don't mind lending it to me for a day or two, Rose. You see, I must go home this morning, but I will send it back to you.'

Sitting down on the edge of the bed to draw on her high boots, Sophie missed the expression that crossed Rose's plump face.

'Well, at least these should ensure no one's modesty is offended.'

Rose smiled faintly.

Sophie moved to the mirror and fluffed out her untidy hair. 'I don't think I know where to start,' she muttered ruefully.

'I've brung my comb. Shall I give ye a hand?'

'Would you? Oh, thank you.' Sophie hurried to sit down. 'Nancy—that's my maid—always says I haven't the least notion of how to dress hair!' Sophie grinned. 'She's right, too; all I do is make my eyes water!'

'Such pretty hair,' Rose murmured, deftly drawing the wooden comb through the tangled mass of curls.

Sophie twisted round to gape at her. 'You cannot think so! It is a dreadful colour!'

'Well, it is very red, to be sure, but I wish my hair was so thick and shiny. I'd swap my mouse-tails with ye any day,' Rose chuckled, pulling a brown strand free from the mob-cap she wore.

This compliment left Sophie speechless.

'There, I'm done.' Rose stood back and gave her handiwork a critical look. 'Aye. Ye'll do.' She nodded decisively. 'Now will ye come and break your fast? I made some poddish earlier for the men and it should be still hot.'

Sophie obediently followed her into the living-room. 'Have the others breakfasted already?'

'Aye.' Rose sounded surprised. ''Tis gone seven. But I let you sleep on; Kirk said not to disturb ye too early.'

Sophie blinked. At home she never rose before eight.

'I'll put on some elding to brighten the fire,' Rose announced, pausing by the wooden bench which stood fixed to the wall by the hearth.

Seeing Sophie's slightly puzzled expression, she laughed. 'That's what we call fuel hereabouts. We have lots of special names for things in the dales.' She waved a hand to the bench. 'This is called a scone and the corridor behind it is known as the mell. It acts as a screen to cut out draughts, ye see.'

Sophie nodded, trying to look interested. What she really wanted to know was where Kirk could have got to, but she didn't like to interrupt her new friend, who was now in full flow.

'The big passageway ye entered by is called the hallan. It separates what we use as living quarters from the down-house, which is the service area. I'll show it to ye later if ye like, but first ye had best have your breakfast,' Rose concluded briskly, pulling out several bricks of peat from beneath the scone and arranging them carefully on the glowing embers.

'Ye'll find a bowl and spoon in that cupboard,' Rose said, pointing it out to Sophie.

While Sophie found these items Rose drew on the adjustable chain hung from a beam set across the chimney-breast and swung the iron pot it held off the fire. It was full of porridge, and Rose filled Sophie's bowl with a generous helping.

When Sophie declined the offer of ale to drink with it Rose asked if she would prefer some milk, and when she nodded said, 'I'll get a jug for ye from the buttery, then.'

She moved past the massive dining-table to a door Sophie hadn't noticed in last night's gloom. Out of curiosity Sophie followed her and saw that the buttery was a tiny room, lit by a large window let into the thick stone wall.

'It is very cold in here,' she murmured.

Rose grinned. 'It's north-facing to help stop the milk turning.'

Sophie surveyed the great cheese press standing in one corner alongside a large butter churn and a long wooden bench tidily set with assorted crocks and butterhands. Several empty milk pails stood underneath, while on a shelf above various-sized cheeses were maturing.

'It were churning-day last week, so there is plenty of butter, and cream too if ye like it on your poddish,' Rose commented, picking up a jug of milk from the bench.

Sophie refused, anxious to get back to the fire, but to her disappointment Rose would not stay to keep her company while she ate but announced that she had to leave.

'I'd like to chat for a while, but Sam is minding the little ones,' she explained almost apologetically.

'You have other children?' Sophie exclaimed with an involuntary glance at Rose's swelling figure.

'I've four at home.' Rose nodded proudly. 'Three boys and one girl, little imps all.'

'They must keep you very busy,' Sophie murmured half enviously.

She liked children and suddenly it occurred to her that she would enjoy having a baby of her own. Kirk's baby. A bonny little boy, perhaps with hair as golden as a guinea. . .

Sophie blushed furiously at her thoughts.

'Ye must come to our cottage and meet them. If ye get time, of course,' Rose added hastily.

Something about her tone made Sophie glance at her sharply, but before she could frame a question Kirk walked into the room.

'I'll be off, then,' Rose announced with what sounded suspiciously like relief, and she whisked out of the room with a speed that belied her condition.

'Good morning. I hope you slept well.'

Kirk smiled at her and Sophie forgot her suspicions in the sheer pleasure of gazing at him.

'Like a babe.' Her wide mouth curled up at the corners as she replied.

'I see Rose brought you a dress. I was sure she would want to help.'

'Yes, she was very kind.' Ruefully Sophie reflected that yet again he was seeing her unflatteringly garbed.

'Have you eaten?'

Sophie indicated her bowl of porridge. 'I've almost finished.'

'Don't hurry.' Kirk sat down opposite her.

Sophie spooned up the last mouthful and swallowed it hastily. 'But we have to leave soon,' she pointed out.

A shadow passed over Kirk's clear-cut features.

'Actually, there is a slight problem,' he murmured.

'I knew it!' Sophie's expression hardened. 'I could tell Rose was concealing something.'

'Hang on, sweetheart,' Kirk said, half laughing. 'Damme, if I ever knew a girl so hot to hand!'

Sophie flushed. 'I'm sorry.' She shrugged awkwardly. 'I know I am too impetuous, but there is something wrong, isn't there?'

'I'm afraid so. Sultan's left hock has developed a slight strain. I've put a poultice on it, but he won't be fit to ride for a couple of days.'

'Oh, no!'

'What's worse, Ned left early to pick up some supplies in Keswick.'

'Don't they have more horses to spare?' Sophie asked hopefully.

Kirk shook his head, frowning. 'It's partly my fault. I should have asked Will last night if I could borrow a mount, but we got talking of other matters and I assumed there would be plenty of time to sort something out this morning.' He gave her a rueful grin. 'But then I overslept.'

Sophie was about to remonstrate when it occurred to her that he had still got up long before she had done, so instead she asked him if he knew when Ned would be back.

'Probably not until late afternoon. Will said he was planning to eat his dinner at the Queen's Head inn.'

'Damn!' Sophie was betrayed into an unladylike exclamation. 'Nancy will be worried sick by now.'

Kirk saw how her great dark eyes clouded and said abruptly, 'We could always walk.'

Sophie stared at him, open-mouthed. Then, realising it was hardly flattering, she snapped her lips shut as he continued, 'It isn't so very far. We could probably do it in less than three hours.'

'You would come with me?' Sophie couldn't keep a note of gladness out of her voice.

He grinned at her. 'I was planning to ask Ned to escort you, since I didn't think I would be a very welcome visitor, but in the circumstances. . .' He shrugged. 'It's the least I can do.'

Sophie immediately decided that she would persuade him to leave her once they got in sight of the gatehouse.

It will only cause more trouble if Pelham thinks I have been with Kirk, she thought. She bit her lip. Last night sleep had claimed her before she'd had time to review the impossible situation she now found herself in with regard to the baronet, but she couldn't keep postponing a decision.

What am I going to do? It was difficult enough, heaven knows, to reconcile myself to marrying him when I wasn't certain of the depths of my feelings for Kirk! Now I know I love Kirk I don't think I can go through with it, not even to please Uncle Thomas.

Sophie winced. The scandal was going to be immense.

Kirk's deep voice broke into her troubled thoughts.

'You'll need to wrap up warmly. It has turned very cold and that pelisse of yours isn't going to keep the wind out.'

'It wasn't designed for walking on these fells,' Sophie retorted tartly.

Kirk grinned at her. 'Come on. Let's have a look in the down-house. Will keeps all sorts of spare garments in there. We might find something to fit you.'

Relinquishing all hope of ever looking presentable, Sophie agreed to this plan and followed him out across the wide passageway Rose had called the hallan and into a large chamber open to the rafters.

It was full of interesting-looking objects whose use Sophie hadn't the faintest idea of, but then she spotted something she did recognise.

A spinning-wheel stood against one rough wall, and she reached out a hand to touch it. 'I've always wanted to try one of these,' she murmured.

Kirk looked up from sorting through a rack of cloaks hung up near the door. 'That used to belong to Will's wife,' he informed her. 'But you should ask Rose to give you lessons if you are interested. She makes fine cloth.'

He turned his attention back to his search and Sophie wondered wistfully if she would ever get the chance. In spite of the differences in their station she had liked Rose, and instinct told her that they could be friends if only they had the chance to spend any time together.

But would she ever come to Watendlath again? Her future seemed so uncertain!

Yesterday Kirk had said he wanted her, but he had not spoken of love. Coming to terms with her own feelings had been a marvellous release, making her feel happier than she had done in weeks, but now that her first euphoria was over Sophie suddenly realised with a sense of shock that nothing else had changed.

How could she have been so blind? Happiness had dazzled her into thinking that all might be well if only she could withdraw from her unwanted betrothal, but how did Kirk feel? He desired her, but was that all?

He cares about me; he doesn't want me to become entangled with Pelham, she told herself stoutly.

But he is a kind man. His concern might stem purely from chivalrous motives, answered the obstinately honest voice in her head.

He likes me. I know he does!

Yes, but does he like you enough to give up his carefree bachelor existence? Because that's what you want, isn't it, Sophie Fleming? You want to marry him and nothing less will do!

Sophie shivered.

'I'm sorry, I know it's cold in here,' Kirk apologised. 'Anyway, I think I've found something which will help.' And he held out a stout hodden cloak to her.

Sophie took it with a silent nod.

She was very quiet as they completed their preparations, and Kirk began to feel slightly worried. Was she so nervous about having to explain her absence to Stanton? I won't let her face him alone, Kirk vowed to himself.

Aloud, he said, 'I'll write a quick note for Will in case we don't see him on our way and then we'll be off.'

Kirk lifted down a ponderous family bible from the recessed shelf above the small window which gave light to the hearth. Beneath it lay a supply of writing-paper, which somehow didn't surprise Sophie. The Hyndes were not the simple, illiterate farmers one might expect to find in such a remote spot.

She sat down to wait on a stool by the fire. Staring into the flames, she remembered that Kirk had said that they did not claim to be gentlemen, but Will's conversation at supper last night had shown he had a sound grasp of what was going on in the wider world beyond Watendlath.

'Education is much prized here in the dales, though not, I must admit, for women,' Kirk remarked, looking up from where he was sitting at the dining-table and guessing at her thoughts with the perception she found so uncanny.

He laid down his pen. 'It goes hand in hand with their fierce sense of independence. You won't find statesmen like Will showing any deference due to rank or position. They judge a man by his actions, and birth or wealth alone will not win their respect.'

'You really despise Pelham, don't you?' Sophie exclaimed impulsively.

Kirk shrugged. 'I won't deny that I was thinking of him,' he admitted. He gave her an intent look. 'How much do you know of Stanton's background?'

Startled by the unexpected question, Sophie spread her hands wide in an uncertain gesture. 'Not very much.'

'They aren't a local family, you know. His grand-father was a Derbyshire blacksmith who made good and brought his family here when he retired. His wife hailed from Cockermouth and apparently enjoyed the idea of returning north as a lady, but she filled her son's head with such grandiose notions that he ended up building that absurd house.'

Kirk's well-cut mouth curled derisively. 'He also decided to send his son away to school to become a proper gentleman. I dare say Pelham went through hell, but when he came back he'd lost his accent and was more inclined to despise the rest of us than ever.'

Sophie winced at the memory he evoked of Sir Alan's soirée. That was the first time she had begun to realise how snobbishly arrogant her suitor was, but foolishly she had ignored her misgivings.

'Unfortunately for him, even after his father died and

there was no evidence left to remind them of his lowly origins, the local gentry still regarded him as an upstart and wouldn't accept him as their equal. That's when he removed to live more or less permanently in London. From what I can gather, he was able to play the fine lord there to his heart's content, but he became addicted to the gaming-tables.'

He gave Sophie a level stare. 'And that's why he's hanging out for a rich wife.'

She bit her lip. 'I'm beginning to believe you.'

Kirk's heart gave a joyful leap. 'Then you'll reconsider your decision to continue with this betrothal?'

Sophie hesitated. 'I think I must,' she muttered in a low voice, fidgeting with a fold of brown kerseymere and avoiding his gaze.

She longed for the courage to tell him the real reason why she doubted if she could go through with the marriage, but pride forbade her to make the first move. She would not shame herself by appearing eager for his kisses! It was bad enough having to admit that she'd been wrong.

'I'm glad.' Kirk carefully refrained from saying more. One wrong word and he might undo all the good he had achieved.

He stood up and placed the note where Will was sure to find it. 'It's time we were leaving.'

Sophie nodded, but she got to her feet with a strange reluctance. Now that the moment had come, she found herself wanting to stay. For a few brief hours she had been happy here!

Outside, the cold struck Sophie like a blow.

'No one would think it was March,' she gasped.

'Take my arm.' Kirk moved so that he was sheltering her from the icy wind.

Sophie smiled at him gratefully. 'Thank you. I think I've caught my breath now.'

The wind got worse as they left the shelter of the porch, and, even huddled within the thick hodden cloak, Sophie shivered.

'Oh, Kirk, how beautiful!'

Last night it had been too dark to catch a glimpse of her surroundings, but now the magnificence of the scenery made her forget the temperature for the moment.

Ahead lay a narrow, ancient stone bridge, its graceful arch spanning a turbulent stream. Beyond it, Sophie could see a swirling waterfall, descending in a ladder of pools from a small round lake whose rippling waters reflected back the pewter-dark sky.

In the distance hills arose, and on their greening lower slopes she spotted a flock of greyish-fleeced sheep.

'Those are Will's Herdwicks,' Kirk informed her. 'Tough little devils they are too.'

'I should think they need to be,' Sophie replied, noticing how the hilltops were still smothered in winter snow.

She turned to watch the stream, which she knew was often called a beck, tumble away down the valley.

'Is that the way we rode up here?' she asked, marvelling at the narrow chasm.

Kirk grinned. 'Aye. Quite a sight, eh?'

Sophie nodded wordlessly. The whole valley seemed to hang like a jewel in its cup of hills, isolated from the rest of the world.

But it wasn't completely cut off, she realised, spotting a narrow trail up the fell away to the east. 'Where does that lead to?'

'It's the pack-horse route over to Armboth,' Kirk said. 'There's another out to Rosthwaite too,' he added, pointing out a track Sophie had missed. 'But neither of them is of any use to us. I'm afraid we have to go back the way we came.'

Sophie had been afraid he would say that. Suddenly the scenery lost its power to charm away the vicious cold, and she sighed.

But as they began walking she started to warm up and strode out more vigorously, trying to match Kirk's long stride. The journey didn't seem quite so daunting now that they were on their way.

'At this rate we'll be at the Hall before noon,' she said cheerfully.

Kirk glanced up at the grey sky. 'Providing it doesn't snow.'

Sophie's expressive face fell. 'Snow,' she echoed in disbelief. 'But it's spring. It can't snow!'

'I'm afraid it can,' Kirk retorted grimly. 'And, if it does, there'll be the devil to pay with this wind. We'll just have to hope it holds off long enough for us to reach our destination.'

He smiled down into her suddenly anxious face.

'Don't look so concerned, sweetheart. I wouldn't have started out if I thought we couldn't make it in time. Only fools take risks on these fells.'

'But how will you get back if there's a blizzard?' Sophie demanded, ignoring his attempt to comfort her. 'I know you wouldn't accept Pelham's hospitality, even if he were to offer it!'

Kirk looked amused. 'No, I wouldn't,' he agreed with a slight shrug of his broad shoulders.

Sophie would have argued, but he forestalled her. 'There's no guarantee it will snow. But if it does, let me worry about it.'

Sophie could see he had made his mind up, and since he was probably even more obstinate than she was herself she knew she wouldn't get any sense out of him on the subject, so she merely sniffed eloquently.

When the going got rough soon afterwards she was glad she had saved her breath. She wasn't used to walking in such conditions and her boots weren't strong

enough. Every sharp stone on the rutted path seemed
to cut into her and her weak ankle was beginning to
ache abominably.

I shall have blisters, she thought ruefully, her pace
slowing as they reached a particularly rough patch.

Kirk turned to offer her a helping hand, but she
waved him on.

'I think I shall do better on my own for a minute,' she
said rather breathlessly, not wishing to admit she was
finding it hard to keep up.

Guessing what was going through her mind, Kirk did
not insist, but tactfully walked on as slowly as possible.

I wish I could tell her how I admire her spirit, he
thought. Most women would have been complaining
long since! She hadn't even moaned about wearing a
dress he knew she hated.

Kirk grinned briefly to himself. Once he'd thought it
impossible to find a woman who was prepared to ignore
her looks when necessary, but he hadn't known Sophie
well then.

But it would be foolish to pay her compliments, his
conscience warned. Already you have become far more
involved than is wise. Your duty is to Ingram's memory,
and she is a distraction you can do without.

Wrapped up in his thoughts, Kirk failed to register
that someone was coming up the valley.

'Kirk? Kirk! Kirk Thorburn!'

The shouts echoed from the rocks, startling Sophie,
who ran forward, her sore feet forgotten. She clasped
Kirk's arm, staring in alarm at the heavily swathed and
bundled-up figure staggering wildly up the track
towards them.

'Who is it?' she gasped. 'Do you know who it is?'

Kirk stiffened.

The figure came nearer, becoming recognisably
female.

'Kirk! Oh, God, it *is* you!'

'Do you know her?' Sophie demanded, but, to her dismay, instead of answering Kirk shook off the restraint of her anxious hand on his arm.

He walked slowly forward like a man in a dream.

The woman stopped, dropping the small valise she carried. Then, as she waited for him to reach her, she threw back her enveloping hood to reveal a face of surpassing loveliness.

Watching in thunderstruck amazement, Sophie saw her throw her arms around Kirk's neck.

'Oh, darling, how I have missed you!' she cried, reaching up to kiss him.

CHAPTER EIGHT

AFTER what seemed an eternity, Kirk disengaged the girl's arms from around his neck and stood back.

'That's enough,' he said gruffly.

A trill of silvery laughter answered him.

'Dear me! Haven't you forgiven me yet, my love?'

There was a mocking note in the husky contralto voice, and the frown on Kirk's handsome face deepened.

Recovering from her astonishment, Sophie moved forward to join them.

The girl's violet-blue eyes scanned her up and down with rapid calculation and then her pink rosebud mouth curled dismissively.

Sophie gritted her teeth. 'Won't you introduce us, Kirk?'

'Miss Sophie Fleming. Miss Rebecca Hurst,' he said as though the words choked him.

'How formal you have grown, Kirk! It used to be Becky, remember.' The husky voice was caressing and she tapped him meaningfully on the arm.

'That was a long time ago.'

The curtness of this reply was not lost on Sophie, and the anguish gripping her heart eased. He doesn't care for her, she decided with relief.

The beautiful stranger didn't seem put out by Kirk's coolness.

'A lifetime,' she agreed, 'but some things don't change.' She smiled sweetly. 'You are just the same.'

'Don't count on it, Becky.'

Now where have I heard that name before? Sophie thought anxiously. Her brain wouldn't oblige. It was too blasted cold to think, yet she was sure it was important if only she could remember.

'Why have you come back?' Kirk's tone remained as unpromising as the weather. 'Your family moved away years ago.'

Sophie thought she detected a look of remorse flash over the blonde's perfect features, but it vanished so quickly that she couldn't be sure she hadn't imagined it.

'I'm here to see Rose.'

Kirk stared at her hard. 'Does she know you are coming?'

A petulant shrug answered him. 'As a matter of fact, I didn't have time to write to her, but I know she will be more welcoming than you!' The violet eyes turned defiant. 'She was always a good friend of mine.'

Sophie's curiosity deepened. There were undercurrents here she didn't understand.

'Rose has always been too tender-hearted,' Kirk said. 'But this time you've made a mistake, Becky. She can't pander to your whims. She's with child and the babe is expected soon.'

Becky paled as the implications of his remark sank in.

'But I *need* a place to stay,' she whispered, almost seeming to shrink in on herself.

After a moment of tense silence she straightened, her slight figure becoming rigid. 'Kirk, don't try to stop me,' she said tightly, the flippancy draining from her manner. 'I want to come home!'

'You made your choice ten years ago.' Sophie had never imagined that Kirk's attractive voice could sound so harsh. 'It's too late to change your mind now. Go back to London and your inamorato.'

Bitter laughter answered him.

'You fool, why do you think I'm here? He has thrown me out. I've nowhere else to go.'

In spite of her initial dislike, Sophie felt a stirring of

sympathy for the older girl as tears began to stream down Becky's face.

'Do you really expect me to feel sorry for you?' Kirk demanded with a fury that made Sophie wince.

She had never seen him look so angry and she wasn't in the least bit surprised when Becky began to cry in earnest.

'You are cruel, Kirk Thorburn!' she sobbed wildly. 'Cruel to hold a grudge after all this time! But I won't let you stop me.' Her face turned even more pale. 'Don't you understand? I can't go back, I can't!' she screamed on a rising note of hysteria.

'Kirk.' Sophie laid an urgent hand on his arm. 'I don't know what this is all about, but I do know she is badly over-wrought. Please don't provoke her further, I beg you.'

His mouth tightened. 'She always threw fits of temper whenever she couldn't get her own way,' he said savagely. 'It is all affectation. She can cry at will.'

Sophie tugged at his sleeve. 'Please.'

He jerked his head in reluctant assent, but it was already too late.

With one last hysterical sob Becky collapsed into a deep faint, and only Kirk's swift reactions enabled him to catch her as she fell.

'Damn!' Kirk said with feeling. 'What the devil do we do now?' He glared down at the fragile burden he held in his arms. There were deep shadows beneath the closed eyelids and he could feel an unhealthy heat emanating from the waxen skin. 'I think she might be genuinely ill.'

Sophie hesitated for a fraction, but even as she struggled to reconcile her obvious Christian duty with her desperate desire to return to Stanton Hall a feather-light snowflake drifted down from the leaden sky to brush her cheek.

'We'll have to turn back,' she answered wryly,

picking up the abandoned valise. 'There is nothing else we can do.'

'Come away in.' Will Hynde wasted no time in asking questions when they appeared on his doorstep, but took the valise from Sophie's weary hand and bustled ahead to build up the fire.

'Lay her down there, lad,' he said, turning to point at the scone-bench as they followed him into the room. 'I'll fetch a blanket. . .'

Sophie saw his expression change.

'Good God, Parson Hurst's daughter!' Will's gaze flew to Kirk's face. 'What's she doing here?'

Kirk said laconically, 'You'll have to ask her.'

'I'll not have that strumpet in my house!'

Sophie blinked in surprise.

'Come, Will, can't you see she's ill?' Kirk laid the unconscious girl down and straightened to face his friend.

Strumpet? Becky?

Sophie's brain worked furiously and the elusive memory clicked into place.

'She's the one, isn't she? The girl who was the cause of your leaving home?'

Her outburst interrupted their heated discussion.

Kirk answered her anxious gaze with a tiny shrug, but Will said bluntly, 'Aye. She blamed Kirk for her condition, the little trouble-maker——'

'Leave it, Will,' Kirk said sharply. 'It's water long since under the bridge.'

'Nay, I'll not be silent this time, lad.' Will ignored the interruption. 'I kept my mouth shut to please ye once before, but I'll not see that slut blacken the Thornburn name again. Your father was my good friend and I owe his memory that much at least!'

Becky began to stir, and Will glared at her. 'Ye should have denied her insinuations at the time.

Because ye did not wish folk to think her a whore, everyone assumed she was telling the truth. When ye left in such a hurry it only confirmed their belief that ye were responsible.'

'I thought I was acting for the best.' Kirk's expression hardened. 'It turned sour at the end, but she meant a lot to me once, Will, and I won't see her insulted. If you intend to turn her out, I must warn you that I'll leave too.'

Sophie winced at Kirk's implacable tone. He hadn't seemed pleased to see Becky, but now he was defending her. Perhaps his love for her hadn't faded as much as he claimed.

Will snorted. 'Ye are a fool, lad!' He shook his balding head. 'Oh, very well, she may stay here until she recovers, but don't expect me to wait on her.'

'Thank you.' Kirk smiled at him.

'Mind, once she is on her feet again I won't house her,' Will added sternly. 'She's nothing but trouble, and ye'd do well to remember it, lad.'

This warning delivered, Will stomped out of the room, his slight figure stiff with indignation.

Sophie let out the breath she didn't realise she had been holding and Kirk flashed her a rueful smile before moving to check on Becky, who seemed to have slipped into a restless sleep.

'She is hot. I think she would do better out of this damp cloak,' he said, feeling Becky's forehead.

'Oh, let me do it!' Sophie exclaimed, watching him struggle to remove Becky's thick outer garments.

When she had performed this task with a neat dexterity that made Kirk stare Sophie said, 'I'll fetch some pillows and a blanket from Will's room.'

Returning swiftly, she covered the older girl up, noting with a faint envy how beautifully Becky's expensive silk gown clung to her voluptuous curves.

'There. At least she won't catch a chill.' Sophie

stared thoughtfully at the sleeping girl. 'I wonder what is wrong with her. Still, her fever isn't very high and she doesn't show any other signs of illness that I recognise, so I don't think it can be very serious.'

'If she's been travelling in this bad weather she's probably more exhausted than anything else,' Kirk commented. He surveyed Sophie and added tersely, 'And so will you be if you don't sit down, my girl.'

Sophie grinned, but obediently sat by the fire.

'Here, drink this.'

Sophie took one of the tankards of mulled ale he had prepared while she had been out of the room.

'Thank you.' She sipped it gratefully, relishing the glow it spread through her weary limbs.

'It is I who should thank you,' Kirk replied with engaging frankness. 'Becky looks much more comfortable now. You are very efficient. Where did you learn the knack of nursing people so well?'

'My uncle has been poorly on several occasions these last few years,' Sophie said, cupping her long, slim fingers around her tankard. 'Nothing serious. I wouldn't claim to be able to deal with any real illness, but I do know enough to make myself useful in the sick-room.'

Kirk nodded thoughtfully.

There was a short silence and then Kirk said abruptly, 'You must wish the lot of us at the devil. You would be safely back with Nancy by now if we hadn't met Becky.'

'It can't be helped,' Sophie muttered gruffly, inordinately pleased by the fact that he was thinking of her in the midst of his own problems.

'None the less, I am sorry. It wasn't my intention to embroil you in my affairs, Sophie.'

'Oh, don't apologise yet,' Sophie retorted with a tartness that concealed her true feelings. 'You might as well save your breath until I have agreed to help you nurse her.'

'Ah.' Kirk let out a low whistle. 'How did you guess what I intended to ask of you?'

'I'm not entirely stupid, you know,' Sophie declared with an impatient toss of her head. 'She can hardly stay up in the loft with the rest of you, but there is a truckle-bed in Will's chamber. I'll sleep on that and she can have the big bed.'

'You won't mind sharing the room with her?'

Sophie shrugged. If she were honest, she would have to admit that she hated the idea. She didn't want anything at all to do with Kirk's former love, but common humanity bade her answer, 'Someone will have to see to her if she requires nursing in the night.'

'I could ask Rose.' Kirk proffered the suggestion.

'Don't be absurd.' Sophie glared at him. 'Rose's cottage must be full to bursting with all those children. Becky wouldn't get the peace and quiet she needs, and besides, it would be too much for Rose.'

She shook her red curls. 'It will have to be me.'

'I'll help as much as I can.'

Sophie's mouth twisted. 'Not at night, though, Kirk. It wouldn't be proper for you to share Will's bedchamber with me.'

'Of course not,' Kirk agreed meekly, but there was a sudden bright gleam in his Viking eyes that made Sophie swiftly lift her tankard to hide her face in case he suspected how much she would have liked to spend the night in the same room with him in other circumstances.

'I wish there were somewhere else available, but you are right about the loft being impossible,' Kirk said, putting down his own empty tankard. 'It is open to the rafters, and although the cracks between the roof-slates have been mossed in they are liable to start dripping once the snow settles.'

'It would be too cold anyway,' Sophie murmured absently, her wayward thoughts still occupied by the enticing vision of a night in Kirk's arms.

Kirk stood up. 'I think I'd better go and make my peace with Will. He could probably do with some help in getting the flock to safety.'

'Do you suppose this snow will last long?' Sophie forgot her fantasies, her mind jumping anxiously ahead.

'I doubt it.' He gave her a reassuring smile as he pulled on his damp cloak. 'Try not to fret, sweetheart. You'll only wear yourself out by worrying needlessly over something you cannot change.'

It was on the tip of Sophie's tongue to retort that *he* was a fine one to hand out such advice when he could not let the matter of his brother's death drop, but the look in his eyes stopped her.

'Go on, go and help Will,' she said quietly, touched by this fresh evidence of his concern. 'I'll look after Becky.'

'Good girl.' Kirk put out his hand and let it linger in a brief caress against her cheek.

He very much wanted to draw her into his arms and chase away the shadows that clouded her dark eyes, but he knew it would be folly, so he quickly withdrew his hand and with a silent nod of farewell strode from the room.

Sophie watched him go, feeling oddly desolate. It was all she could do to curb the desire to call him back. She felt bereft and lost without his comforting presence.

'Idiot!' She muttered the word in contemptuous self-castigation and resolutely turned away to see how her patient did.

By supper time Sophie was regretting her decision.

Becky had awoken shortly after Kirk's departure and her mood had been sullen. She complained continually, and nothing Sophie did for her was right.

'Do you expect me to eat this rubbish?' she had demanded angrily when Sophie had set bread and cheese before her a little after noon.

'The men did not complain, and they'd been out working in bad weather,' Sophie retorted.

Becky sniffed disdainfully. 'Will Hynde is a peasant,' she declared. 'He wouldn't know good food if he saw it.'

Gritting her teeth, Sophie removed the tray she had prepared. 'As you wish, but there isn't anything else,' she warned.

'Why not? Do you intend to starve me?'

Sophie let this gibe pass, refusing to let the petulance in Becky's tone upset her. 'Will didn't have time to cook dinner.'

'What happened to Mally?' Becky saw her look of incomprehension and added impatiently, 'She used to be the servant here.'

Sophie remembered Will apologising for not being able to offer her a maid to assist her. 'I think she left to get married. Will mentioned that he had tried a couple of others, but nowadays he prefers to manage on his own. Rose told me that she helps out in the dairy and with the laundry and——'

'Oh, never mind all that!' Becky interrupted rudely. 'If Will was busy, why didn't you cook the meal?'

Sophie resisted the temptation to point out that she had been kept busy sorting linen and organising the necessary changes to Will's bedchamber. Any explanation would doubtless be interpreted as an excuse.

'And you've let the fire die down! I shall freeze to death.'

The room was still warm, but Sophie decided to humour her, and placed more elding on the fire.

'Thank you.' Becky's tone was wreathed in sarcasm.

'Would you like something to drink?' Sophie ignored this provocation.

Becky nodded grudgingly and Sophie brought her a cup of cool milk.

She drained it and then burst out abruptly, 'Who are

you anyway and what are you doing here? I've never heard of any Flemings living in Watendlath.'

'My home is in Kendal,' Sophie answered with more composure than she felt. 'I came up here to visit. . .a friend——'

'You came to visit Kirk?' Becky demanded, seizing on Sophie's slight hesitation.

'No!' Sophie moderated her tone. 'No. I encountered him by accident and when the storm broke he suggested taking shelter here.'

'Really? How very convenient!'

Becky's pansy eyes rolled disbelievingly and Sophie experienced a flicker of alarm. Was Becky a naturally suspicious person or was it that her story sounded weak? If a stranger did not believe her, then what chance was there that Pelham would accept it as true?

Fortunately for Sophie's nerves, Becky soon lost interest in her and returned to her own affairs.

'I don't understand why Kirk couldn't take me to Rose's cottage,' she announced petulantly.

'He told you why.' Sophie strove for patience. 'Rose must not be bothered with guests in her present condition.'

'He knows Will dislikes me.' Becky ignored Sophie's answer, a sulky pout disfiguring her perfect rosebud mouth. 'I don't want to stay here.'

'There's nowhere else.' Sophie tactfully forbore to mention Will's reaction.

'Oh, how I wish Haraldsgarth was still as it used to be!' Becky let out a plaintive sigh.

'You know about the fire?' Sophie enquired sharply. 'I thought you were living in London.'

Becky's lovely face assumed a secretive expression. 'I was.' She paused for a moment and then continued airily, 'I saw the ruins on my way up the dale.'

This explanation rang false to Sophie, but before she

could say another word Becky snuggled down into her
blanket and announced she was tired.

'I want to sleep,' she declared imperiously. 'Go
away.'

Seething, Sophie removed the dirty cup and withdrew, seeking refuge in the down-house.

If she speaks to me like that again, I'll. . . I'll. . .

The angry voice in her head stuttered to a halt.

What could she do? She had promised Kirk she
would help him, and, in any case, she was trapped here
until the snow stopped.

Even then, I'll probably not be able to leave until it
melts, she thought to herself gloomily. My ankle won't
stand that rough walk in the snow.

All she could hope for was that the weather would
improve before Nancy was driven frantic. As for
Pelham, well, she doubted if he would really care
whether she was lost on the fells or not.

She swallowed a painful lump in her throat. Kirk had
been right. Pelham only wanted her for her money. All
those compliments were just a ploy to turn her up
sweet.

A little sigh escaped her. If she were honest with
herself, she had known the truth almost from the start,
but she had let his flattery lull her into thinking that she
could make a success of their marriage.

Perhaps if she were as beautiful as Becky things
might have been different. . .

Stop it, Sophie Fleming, stop this deplorable self-pity
at once, her conscience said firmly. Don't forget that
Pelham thinks you beneath him and his pride is such
that a face like Helen of Troy's would not change his
views. Anyway, do you really want him to be in love
with you?

No, I don't, I don't even like the man, she realised
with a start of surprise. His mouth is thin and hard and

his eyes are like chips of hazel ice. Why did I never realise it before?

Because you were too dazzled by his sophistication, she answered herself, shivering slightly. She wanted to push the painful revelation away, but an innate honesty warned her not to ignore the truth.

I wouldn't be in this mess now if I had trusted my instincts, she thought ruefully. I ought to have told Uncle Thomas no at the beginning.

Instead, she had taken the easy way out, only to find herself trapped.

Sophie shuddered. What was she going to do?

'Sophie? Sophie, why are you in here? It's cold enough to freeze your marrow.'

'Rose! You shouldn't have come out in this weather!'

Rose shook her head. ''Tis only a step from my cottage,' she said stoutly. 'Kirk called to tell me that Becky was here and taken bad.'

'Yes, but she's sleeping now,' Sophie explained.

'Then we'd best try to be quiet, since we can't stop out here,' Rose said practically.

She turned to lead the way back to the living-room, and Sophie followed obediently. To her relief, Becky didn't stir at the sound made by Rose's clogs on the flagged floor.

'She don't seem too bad. Just a touch of low fever, I reckon,' Rose stated, removing her shawl and draping it over a stool by the hearth to dry.

'That's my thought too.' Sophie was glad to have her diagnosis confirmed.

'Dad don't keep much in the way of remedies,' Rose continued quietly, searching in the wicker basket she carried on one arm. 'So I've brung ye a few things ye might need.' She held up a stubby brown bottle. 'This is sorrel-leaf tea, 'tis champion for cooling a fever. Ye can give her some when she wakes.'

Delving into the basket again, she produced a stone

jar. 'Beef jelly,' she said. 'Sounds as if she needs building up.'

Her thick eyebrows drew together. 'Ye look as if ye could do with some an' all, Sophie, lass. Has she been playing her tricks off on ye?'

Sophie gave a shaky little laugh. 'You are very perceptive, Rose,' she answered, careful to keep her voice low.

'I don't know about that, but I know Becky used to enjoy causing a stir.' Rose shook her head disapprovingly. 'Don't let her aggravate ye.'

'Was she always so petulant, Rose?' Sophie asked impetuously.

Rose hesitated and Sophie added quickly, 'Forgive me, you are her friend. I shouldn't have said anything.'

'It's true enough we were friends in the old days, but even then I don't think I was blind to Becky's faults,' Rose announced with a faintly rueful smile. 'Aye, she was often rude and ungrateful, but she could be very charming when she wanted and, well. . .somehow ye ended up forgiving her bad moods.'

Rose's smile deepened.

'She was so very pretty, ye see. Like something out of a picture-book.'

'Weren't you jealous?'

Rose chuckled. 'More times than I can count! Mind, there were compensations. Becky was an only child and her parents spoilt her. Parson might rant about self-denial in the pulpit, but he never refused her anything. Oh, the cakes and sweetmeats she used to share with us when we were children!'

Rose shook her head with a little chuckle at the memory.

'Was Kirk interested in her then?' Sophie asked, trying desperately to sound casual.

Rose gave her a sharp look, but answered readily enough. 'Nay. Like most lads, he thought us girls nothing but a plaguy nuisance. It wasn't until after he came home, when he'd finished at the grammar school in Cockermouth, that his attitude changed. While he'd been away Becky had grown up.'

An expressive shrug shook Rose's plump shoulders.

'They began courting soon afterwards and everyone thought they would make a match of it. Kirk was mad for her! She led him a merry dance, but he put up with her whims. I just hope he's learnt more sense than to fall for her again, or else he'll rue the day, if I know Becky.'

Sophie nodded, striving to suppress the irrational jealousy which tore through her. Was Kirk really as immune to Becky's charms as he claimed?

'Ye know what happened next? About the babe, I mean?'

This demand forced Sophie to pay attention. 'Kirk says he was not the father.'

'Not many folk believed him, I can tell ye,' Rose retorted. 'Dad did and so did me and Ned, 'cos we knew Kirk. He's no liar, but we couldn't understand it. There'd never been any hint that Becky was seeing anyone else.'

'Do you think Kirk knew who it was?' Sophie fiddled with the bottle of sorrel-leaf tea that Rose had handed to her.

'I'm not sure. Sometimes I think he did guess, but wild horses couldn't drag a word out of him on the subject.' Rose sighed. 'Gossip is a nasty business. 'Tis a thousand pities that his return home has been tarred with the same brush.'

'Do you believe Sir Pelham Stanton had Ingram murdered?'

Rose's eyes widened. 'That's a blunt question, lass.'

'I have a particular reason for asking.' Sophie strove to keep her voice level. 'A private matter, you understand.'

Rose gave her a curious look. 'Well, for your sake, I hope it ain't that Stanton is a friend of yours, Sophie, for he's not well thought of in these parts. He's a hard landlord and most folk hereabouts dislike that crowd of off-comers he's imported from London to serve him. They're a bad lot, and aye, I reckon Kirk might be right. I wouldn't put it past one of them to carry out Stanton's dirty work for him.'

'I see,' said Sophie in a rather breathless voice.

Anxious to avoid Rose's searching gaze, she moved towards the fire.

'I'll warm this tisane for Becky,' she murmured over her shoulder.

'Aye. Well, I'd best be going or else they'll be wondering what has become of me,' Rose replied. She picked up her shawl and wound it tightly around her and Sophie prepared to escort her to the door.

'Nay, carry on with what ye are doing; I'll see myself out.' Rose took a few steps and then paused. 'You'll send word if ye need any help?' she said.

'Of course.'

Rose nodded briskly and was gone.

After her departure, Sophie was uncannily aware of the silence, broken only by the spluttering of the fire.

Rose meant more by that offer of help than it sounded, she decided, sure that Rose had somehow guessed she was deeply involved with the master of Stanton Hall. If only she'd had the courage to explain. . .

But Rose's fierce condemnation of the baronet had shaken Sophie. It was further proof, if any were needed, of the truth of Kirk's claims and the foolishness of her own behaviour in accepting the suit of a man she hardly knew.

Sophie sighed. What a dreadful tangle it all was!

Becky groaned, and the sound immediately roused

Sophie from her contemplations. She hurried over to the bench, but Becky was still asleep, although restless.

Realising that her patient would soon be awake, Sophie finished warming the sorrel-leaf tea and poured it into a cup. Once it was ready she decided she might as well prepare the strengthening broth Rose had brought too. Becky hadn't eaten anything earlier, but perhaps she could be tempted to try this.

It didn't take long to empty the contents of the jar into a saucepan and suspend it over the fire, but Becky continued to sleep on, so Sophie sat down again.

Staring into the flames, she found her thoughts kept returning to what Rose had said, and in an effort to banish them she leapt to her feet. Casting about for some task to keep her occupied, she began to light the candles, for it was growing gloomy.

The winter dark made it seem later than the actual hour, but, even so, if Will didn't appear soon it would be another cold meal.

Perhaps I should prepare supper.

The idea, sparked by Becky's demand, planted itself in Sophie's head. Surely Will wouldn't mind if she helped? And it would give her something to do.

After checking once more on Becky, Sophie set to work.

She found root vegetables stored in the down-house and enough ham to create savoury stew. Peeling the vegetables and slicing them was a routine that soothed her strained nerves, but she couldn't help wishing for the sophisticated kitchen range she was used to in the Stramongate once her preparations were complete.

'Oh, well, if it burns, it burns,' she muttered, filling the kail-pot with her concoction. On its three short legs it could be positioned to stand neatly over the fire, but Sophie suspected that its contents would need frequent stirring to prevent a disaster.

She had just finished when Becky woke and demanded a drink.

'What is this disgusting stuff?' she snapped, thrusting the half-full cup back into Sophie's hands.

'Sorrel-leaf tea. Rose brought it over for you. She says it is good for combating fever.'

Becky squirmed. 'It's horrid.' To Sophie's surprise she evinced no further interest in the news that Rose had visited but said impatiently, 'Bring me something else, for God's sake.'

Realising that it would probably do more harm than good to insist, Sophie acquiesced and offered warm broth instead.

Becky drank it greedily and then lay back against the pillows Sophie had propped behind her.

'I want to go to bed,' she said pettishly. 'My neck aches and I cannot get comfortable lying here.'

Sophie hesitated. Will's chamber was cold.

'Oh, don't fuss,' Becky cried irritably when she said so. 'Surely there are enough blankets, and you can warm the bed for me with a hot brick, or are you too stupid to see how easily the thing can be done if only you will make shift?'

Sophie compressed her lips, swallowing down her anger.

'You could try asking more politely if you want people to help you,' she said tightly.

'Oh, indeed! I must remember that in future in case I should meet anyone worthy of my regard.'

The big pansy eyes mocked, and Sophie was on the point of losing her temper when she heard the sound of approaching footsteps that had been previously drowned out by Becky's taunting voice.

'Kirk! Oh, Kirk, come and tell this fool to do as I say!'

Sophie spun round to meet Kirk's startled gaze.

'She won't let me go to bed, and I am so tired!'

Becky stretched out her arms to him in a pretty gesture of appeal, and Sophie experienced a flicker of jealousy as Kirk's expression softened.

He moved closer to the bench and took one of Becky's trembling hands. 'Don't upset yourself,' he said in a far gentler voice than any he had used previously to her.

Sophie suppressed a sniff of indignation. Surely he wasn't going to be fooled by this piece of nonsense? Granted, Becky looked the picture of distressed frailty, but Sophie was rapidly coming to the conclusion that there was nothing much wrong with her other than an over-developed taste for dramatics!

'It is cold in the chamber——' she began, but Kirk interrupted her.

'I'll fetch a brazier to warm it once you've got the bed ready,' he said without turning his head.

Sophie stared at his broad back, experiencing a most unladylike desire to hammer her clenched fists against it. Oh, why couldn't he see sense?

Her stomach plummeted.

Was history about to repeat itself? Rose had said that he could never resist Becky's wiles, and Kirk's ridiculous behaviour seemed proof that she was right, in spite of his assertions that the lovely blonde no longer meant anything to him.

Over Kirk's shoulder Becky flashed her a smile that reminded Sophie of nothing so much as a cat who'd got at the cream-bowl. 'Well, go on, then,' she said sweetly.

Sophie spun on her heel and marched out of the room.

'You needn't bother trying to finish. I know it is inedible!'

Sophie thrust an errant lock of hair behind her ear and glared at Kirk Thorburn.

They were alone in the living-room. Will and Ned

had retired early to bed, Will worn out by his exertions in getting the Herdwicks to safety and Ned by the struggle to return to the dale in thickening snow.

He had brought a copy of the *Cumberland Pacquet* with him, along with sundry provisions, and over supper the two Hyndes had discussed a lurid report which claimed that the imprisoned Queen of France had gone mad with grief, locked away from the world in her bleak tower in the temple gardens, but even this shocking news failed to pierce Sophie's gloomy abstraction.

Earlier in the evening Kirk had closeted himself with Becky, emerging only when supper was ready. Then, to Sophie's chagrin, he had excused himself to attend to Sultan.

'Well, I suppose we'd best sit down and eat like the lad said,' Will announced in a cheerful tone, breaking the moment of awkward silence after Kirk's departure. 'There's no sense in waiting when it smells so good.'

Sophie finished ladling the stew into bowls and handed them round, but she did not immediately sit down. 'Please don't let it grow cold on my account. I'll be back as soon as I've seen whether Becky wants any.'

Will's smile faded as he acknowledged her remark with a curt nod.

It didn't surprise Sophie that Becky spurned the simple fare on offer. Instead she asked for a cup of milk and drank it thirstily.

'Will you try some more of Rose's sorrel-leaf remedy?'

'No!' Becky pulled a face.

'Then I'll leave you.'

Becky's mouth fell open and Sophie experienced a spurt of satisfaction as she turned away.

Let that be a lesson to you, she thought savagely. If the older girl was determined to be rude and hostile, then two could play at that game. She would do her duty, but no more!

She could feel Becky's eyes boring into her back, but her relief at quitting the chamber was short-lived.

'Oh, heavens, it's much too salty!' she exclaimed after taking one mouthful of the meal she had so laboriously prepared.

'Is it?' Will enquired. 'Tastes all right to me.'

Sophie shot him a suspicious glance.

'Aye, I like a bit of a bite to my stew,' Ned said, a rare grin tempering his usual laconic brevity.

Sophie blinked away a sudden tear as she watched them manfully ploughing their way through to the bottom of their bowls.

They were trying to be kind to her, and Sophie responded by doing her best to reply sensibly to any questions put to her during the discussion that followed, but she found it hard to concentrate. She was too achingly aware of Kirk's continuing absence.

Was he trying to avoid her?

She pushed aside her unwanted stew, her appetite destroyed. Even if it had turned out as well as she had hoped, it would have choked her.

The Hyndes had almost finished by the time Kirk came in, and although he apologised for taking so long Sophie sensed his mind was far away.

Will took a last pull at his ale and rose, yawning, to his feet. 'If ye'll excuse me, I'm away to bed. It's been a hard day.'

Ned nodded and also stood up. 'I'll come with ye, Dad.'

When they had gone Sophie filled a bowl and banged it down on the table.

'Your supper is ready if you want it,' she said coldly.

Kirk sat down promptly and smiled at her. 'Thank you.'

Sophie meant to turn away, but she couldn't prevent

herself from watching as he raised the spoon to his
mouth.

Kirk half choked. 'It's a little. . .hot.'

'Hot! You lying hypocrite, it's damned well burnt,
and no wonder!' Sophie planted her balled fists on her
hips and glared at him.

'If it is, then it's my own fault,' Kirk answered mildly.

His unexpected meekness was the last straw.

Sophie exploded.

'Have you quite finished?'

Temporarily out of breath, Sophie nodded
truculently.

Kirk laid down his spoon.

'You're right. It is too salty, but I hadn't intended to
say so.'

His frankness took the wind out of Sophie's sails,
and, seeing that she was beginning to calm down, Kirk
continued in the same level voice, 'You see, I knew you
had gone to a great deal of trouble to cook something
for everyone when you were already busy looking after
Becky.'

Sophie blinked. She didn't think he'd noticed!

'I'm sorry if you found my prevarication offensive.
That's the last thing I wanted; I owe you too much
already.'

Kirk regarded her steadily, and Sophie began to
blush.

'I forgot to allow for the fact that the ham would be
salty,' she muttered, sheepishly regarding the tips of
her boots.

'Damn the stew!' Kirk sprang to his feet and came to
put his arms around her. 'It doesn't matter a toss. All I
care about is that you shouldn't be upset.'

Summoning all her will-power, Sophie placed her
hands flat against the broad plain of his chest and
held him off.

'Oh, really? In that case, why have you been avoiding me, Kirk Thorburn?'

'Avoiding you? What maggot has got into your brain now, you little shrew?' Kirk demanded, looking so stunned by this accusation that Sophie quite overlooked his unflattering appellation.

'You spent half the evening in there,' she cried, waving an agitated arm in the direction of Will's chamber, 'and then you disappear into the stables! Is it any wonder I should think you were avoiding me?'

Kirk tightened his grip on her narrow waist.

'I think this cold weather has turned your wits, my girl,' he declared.

'Oh. . .oh, you. . .' Sophie squirmed in his hold.

She opened her mouth to continue the argument, but Kirk swiftly put a stop to her protests by the simple expedient of kissing her.

At the touch of his lips, Sophie's anger melted. The tension went out of her taut limbs and she allowed herself to relax into his embrace, accepting the comfort of being held in his strong arms.

She clung to him, relishing the warmth of lips against her own, but to her disappointment Kirk did not seek to deepen the kiss, but released her after an all too brief moment.

'I'm sorry I flew into a temper,' she whispered, gazing into his vivid eyes.

He was still standing very close, and Sophie saw a muscle flicker at the corner of his mouth, but there was no trace of amusement in his voice when he answered her.

'There's no need to apologise. I should have had more sense and waited until after supper to attend to Sultan, but I wanted to be sure of a moment alone with you. You see, I have an idea to suggest to you.'

Sophie gazed at him anxiously. 'Is it about Becky?' she blurted.

'Becky?' Kirk's expression was puzzled. 'What has she got to do with it?'

'You don't deny that you spent a long time with her this evening?' Recovering herself, Sophie tilted her chin. 'Or that you took her part this afternoon?'

'Did that rankle?'

'You practically ordered me out of the room!'

Kirk coughed ruefully. 'I never meant to treat you like a servant, sweetheart. I just thought it would be easier on everyone if Becky was safely tucked up in bed before supper.'

He grinned suddenly. 'But if I'd tried to suggest it, Becky would have been determined to remain on that bench all night! That's why I wanted to hurry, before she changed her mind.'

Sophie nodded. His explanation made sense, but somehow she didn't feel reassured. You are turning into a jealous woman, Sophie Fleming, she thought to herself with rueful dismay.

'Surely you didn't imagine there was anything more to it than that?' Kirk stared at her hard.

'No, of course not,' Sophie lied quickly.

'Good.' Kirk heaved a sigh of relief.

Sophie thought it prudent to change the subject.

'Would you like something else to eat? I can easily——'

'Thank you, but no. I'm not hungry,' Kirk interrupted with one of his charming smiles, and then, putting his arm around Sophie, he steered her towards the settle.

'Let's sit down,' he said.

'What was it that you wanted to tell me?' Sophie asked once they were comfortable.

'I've asked Ned if I can borrow his horse in the morning, and he's agreed, so I intend to try and get a message through to your Nancy.'

'But Kirk, it's too dangerous!' Sophie paled and laid

an urgent hand on his arm. 'Ned said he'd had a terrible journey home.'

'He probably did.' Kirk did not appear unduly concerned.

'I don't want you to run any risks!' Sophie's fingers tightened and Kirk gently removed them from his arm.

Holding both her hands lightly in his own clasp, he said, 'I don't intend to, sweetheart, but we both know Nancy will be desperately worried by now, and I feel it is my responsibility to let her know you are safe.'

'But even if you make it to Stanton Hall Pelham won't receive you!' Sophie pulled her hands free, waving them in wild agitation. 'He might refuse to let you see Nancy.'

'Perhaps. But I shall find a way all the same.' He smiled at her, his confidence unimpaired. 'There is no point in trying to dissuade me. My mind's made up.'

Sophie glared at him. 'You are a very stubborn man, Kirk Thorburn.'

'I know,' he replied tranquilly.

CHAPTER NINE

SOPHIE crept noiselessly to drape a thick shawl over the window. The pale light of dawn was instantly cut off and gloom descended once more upon the stuffy bedchamber.

It had been a very long night.

Becky had woken up just as Sophie slipped wearily between the sheets of the little truckle-bed, and at first Sophie had been inclined to think that she was exaggerating her aches and pains in a bid for attention. However, it was soon clear that Becky's fever had taken a turn for the worse.

She had tossed and turned all night, keeping Sophie busy bathing her forehead with cool water and trying to get her to take a few sips of medicine, before finally falling into a deeper sleep only moments ago.

Sophie stretched her weary limbs. Her eyes felt gritty from lack of sleep and she longed to snatch away the shawl and throw the window wide open so that she could feel the sunlight on her face and breathe in some fresh air.

Not that she would ever do such a foolish thing, of course!

The sound of movement coming from the adjoining room informed her that someone else was astir, and with a last look at her patient Sophie slipped from the chamber.

'Good morning. Did you know that the snow has stopped at last —?'

Kirk's cheerful greeting came to an abrupt halt when he saw the dark shadows beneath eyes which lacked their usual sparkle.

'God, you look awful!' he exclaimed.

'Thank you!' Sophie bridled for an instant, but her indignation changed to amusement as a look of horrified dismay swept over Kirk's face.

'And I thought *I* was the tactless one!' she chuckled.

Relieved to be so easily forgiven, Kirk grinned. 'Let me make amends by offering you a cup of tea.'

'Tea?' Sophie shot him a glance of puzzled enquiry.

'I asked Ned to get some yesterday when he was in Keswick, but he forgot to unpack it last night. I reminded him just now.'

Kirk held out the little lead-foil wrapper to her, but Sophie hesitated.

'Oh, don't worry, I gave Ned enough money to pay for it.'

'Then I am in your debt, sir.'

Kirk's grin broadened. 'I dare say I shall think of a way for you to repay me.'

There was a devilish glint in his Viking eyes as their fingers touched, warning Sophie exactly what he was thinking, and she coloured in confusion, snatching her hand away.

'But first things first, eh? I don't know about you, sweetheart, but I'm not at my best in the mornings until I've had my breakfast,' Kirk added wickedly, admiring the way her blushes heightened the fine texture of her pale skin.

Relenting, he continued in a less provocative tone, 'I asked Ned to make sure that the grocer blended the tea while he waited, just in case the fellow tried to eke it out with some cheaper rubbish.'

Realising that he'd been teasing her, Sophie recovered her composure.

'You have a most suspicious mind, Mr Thorburn,' she said with a gravity belied by the dancing merriment in her eyes.

'Very probably.'

There was an unexpected curtness in his voice which baffled Sophie for a moment, and then it suddenly occurred to her that he might think she was baiting him about Pelham.

'Kirk, I. . . I didn't mean to sound as if I were criticising you,' she said quickly.

Kirk's handsome face lost its frown.

'I know you didn't,' he answered softly. 'It's my curst hot temper. Sometimes I say things I don't mean, but I'm not fool enough to deliberately quarrel with you. I value your friendship too much to want to antagonise you, Sophie.'

Sophie's smile lit up her irregular features.

And I don't want any more arguments to spoil things between us either, she reflected, her fatigue vanishing as she basked in the warmth his unexpected compliment had generated.

Kirk put the kettle on to boil while Sophie found the little-used china tea-set and washed everything carefully.

'I shall make a whole pot,' Sophie announced gaily, spooning expensive Chinese leaves with a liberal hand.

'Ned and Will have already gone out,' Kirk warned.

Sophie turned a surprised gaze on him. 'I thought they were still abed,' she murmured.

Kirk shook his head. 'They went to check on the animals, but they'll be back in time for breakfast.' He paused slightly. 'However, Becky would probably enjoy a cup.'

'She is sleeping.' Sophie's tone lost its animation. 'How is she?'

'She was feverish in the night, but she's well enough now.' Sophie shrugged, hating the pang of jealousy that shot through her at the concern underlying his deep voice.

'In that case, we'd better not disturb her.' Kirk spoke

easily, but he wondered why Sophie's mouth had suddenly tightened.

They sat down to drink their tea, and Sophie stifled a yawn. 'Oh, excuse me,' she murmured.

Kirk's puzzlement lifted. Of course! The poor girl was exhausted after nursing Becky all night. No wonder she had seemed out of spirits a moment ago.

'Why don't you step outside for a breath of air while I cook breakfast?' he suggested.

Sophie laid aside her empty cup. 'I'm not sure if I should,' she murmured.

'Don't you trust my cooking?' Kirk challenged.

A rueful grin curled Sophie's wide mouth. 'You couldn't make a worse botch than I did last night.'

Her failure to impress him with her skill was upsetting, but she'd had plenty of time during the long, silent hours of the night to realise that it didn't really matter. With any luck, she would do better next time, and anyway, she doubted if Kirk was the sort of man to care about such things. He was more interested in what people *were* than what they *did*.

I want him to like me for myself and not because I can cook or paint or dance, she thought. He's the only man I've ever met who showed more interest in *me* than my dowry. His good opinion counts because I know he will tell me the truth and not seek to flatter me.

'It is refreshing to find a woman with a sense of humour,' Kirk answered slowly. His engaging smile dawned, unsettling Sophie's pulse. 'Go on, enjoy a stroll while I endeavour to produce a meal worthy of your regard.'

Sophie collected her stout hodden cloak and muffler from the down-house and ventured outside.

Taking a deep gulp of air, she revelled in its cold, crisp sweetness as she walked down the path towards the tarn.

The whole world was swathed in white and the valley

looked like a page out of a child's book of fairy-tales. The hills had become dazzling sentinels guarding the treasure of the shining diamond lake, while the branches of every tree and bush seemed sprinkled with glittering crystals.

The last remnants of the stale fatigue which had enveloped her earlier dropped away, and Sophie lingered for a moment to admire the scene before taking the track that led to where Rose lived.

It was a small white-washed cottage with no feature to distinguish it, except for a wooden spinning-gallery under the eaves. Smoke emerging from its little chimney indicated that the occupants were already astir, so Sophie was emboldened to knock.

Rose herself answered the door.

'Why, Sophie. Come in and thaw yeself out by the fire.'

What seemed a dozen curious pairs of eyes turned in her direction as Sophie entered and a deep silence fell on the little room.

'Sam's out on the fell,' Rose explained, thrusting a poker into the heart of the fire as she spoke.

After a moment the children's shyness evaporated and Sophie found herself deluged with noisy questions, which she did her best to answer.

'Away into the bedroom.' Rose shooed her noisy brood out of the kitchen and pressed a mug of mulled ale into Sophie's hands.

Sophie thanked her. 'They are lovely children,' she added with a sincerity that made Rose beam with pride.

'Is there something I can do for ye, Sophie?' Rose asked after they had chatted for a while.

'Do you have any more of that sorrel-leaf tea?' Sophie was glad that Rose had guessed this was not just a social call. 'I don't want to be a nuisance, but Becky was very feverish in the night and it is all finished.'

''Tis no bother. There's plenty to spare.' Rose's expression grew solemn. 'How is the lass this morning?'

'She was sleeping when I left.' Sophie paused and then exclaimed impulsively, 'I wish I knew whether she means to stay in Watendlath!'

'Have ye asked her?'

'She refuses to talk to me,' Sophie replied with a faint smile. 'I am too lowly to merit her attention. Kirk is the only one she favours with her confidences.'

'And ye are worried that he'll fall under her spell again,' Rose said with a shrewdness that made Sophie gasp.

'I . . . I . . .' Sophie fiddled frantically with a loose strand of hair, but couldn't find the right words to refute this claim. After a moment she gave up the struggle. 'You are right, of course. How did you guess?'

'Your face gives ye away, lass.'

'Oh, dear, are my feelings for him so very obvious?' Sophie let out a squeak of dismay.

'No more than his.' Rose began to chuckle. 'Eeh, a blind man on a galloping horse could see that the pair of ye are smitten! Ye were made for each other, even if that great looby ain't realised it yet.'

Sophie couldn't help laughing. 'Oh, Rose!'

Her wry amusement quickly faded. 'I wish it were so simple, but there are. . .complications.'

'Ye mean Stanton, I expect.'

Sophie stared at her in amazement.

'Kirk mentioned that ye were betrothed to him,' Rose explained.

'I see.'

'Nay, don't take offence, lass. Kirk knew Sam would be busy yesterday on account of the snow, so he called to see if I needed a hand with anything, and I asked him how matters stood with his search for Ingram's murderer. He happened to let slip how ye had agreed to marry Stanton to please your uncle, but once he'd realised what he'd said he swore me to silence, so ye needn't think he's been going around telling your private business to all and sundry.'

Sophie relaxed. 'I would have told you myself, but it was. . .well. . .awkward.'

'I wouldn't have wrapped my opinion about that rogue in clean linen even if I'd known about your betrothal,' Rose declared with characteristic bluntness. 'Ye'd be a fool to marry him, Sophie.'

'I know, but it's not as easy as you might imagine to withdraw from such a contract,' Sophie sighed.

She might have said more, but just then a yell rose in protest from the bedroom, followed in swift succession by several further cries and the sound of scuffling.

'I must be going.' Sophie got to her feet even as Rose moved to quell the riot.

'I'll fetch that medicine over later.' Rose nodded.

Thanking her, Sophie flung her cloak over her shoulders and hurried back to the farm.

A delicious smell of frying bacon greeted her.

'Come and join us, lass,' Will hailed her from his position at the head of the table.

Unconsciously, Sophie had been hoping that she would find Kirk still alone, but she stifled her disappointment and sat down to partake of the excellent breakfast set before her.

'Aye, we rear good pigs here,' Will said, casting a complacent glance at the sides of meat hanging up to dry in the dim, smoky recesses of the canopy when she complimented him on the bacon.

'And Kirk's cooking has improved,' Ned chimed in unexpectedly. 'He used to burn everything when he first got home.'

Sophie glanced mischievously at Kirk, who exclaimed, 'Ned, you traitor!'

'Did I say something wrong?' Ned's broad, honest face wore a bewildered expression.

To the astonishment of the Hyndes, both their guests
burst out laughing.

'A private jest,' Kirk explained when he had
recovered his breath.

'Aye, well, we'd best be getting back to work,' Will
announced, a sudden suspicion forming in his mind as
he watched his young friend smile across the table at
the lively redhead he'd brought to the dale.

Will chivvied Ned to his feet, ignoring his son's
protests.

'Ye bide here and keep Miss Fleming company. We
can manage,' he insisted when Kirk offered his services.

Kirk yielded with a smile and Will went off, pleased
to see him in such good spirits. The lad had been right
moped since his return; not that anyone could blame
him. Ingram's death had been a shocking business, but
the lad was too young to wrap himself up in nothing but
gloom and fury. If that attractive lass had given Kirk's
thoughts a new direction, then he for one approved!

'I'd like to stay and talk, Sophie, but I think it's time
I set out if I'm to get back from Stanton Hall before it
grows dark,' Kirk said, once the door had closed behind
the Hyndes.

Sophie had blithely forgotten all about his intention
to go and see Nancy, and she gazed at him in
consternation.

'Do you really think it is wise?' she said desperately.
'The snow has stopped. Surely we could both go
tomorrow?'

'I hope so, but in the meantime your disappearance
will be causing anxiety.' Kirk shrugged. 'I dare say
Stanton will try and have me thrown out, but I reckon
it's worth the risk.' He was tempted to add that almost
anything would be worth it to lessen the anxiety he
could read in her lovely eyes. Even when she was
laughing, as she had done a moment ago, that shadow
remained.

Damn it, but he hated to see her unhappy!

'I must go,' he said, rising to his feet. 'Call it a quirk of my nature if you like, but I should feel I have failed if I did not try.'

'Then at least promise me that you will not attempt to see Pelham,' Sophie implored. 'You can leave a message at the gatehouse.'

Kirk hesitated.

'Please, Kirk. Pelham is suspicious of you and it will not help my position if he learns that I have been in your company before I get the chance to explain matters.'

'Then you still intend to marry him?'

The words exploded from his throat, but Kirk cursed his impatience when Sophie paled and dropped her gaze. He had promised himself that he would not harry her for a decision!

'Forget I asked,' he said gruffly. 'Very well, then, I'll do as you suggest, but only if you will write a note for your maid. That way we won't have to rely on the gatekeeper's memory.'

'Of course!' Sophie flew to find pen and paper.

'You won't give your name, will you?' she said anxiously, handing him the hastily scrawled missive.

It went against the grain, but Kirk consented to this stipulation.

His preparations for the journey were soon complete.

'I'll be back before dusk,' he announced with such cheerful confidence that Sophie took heart and managed to wave him off with a creditable attempt at a smile.

Indoors again, she checked on her patient and, finding Becky still asleep, she set to work on the household chores. The novelty of sweeping floors and washing dishes quickly wore off, but she persisted until every task was eventually accomplished, though not without some unladylike mutterings.

'Perhaps I ought to attend to you too,' she said aloud, eyeing a pile of shirts awaiting mending.

Sewing was not a task Sophie enjoyed, but she knew herself well enough to know that her imagination would run riot if she did not find something to keep her occupied.

'What a pity Will's taste in reading doesn't include novels,' she sighed, settling herself under the canopy and picking up the first shirt.

'Damn!'

A splatter of black sooty liquid dropping from the open chimney some minutes later made Sophie jump in alarm.

'No wonder Will jokes about needing to keep his hat on!' she groaned, surveying the dirty mark the *hallan-drop* had left. 'Now this needs washing, and I had only just finished repairing it!'

Her lukewarm interest in the job completely destroyed, Sophie put the rest of the mending away, but before she could start to launder the spoilt shirt a cry from the bedchamber alerted her to the fact that Becky was awake.

'Here, sip this. Slowly, now.'

Sophie held the cup to Becky's cracked lips and patiently helped the older girl drink a little water.

'That tastes so good. Thank you.'

The animosity which had formerly marked the husky contralto voice was missing, Sophie noticed.

'Could you manage to eat something?'

'Later, perhaps.' Becky shook her blonde head.

'Very well.' Sophie gently lowered her back against the pillows and after a moment's hesitation enquired if Becky would like to wash her hands and face. 'It might make you feel a little more the thing.'

This offer was eagerly accepted, and when Sophie had helped her to complete her toilette Becky let out a

sigh of relief. 'I was beginning to feel filthy,' she said
with a slight chuckle.

It was the first time Sophie had seen her smile, except
for that hateful superior smirk!

'I'm glad you are feeling better,' she said and meant
it.

Becky heard the sincerity in her voice, and a faint
blush stained her wan cheeks. 'Thank you for nursing
me,' she muttered. 'If things had been the other way
around I would have probably thrown that sorrel-leaf
tea over you, not looked after you with such unstinting
care and patience!'

Sophie grinned. 'I must admit I was tempted!'

The lines of strain around Becky's taut mouth eased
and she gazed at Sophie with a winning frankness.

'I'm sorry, I didn't mean to behave so abominably.
It's just that feeling ill on top of all my other problems
was the last straw, and I took my wretchedness out on
you.' A charming smile lit up her perfect features.
'Please say that you forgive me. I promise I will conduct
myself with more decorum from now on.'

Sophie wondered how sincere this volte-face was, but
said pleasantly, 'I'm willing to start afresh if you are.'

'Wonderful! I'm sure we are going to be great
friends,' Becky exclaimed brightly.

There was something almost childlike in the appeal
of those big eyes and that dimpling smile. It made it
difficult to resist her charm, Sophie thought. Moreover,
a truce would certainly help while they had to remain
cooped up here, but she strongly suspected that Becky's
mood might just as easily turn hostile once more if it
suited her purposes.

'Is there anything else I can get you or would you
prefer to rest now?' Sophie asked, removing the basin
and towel.

'Actually there is something.' Becky waved her

towards the rocking-chair. 'Have you time to listen? I would welcome the advice of another woman.'

Don't trust her, Sophie warned herself as she sat down. Remember what Rose said! No matter how charming she may seem, she is a determined manipulator, willing to use other people to gain her own ends.

'You are a stranger and somehow I feel more comfortable talking to you about my problem than someone I know,' Becky began slowly.

'Perhaps it's because you hope I may be able to offer you an unprejudiced view,' Sophie answered, understanding exactly what the older girl meant.

'Well, I certainly stand in need of advice! If I lie here worrying any longer I swear I shall end in Bedlam!'

Sophie nodded. She had spent too much time pondering her own situation lately not to feel a kindred sympathy.

'You see, I am virtually penniless, but yesterday I received an unexpected offer from Kirk.'

Sophie stiffened.

'Oh, I don't mean that kind of offer!' A trill of laughter escaped Becky, and Sophie blushed, angry that she had betrayed herself. 'Once upon a time. . . Ah, but that's another story, as they say!' Becky shook her head in a pretty gesture. 'No, he has offered me money, not marriage.'

'Why?'

The bluntness of this question didn't disturb Becky.

'I don't know. Such kindness is the last thing I expected.' She gave Sophie a direct look, devoid of her usual coquettishness. 'Don't you find it strange?'

'Have you asked Kirk his reasons?'

'He says it is to help me get settled in a new life.'

'Perhaps he is fond of you.' Sophie managed to force the words out, although they nearly choked her.

'After the way I treated him?' Becky laughed, but it was an unpleasant sound.

After a moment she continued, 'I take it you have heard the story of my wanton past.'

Sophie nodded, hardly knowing how to answer.

'I thought as much. Puritans like Will Hynde won't ever let me forget!' The petulant note was back in Becky's voice, and Sophie studied her fingernails in embarrassment.

'Not that his opinion matters. He never liked me anyway.' Becky shrugged. 'But I don't understand why Kirk has changed his attitude. When we met the other day I was hoping he might have forgiven me, but he was still angry, almost as angry as the last time we met.'

A wry grimace twisted Becky's rosebud mouth.

'We quarrelled bitterly. He wanted me to tell my parents about the baby, but I refused. Papa was indulgent; he would have overlooked most misdemeanours, but how could he condone such a sin? To have shown mercy would have made him the laughing-stock of the district!'

A little sigh escaped her. 'I meant to leave Watendlath before my condition became obvious, but unfortunately my mother guessed the truth. She became hysterical and Papa came rushing in to see what was wrong. In the recriminations that followed I blurted Kirk's name.'

'You could have retracted it later and told your parents who the real father was.'

'I dared not!' Becky shuddered. 'I knew he would deny it. He had no wish to marry someone like me.'

Sophie stared at her in astonishment.

'Not all men are as honourable as Kirk Thorburn, you know,' Becky snapped. 'My lover was rich and I found his world exciting, but even then, green though I was, I knew he would never accept responsibility for my predicament. In fact he had already warned me that if I breathed a word of our affair he would make sure that

my name became a byword! I had no choice but to
blame Kirk!'

Sensing that argument would only increase Becky's
distress, Sophie remained silent, and after a short pause
Becky resumed her story.

'I didn't want to harm Kirk. I was fond of him — who
could not be? — but I knew if I didn't pretend he was
responsible my parents would give me no peace, and I
needed time until my lover could help me get away.'

'Was that when you went to London?'

Becky nodded. 'It was wildly exciting. He installed
me as his mistress in a grand house where I lived like a
queen! I had fine clothes, jewels —— '

'But what about the baby?' Sophie couldn't contain
her curiosity.

'Oh, I miscarried and lost it,' Becky replied with an
airy unconcern that took Sophie's breath away.

'Didn't you mind?' she gasped.

Becky tossed her head. 'I didn't want it, you know!
Perhaps if Sir. . . I mean my lover. . .had been pleased
about my condition I would have felt differently. In fact
he made no secret of his relief, so I could see no point
in staying at home moping and pretending to grieve
when he wanted me to accompany him to parties. . .'
She halted, catching the look of disgust that flashed
across Sophie's expressive face.

'No doubt you think me very unprincipled to abandon all the beliefs that my parents had taught me, but
life in London was different! It was all so sophisticated
and new and I was fascinated by. . .' She paused, a
little uncertainty entering her manner. 'I have never
spoken his name to anyone in Watendlath.'

Sophie stifled her curiosity and said briskly, 'It
doesn't matter. I wouldn't know him anyway.'

'No, of course.' Becky let out a faint sigh of relief. 'I
know my secret departure hurt my parents, as well as
causing a great deal of bother for Kirk, but I didn't

regret my decision. I was in love! The man I had chosen could be very reserved and haughty, but I was happy with him, even when the passion between us eventually faded and I knew he was no longer entirely faithful to me. By that time I had my own circle of friends, and fidelity didn't seem to matter. He continued to keep me in great style and I still enjoyed all the pleasures London had to offer.'

'Then why did you decide to come back?' Caught up in the older girl's story, Sophie had forgotten the cry of despair Becky had hurled at Kirk at their first meeting.

The pansy eyes darkened.

'He swore to me that he would never cast me off. I knew that one day he must marry to provide himself with an heir, but I thought that need not change our relationship — in fashionable circles no one blinks at a man keeping a mistress — but then a few months ago his manner towards me began to change. Nothing I did pleased him! He was tense and sullen, refusing to buy me trinkets if I asked.'

Becky pouted.

'Finally, just before Christmas he declared that he would no longer pay my bills, and when I asked him how I was to keep up the house and servants he coolly informed me that he meant to let the lease run out!'

'At first I thought he was joking, but he answered my protests with a curt shake of his head, saying that he intended to marry and that he could no longer afford to keep me. I knew he had money troubles — what fine gentleman does not? — but I hadn't realised things were so bad.'

Becky let out a bitter laugh. 'Do you know I actually offered to move to a smaller house and practise economy? But he laughed in my face and told me he was tired of me. "Any man is entitled to a change after ten years", that's what he said. Is it any wonder that I began to hate him?'

Sophie gulped and wondered what she could say. 'Now that your feelings for him have altered, perhaps it is better that you should seek a new life,' she ventured at last.

'I'd be glad to, if I had the money. Do you know I had barely enough in my purse to cover the stage fare? He made me return every piece of jewellery, every trinket of value! He even ordered my maid to parcel up my clothes for sale before he dismissed her. I was left with nothing but the garments I stood up in!'

Becky shook her head in angry disbelief.

'I knew he was secretive and could be cold, but to do such a callous thing after all the years we had been together. . .! When the lease on my house finally ran out a few weeks ago I would have been reduced to sleeping on the streets if a friend had not helped me!'

She shuddered dramatically.

'The whole business made me feel so sick that all I wanted to do was to lie down and die! I longed to get away from him and away from London, where everyone knew of my humiliation.'

A sigh escaped her. 'Watendlath suddenly seemed very desirable.'

'Only now you are having second thoughts?' Sophie queried perceptively.

'It was folly coming back.' The big violet eyes turned to her with a miserable expression in their depths. 'I simply can't settle to living a quiet country life, even if the people around here would accept me back into the fold. Lord, I should have realised it before I set foot in the coach! After all, it was the main reason I rejected Kirk in the first place. He is the sort of man any girl might want to marry, but he would hate to live in a city. He wanted to stay at Haraldsgarth. I wanted excitement, gaiety! Now that I have tasted that kind of life I don't think I can give it up. It's in my blood.'

'Then you had better take his money and go back to

London.' To hear Becky casually dismiss Kirk's love
when it was all she longed for made Sophie boil, and
her voice was so sharp that Becky blinked at her.

'But don't you see? It wouldn't be fair to take
advantage of Kirk a second time,' she explained. 'I
know I am selfish, but I am not a complete monster! I
can't let Kirk make such a sacrifice for me.
Haraldsgarth is ruined. He cannot afford to help me
out.'

Sophie began to choke with harsh, jerky laughter.
'Your sentiments do you credit; but you are sadly
misinformed. Kirk acquired considerable wealth in the
Bahamas. He is a rich man now.'

Becky goggled at her. 'I had no idea!' she gasped.

Struggling to control her unseemly mirth, Sophie
didn't perceive the significance of Becky's sudden fit of
silent abstraction until Becky lifted her downcast gaze
and said, 'How very interesting! Thank you, Sophie.
You have put quite a different complexion on matters.'

There was a distinctly acquisitive gleam in the pansy
eyes, and Sophie could have kicked herself as she
realised her mistake.

Why, oh, why had she opened her big mouth?

By the time the afternoon shadows were drawing in,
Sophie's anxiety regarding Becky's intentions was sub-
merged in a greater fear for Kirk's safety.

Providing a noonday meal for everyone had been a
distraction, and Rose's promised visit had also helped,
but now it was nearly dusk and her imagination kept
conjuring up visions of Kirk lying injured and helpless
in the snow.

'I think I'll take a turn by the lake before it gets too
dark,' she announced abruptly.

Ned gazed at her in open-mouthed surprise, but Will
merely nodded.

'Aye, you do that, lass. Mind you don't stay out too

long, though. I reckon it's going to be another cold
night and it'll be like glass underfoot once the sun goes
down.'

Sophie nodded. During the day the top layer of snow
had thawed, but it would freeze again once the temperature dropped.

Out by the tarn Sophie felt her over-stretched nerves
beginning to relax. The wind had dropped and the sky
was a miracle of golden fire as the sun flamed to its rest
in a sunset so spectacular that it was almost enough to
make her forget how cold the temperature still was.

Sophie took a deep breath. It was utterly peaceful;
only the faint pee-wit cry of a curlew in the distance
disturbed the silence. A perfect time and place to
dream of love!

She lifted her face to catch the last rays of the sun,
and somehow it was no surprise to see a lone horseman
riding down the track. It was in keeping with the magic
of the hour that Kirk should be returning safely,
dissolving her nightmare fears.

Excitement shot through her as she waved to him,
and she had to bite back the urge to laugh aloud as he
raised an arm in acknowledgement.

'Kirk! I'm so glad you are back!'

Sophie greeted him with a warm smile as he
dismounted.

'Sophie.' Kirk swept her a courtly bow that hid his
dismay. How strained and pale she looked!

'How do you like Watendlath now?' he enquired
lightly, waving an arm to encompass the scene around
them.

'It's beautiful. I never realised how dirty snow looks
in the streets of a town until now.'

Kirk laughed, but his attention was diverted when
she raised a hand to push back a lock of hair that had
strayed from the confines of the muffler she wore.

'Here, take these,' he said, stripping off his gloves. 'Your hands look frozen.'

Sophie glanced down and was horrified to see how waxen her bare hands appeared, apart from the chapped and reddened knuckles. To make matters worse, she had broken two of her long fingernails into the bargain.

Feeling embarrassed, she nevertheless managed a feeble grin. 'I'm not used to housework.'

Kirk's mouth tightened and, wondering if she'd said the wrong thing yet again, Sophie quickly moved to take the gloves he was still holding out to her.

One of them slipped through her cold fingers and fell to the ground. She stooped hastily to retrieve it and felt herself beginning to slither on the icy path.

The squeak of alarm died in her throat as Kirk caught her in his strong clasp and steadied her.

Her pulse began to hammer and she stood very still, not daring to move.

'This reminds me of the time we were skating in Kendal,' Kirk said in a voice that was suddenly hoarse.

Sophie lifted her head, and as he gazed down into her vivid little face Kirk's arms tightened of their own volition.

'I remember. We quarrelled like a pair of shrews,' Sophie said shakily.

A slow smile dawned on Kirk's handsome features.

'We have wasted a lot of time arguing. Very foolish of us, don't you agree? We could have found out we were friends so much the sooner.'

His words brought a shine of happiness to her dark eyes, and the smiling curve of her generous mouth proved so irresistible that he abandoned the last vestiges of common sense and gave in to his urge to kiss her.

The touch of his warm lips made Sophie's senses swim. She clung to him tightly, and Kirk's initial intention faded. Instead of releasing her, he deepened the kiss, and found she answered his growing passion with a matching fervour.

Sophie twined her fingers into the golden mane that curled crisply on to the back of Kirk's strong neck, pressing herself even closer to him. He let out a growl of pleasure, and every single nerve in her body stirred with heady delight as his tongue demanded admission into the intimacy of her mouth.

The taste of him left her giddy with longing. The potent male smell of him was in her nostrils. The animal warmth of his big, strong body lapped around her, banishing the cold weariness frozen into her bones. She was alive for the first time in days. . .and consumed by desire!

'I think we had better go in. You'll freeze to death if we linger.'

Kirk reluctantly broke their embrace, trying to mask his emotions with a smile, but his breathing remained ragged.

Sophie laughed a little shakily. How could he think she felt the cold while in his arms?

They moved slowly away from the tarn, Kirk leading his horse by the reins. The treacherous path required close attention, and Sophie had recovered her composure by the time they reached the shelter of the stable, where Kirk unsaddled Ned's roan and rubbed him down.

Once this task was accomplished he said, 'I need to take a look at Sultan. Perhaps you ought to go in.'

Sophie gazed at him in surprise. She had been expecting him to explain what had happened at Stanton Hall.

'Don't worry. I left your note as we planned,' Kirk replied when she ventured to ask how his mission had fared. 'Apart from that, there's nothing to tell.'

It cost Kirk a great deal to sound offhand when he

longed to reassure her, but he had come to the conclusion that it was about time he put a little distance
between himself and the delectable Miss Fleming.

Damn it, all he really wanted to do was catch her up
in his arms and kiss her again, but the walk back from
the tarn had given him time to think.

It was not the act of a gentleman to lead a lady on,
and until this business of finding Ingram's murderer was
over and he was free to decide his own future he had no
right to treat Sophie in such a cavalier way. No matter
how he might long to kiss her, it simply wasn't fair when
he was in no position to offer marriage until he had
fulfilled his duty to his dead brother.

Sophie turned to go and then hesitated. Perhaps she
had imagined that coolness in his tone.

'I'd like to stay and watch, if I won't be in the way,'
she murmured, swallowing her pride.

'Of course.' Kirk nodded politely. 'Why don't you
stand over there where you won't get your skirts dirty?'

Sophie's spirits plunged. This time there was no
mistaking the reserve in his deep voice!

Taking up the position he had suggested, she watched
him attend to the great bay stallion, her thoughts in a
turmoil. Why had he turned cold? Could her ardour
have embarrassed him? From conversations with
friends like Charlotte Fletcher, she knew many men
didn't like a girl to be too forward.

'They like to do the chasing, not the other way
round,' Charlotte had declared with an authority
Sophie saw no reason to doubt.

A hot flush mantled Sophie's cheeks. Did Kirk think
she was fast? She pressed a clenched fist to her mouth.
Of course he must! After the shameless way she had
behaved, it would be a miracle if he thought anything
else!

And yet. . . He had never shown any sign of disliking

her fervent response to his caresses before, so perhaps there was something else.

Becky.

She was so beautiful! Had her own attractions paled to nothing beside that glamorous allure?

It was a depressingly logical conclusion.

Desire is not the same thing as love, Sophie reminded herself bitterly. It was perfectly possible that Kirk might want to enjoy Becky's lush body even though he no longer cared for her.

But he kissed *me*, not her, Sophie told herself frantically.

You were there, replied the inexorable voice in her head. Kirk might not be the womaniser you once thought him, but he is a man, not a monk! What did you expect him to do in those circumstances after the way you've been throwing yourself at him ever since you met?

Sophie shivered.

And Becky, how would she react if Kirk offered her a *carte blanche*? She had made no secret of her attraction to him. No doubt she would welcome him as a lover, particularly as he was now rich enough to give her the things she wanted!

Shocked by the meanness of her thoughts, Sophie gasped, and Kirk turned round abruptly.

'Is something wrong?'

'No, no. . .nothing.'

'You're shivering.' Kirk wiped his hands clean on a rag. 'Come, let's go inside. I've just about finished here anyway.'

He offered her his arm, but to his surprise she drew away.

'I think you still have some liniment on you. I don't want to get this cloak dirty,' Sophie said hastily.

Kirk's eyebrows rose, but he accepted this feeble excuse without comment.

Sophie's spirits sank even lower, and it was a relief to regain the farmhouse, where her tongue-tied silence might go unnoticed.

'Eeh, but the pair of ye look frozen to the marrow!' Will exclaimed. 'Ye could do with warming up, but supper is nowhere near ready.'

Kirk repressed a smile. 'It doesn't matter in the least, Will. I must go and change out of these damp clothes in any case.'

A frown of concentration appeared on Will's wrinkled nut-brown face.

'What do ye say to a bowl of powsowdy while we are waiting?' he declared triumphantly. 'I can have it ready in two shakes of a lamb's tail.'

Not wishing to offend his friend, Kirk accepted, and Will crossed to the spice cupboard built into the wall by the hearth. Here cinnamon and nutmeg were stored along with the household's block of salt to keep dry, and Sophie watched with interest as Will carefully grated and measured out the amount of spices he required.

'Off ye go, lad, or ye'll be catching a chill,' Will admonished, and Kirk left to climb the slate stairs to the loft while Sophie made herself comfortable by the brightly burning fire.

'Would ye mind toasting this, lass, while ye are sitting there?'

Sophie took the toasting fork Will handed her. He had speared a thick slice of bread on to the prongs and she held it close to the flames, glad to have some task on which to fix her attention.

'Mind ye don't burn it, lass,' Will directed, busying himself with setting a pan of strong ale to heat.

Sophie grinned. Sometimes Will reminded her of her uncle Thomas!

When everything was ready, Will poured the hot ale

into a big basin, and threw in a dash of brandy, followed by the spices and crisp toast.

'That smells good,' Kirk remarked, walking back into the room.

He was wearing a pair of tan breeches and a fine linen shirt beneath a dark brown riding coat, and it struck Sophie afresh how informal attire suited him. He looked so handsome that her heart contracted, and she longed to stroke smooth a wayward lock of hair that had escaped his brush.

Will began handing round piggins of his potent brew as Ned emerged from the down-house, a bundle of elding in his arms.

'Powsowdy! What a good idea, Dad!'

Accepting the little wooden barrel-shaped dish and sipping at the hot drink with a spoon as the others did, Sophie soon understood Ned's enthusiasm. It sent an immediate rush of warmth along her veins and she could feel the tension beginning to drain out of her.

'Do you expect the weather to continue to improve, Will?' Kirk spoke up, laying aside his empty piggin.

'I heard a thrush sing afore Candlemas Day, and that's always a bad sign, but I reckon we're over the worst of it.' Will grinned and added, 'Anyway, for now at least.'

'Then I shall escort Miss Fleming home in the morning.'

Sophie's bright head jerked up and she dropped her spoon, her nerves tautening once more.

'*Tomorrow* morning?' she said shakily.

'Of course. Sultan's hock is healed and we have imposed upon Will's hospitality for long enough.'

There was a cool finality in Kirk's words, and Sophie saw that his expression was determined.

'Ye are more than welcome to stay, both of ye,' Will began a little uncertainly, sensing the tension that had suddenly flared between his guests.

'No, thank you, Mr Hynde.' Sophie strove for composure. 'Mr Thorburn is right. It is high time I left.'

'Can you be ready to make an early departure?'

Sophie forced herself to meet his vivid gaze.

'As early as you wish. Becky is on the mend; she no longer requires the services of a nurse.'

With an effort Kirk kept his face impassive. 'That's good news. I'm glad she is better,' he murmured.

Hellfire, he had forgotten all about Becky! Perhaps he should tell her that he would be away for a short time. In any case, he ought to find out whether she had decided to accept his offer to stake her or not.

To Kirk's surprise, he found he no longer cared either way. He still wanted Becky gone from the dale, but the fury she had aroused in him had faded. It belonged to the past, like the love he had once borne her.

'That makes two of us glad to hear your news, lass.' Will's emphatic declaration interrupted Kirk's thoughts.

'I meant what I said,' Will continued grimly, putting down his piggin. 'If that hussy is better, then she leaves my house.'

Kirk frowned, but before he could speak Sophie intervened. 'I don't think she is fit to travel, not for another day or two at least.'

Will snorted. 'Very well, lass.' He nodded grudgingly.

Relief washed over Sophie. Leaving Watendlath would be hard enough, but she didn't think she could bear it if her last moments with Kirk were tainted by Becky's presence!

'Pray excuse me.' Kirk rose abruptly to his feet. 'Since we are to make an early start, I'll say farewell to Becky now.'

Sophie watched him go.

He has forgotten I exist, she thought sadly, longing to call him back, but knowing it was no use.

For a few lovely moments earlier by the tarn she had allowed herself to dream that Kirk Thorburn might come to love her, but for the sake of her own self-respect it was time to stop pretending. She was nothing more than a momentary distraction in his life, and the sooner she accepted it, the sooner her heart might begin to heal!

CHAPTER TEN

SOPHIE stared in the mirror and let out a sigh. Heavens, what a fright she looked, in spite of her best efforts to refurbish her appearance for the journey ahead.

'What time is it?'

Becky's muttered remark made Sophie spin round. 'Did I wake you? I was trying to be quiet,' she murmured apologetically.

Becky shrugged sleepily and sat up in bed. Her violet gaze took in the new daylight pouring in through the uncurtained window and she grimaced in distaste.

'What on earth possessed Kirk to want to leave so early? This is an ungodly hour!'

Sophie felt much the same, but she recognised the necessity. 'We may get bogged down,' she reminded Becky, who shuddered.

'I'm glad I'm not travelling with you,' she said frankly. 'I shall stay snug in bed. Will Hynde will have to wait on me whether he likes it or not.'

Sophie turned back to the mirror before her hasty tongue could produce a sharp retort.

'Would you like to borrow one of my hair ribbons?' Becky asked a moment later, watching Sophie's struggle to tame her riot of brilliant curls.

She rummaged in the reticule she kept by the bed and held out a length of violet silk. 'You may keep it if you wish.'

This offer was so at odds with Becky's customary lack of interest in any concerns but her own that Sophie stared at her in surprise.

'Oh, I know what you are thinking. I am a selfish beast, but you've been kind to me, Sophie.' Becky had the grace to blush. 'I just wish I had the means to repay you, but my purse is empty.'

'I wouldn't dream of taking your money even if I stood in need of it, which I can assure you I do not!' Sophie exclaimed hotly.

'I'm sorry,' Becky apologised, looking so bewildered that Sophie felt forced to clarify her position.

'I didn't realise that you were an heiress.' Becky stared at the borrowed brown dress, now sadly stained by Sophie's attempts at housekeeping, and laughed rather shortly. 'You certainly don't look it.'

'I know,' Sophie answered lightly, choosing to ignore the note of envy in the older girl's tone.

'If I had your wealth I should cut a dash! What's the point in being rich if no one knows it?'

'You sound like my betrothed,' Sophie chuckled and then regretted this unguarded remark when Becky began to hurl questions at her.

'I didn't mention my betrothal for reasons I prefer to keep private,' she replied evasively.

Becky pouted. 'Forgive me for asking, I'm sure!'

There was a short silence while Sophie finally managed to bind up her curls with the silk ribbon.

'It clashes with your hair,' Becky announced with an air of satisfaction.

Sophie laid her comb down. 'It doesn't matter,' she said dully, too depressed by the thought that in a few moments she would be leaving Watendlath forever to be upset by Becky's envious spitefulness.

A strange expression, almost of remorse, flickered over Becky's perfect features.

'I'm sorry. I shouldn't pick at you when you are feeling miserable.'

Sophie forced a smile. 'Nonsense.'

'I mean, anyone can see that you are in love with Kirk,' Becky persisted. 'It must be very galling for you that he doesn't return your affections.'

Sophie stared at her in dismay, but Becky continued to rattle on.

'Of course, since you are betrothed elsewhere it is probably best that Kirk thinks of you as merely a friend.'

'Did he say so?' Sophie asked through clenched teeth.

Becky's eyes widened innocently.

'Not in quite those words, but his meaning was plain,' she replied with a childlike earnestness. 'We talked about it last night when he came to say farewell.' A delicate blush coloured her cheeks. 'We have come to an understanding, you see.'

Sophie thought she understood only too well and she shivered, suddenly chilled to the bone.

Pride came to her rescue.

'My congratulations on solving your pecuniary difficulties,' she said coolly. 'However, you mistake the matter. I am perfectly content with my betrothal.' The lie slid smoothly off her tongue and she saw a frown crease Becky's brow.

'I doubt if there will be time to prepare a proper breakfast, but I'm going to make some tea. Would you like a cup?' Sophie took advantage of Becky's puzzlement to make her escape.

Will was already down and had the kettle on to boil.

'*Hoo ista*, lass?' He hailed her with the traditional greeting, and Sophie forced herself to smile and reply in a composed manner, as though her heart was not breaking.

She had been right! Kirk no longer desired her. He had denied that she was anything more than a friend. No doubt he was relieved to be free of the strange tug of attraction that had bound them, the oddest pair of unlikely lovers, together.

Will and Ned had finished their morning ale and were gone before Kirk strode into the room. Sophie was

about to make a tart comment on his belated arrival
when she noticed the lines of strain carved around his
deep blue eyes.

He looks like a man who has had very little sleep, she
thought to herself, and the words of censure died in her
throat, to be replaced by a concern she could not quell,
try as she might.

'Are you ready to leave?'

'Don't you want any breakfast?' Sophie exclaimed in
response to this curt greeting.

Kirk shook his head impatiently. 'We have wasted
enough time already.' Seeing her indignant expression,
a crooked grin split his clear-cut features. 'Sorry, *I* have
wasted enough time.'

'A delay of a few minutes more will make no odds,'
Sophie said firmly, pushing a plate of bread and cheese
towards him.

Kirk shrugged. 'You are an obstinate woman, Sophie
Fleming,' he muttered, but he accepted the tankard of
ale and quickly ate a slice of bread.

'Thank you,' he said, wiping his mouth free of
crumbs. 'No doubt I shall be glad of that later on, since
Stanton is hardly likely to offer me any hospitality.'

Sophie had been stacking the used dishes together,
but she halted abruptly. 'What do you mean? I hope
you won't even see Pelham, much less have occasion to
talk to him.'

Kirk returned her worried gaze calmly. 'Of course I
shall have a word with him, Sophie. You didn't imagine
that I would leave you on his doorstep like a parcel, did
you?'

Sophie's eyes widened. 'But Kirk, you can't!' she
protested. 'He will be furious if you dare appear at the
Hall!'

'My dear, you and I both know he is very likely to be
furious anyway,' Kirk answered, his tone softening.

Sophie swallowed hard. She could feel the palms of

her hands grow clammy and knew he had put her secret fear into words. Not normally a timid person, she found herself oddly apprehensive and unwilling to face Pelham's anger, because at heart she sensed that her betrothed was not the cold fish he pretended.

'Perhaps it would be wiser if you remained here at the farm,' Kirk suggested. 'I could deliver a message——'

'No!' Every feeling in Sophie was revolted by the idea of running away from her responsibilities. 'I owe it to him to return. I will not make him a laughing-stock even if I finally decide not to marry him.'

Kirk frowned. In his opinion Stanton didn't deserve such consideration, but he knew that they would only quarrel if he said so.

'Very well, I accept your reasoning, although I think it unwise,' he said curtly. 'But why not wait for a while until the Stricklands return? Then you could travel home with them as soon as you had spoken to him.'

For an instant Sophie was tempted, but she shook her bright head.

'I want to get it over with,' she murmured, reluctant to confess that she could not bear to stay and watch him dote on Becky.

'In that case, I insist on accompanying you,' Kirk announced with a grim set to his mouth. 'My conscience will not permit me to abandon you without first ensuring that all is well. I shall explain that Will found and housed you, but asked me to escort you home, since he could not leave the farm. Stanton won't like it — he hates me — but at least he won't question your story.'

Sophie twisted her fingers together in agitation.

'Come, now, sweetheart, there is no need to look so worried. He is hardly likely to shoot me on sight!'

'What if he tries to set his men on you?' Sophie couldn't respond to his teasing grin, and a little quiver shook her voice.

'I doubt he would be so foolish, but. . .' Kirk shrugged his broad shoulders in a telling gesture. 'I'm not exactly a novice when it comes to taking part in a mill.'

Sophie gasped. 'I won't have you fighting over me!' she exclaimed in accents of disgust, her temper flaring under this new strain.

Kirk raised his brows.

'Don't you frown at me, Kirk Thorburn!' Sophie had endured a very trying morning and she was in no mood to mince her words. 'I find the idea of grown men fighting utterly abhorrent!'

'It's easy to see you don't have brothers,' Kirk replied lightly, trying to defuse her anger, but Sophie's blood was up.

'Nor will I allow you to use me as another bone of contention in your dispute with Pelham,' she declared angrily. 'I am not a parcel, as you so inelegantly term it, and I will not permit you to entangle yourself in my affairs. I do not want you to speak to Pelham on my behalf. You will only make things worse!'

Kirk could feel his temper beginning to simmer. He had spent a large part of the previous night mulling over the difficulties inherent in returning Sophie to the Hall, and her haughty dismissal of his solution rubbed him raw.

'Do you imagine I want to waste my time smiling politely at that scoundrel? I wouldn't offer to do so unless I thought it necessary, you silly chit! Good God, anyone would think you suspected I had some devious scheme in mind, rather than worrying about you.'

'It wouldn't surprise me if you had,' Sophie flashed back at him. 'I think you would use anything or anyone if it furthered your scheme to obtain revenge for your brother's death.' Tears stung at her eyelids, but she ignored them and continued fiercely, 'In fact I sometimes wonder whether you didn't decide to worm your

way into my affections for that very purpose!' She
glared at him. 'Did you hope I might spy on Pelham for
you?'

'You impudent baggage!' Kirk roared, but, even as
he began to deny her slanderous accusation, the incon-
veniently honest voice of his conscience reminded him
he had once thought he might try to see if jealousy
would make the baronet grow careless.

'Perhaps I did briefly entertain such foolish notions
when we first met at that soirée, but I swear to you they
did not last beyond our first conversation,' he said
gruffly.

Too angry to hear the note of apology in his voice,
Sophie failed to realise that the unaccustomed tide of
colour flooding his bronzed face stemmed from embarrassment, and took it for a sign of guilt.

'It was all a trick from the start!' She stared at him,
her great dark eyes stricken. Pelham had tried to tell
her that Kirk might use her as a means of revenge, but
she had buried that warning deep in her subconscious.
'I should have known you would never care a scrap for
a girl like me!'

Oh, how could she have been so foolish? Hadn't she
learnt the hard way that men did not care for her
unfashionable looks or sharp tongue? It was evidence
of her own idiocy that she could have believed even for
a moment that Kirk Thorburn might have tumbled into
love with her in the same crazy way that she had fallen
for him.

'What the devil are you talking about?' Kirk
demanded hoarsely, his conscience pricking him. 'I
have done my best by you, but you have thrown all my
advice in my face.'

'Advice? Damn your good advice!' Sophie could hear
her voice turning shrill, but she couldn't stop herself. If
she couldn't have his love, then at least she would keep
her pride.

'Advice is the last thing I want from you, Kirk Thorburn! Keep out of my life! I shall go back to the Hall and deal with Pelham as I see fit. I do not need your help. You were only pretending to like me anyway——'

'Stop it!' Kirk grabbed her by the shoulders. 'You are talking hysterical nonsense. I have admitted that I might have originally sought you out because of Stanton, but surely you *cannot* think all that has passed between us since was some kind of nefarious plot on my part? My God, I know I haven't always behaved as a gentleman ought to, but that doesn't make me a complete monster!'

Sophie gazed up at him rebelliously and he gave her an infuriated shake. 'Well, do you believe me or not, damn you?'

'I don't know! I don't know what to think any more!' Sophie screamed at him, pulling away so violently that Kirk was startled into releasing her.

Sophie fought for control and managed to quieten her ragged breathing. 'You say one thing, Kirk, but do another,' she murmured wearily, her temper spent. 'One minute you act as if you desire me, the next you are cold. What *am* I supposed to think?'

'Sophie.' He brushed her cheek with a repentant finger. 'I told you once before that I did not mean to hurt you. Please believe that, in spite of my ungentlemanly behaviour.'

The tenderness in his Viking gaze penetrated the shell of anger Sophie had been frantically building around her bruised feelings.

'My own behaviour hasn't always been that of a lady,' she sighed, her sense of fair play returning. 'I encouraged your advances, Kirk.'

'Would you deny me my wicked reputation?' he asked with a wry grimace.

'Nonsense! You aren't some heartless womaniser, I

know that now,' Sophie asserted. 'But that leaves me
with only one conclusion: namely that you care far
more for your brother's memory than whatever it is that
you feel for me.' Sophie lifted her gaze to meet his.
'Your duty binds you, Kirk, and it leaves no room in
your life for me. Becky will suit you far better.'

'Becky?' Kirk's expression changed to one of puzzlement, but before he could question her a flush of hot
colour stained the skin over Sophie's high cheekbones
and her gaze flew in embarrassment to the partition
wall dividing the bedchamber from where they stood.

Was Becky awake? Had she overheard them?

Sophie wished the floor would open up and swallow
her. 'I am going to go and say goodbye to Rose,' she
gasped, whirling beyond the hand Kirk put out to
detain her.

'Kirk, let her go.'

The husky contralto voice carried to Sophie's ears as
she fled, and she knew if she turned back she would see
Becky gliding seductively towards him, her arms out-
stretched in welcome.

'I don't rightly know, Miss Fleming,' Sam
Braithewaite's freckled face wore a frown. 'What do ye
think, wife?'

Rose took her gaze from Sophie's anxious eyes and
nodded briskly. 'I think ye should take Sophie into
Keswick as she asks. You were saying that we need a
few supplies, and there's no time like the present.'

Sam's anxious look melted. 'Aye. Well, in that case,
I'll go and saddle Darkie up.' He turned to Sophie and
added in a faintly apologetic tone, 'Ye won't mind
riding pillion, Miss Fleming, will ye?'

'Not in the least,' Sophie assured him fervently.

When her husband had gone Rose said, 'Are ye sure
ye wish to leave in such haste, lass? I shouldn't wish ye
to change your mind and regret your decision when it's

too late to mend matters. Both of ye have hot tempers, but I doubt if Kirk meant to quarrel with ye.'

Sophie shook her head firmly. 'I won't change my mind.'

The cold air had cleared her head as she walked to Rose's cottage. Before she had completed the short distance she had known what she must do. Kirk had chosen Becky, and for the sake of her own sanity she had to get away.

'I must leave immediately, Rose. Kirk cannot be permitted to confront the baronet. He says he would be able to control his temper, but it would end in bloodshed, I know it would!'

'Aye, I reckon it might at that. They never could abide each other.'

Sophie smiled faintly. 'Will you thank your father for his hospitality?'

Rose nodded. 'Do ye want me to say goodbye to Kirk for ye as well?' she enquired perceptively.

Sophie winced.

Outside, the wind was fresh, and Sophie told herself that it was responsible for the tears stinging her eyes. Stoutly she refused to let them fall and scrambled up behind Sam, striving to control a tremor of fear at the thought of the journey ahead.

'I'm not much of a rider,' she murmured apologetically, accepting his help to settle herself on the pony's broad back.

Thankful to hear him describe Darkie as a placid beast, Sophie bent down to clasp his wife's hand in farewell. 'I'll return your dress as soon as I can,' she informed her. 'Good luck with the new baby and thank you for all your help and kindness, Rose.'

Rose nodded in acknowledgement. 'I hope all goes well for ye too, Sophie.'

'It will.' Sophie forced a note of optimism into her voice and waved farewell with a bright smile.

'Hey up, Darkie!'

Sam encouraged the pony into a trot and Sophie murmured, 'I just hope she can persuade Kirk not to follow me!'

'What's that ye said, Miss Fleming?'

'Oh, nothing, I was merely thinking aloud,' Sophie replied quickly, cursing her lack of self-control.

It was time she pulled herself together. She had to stop thinking about Kirk Thorburn. Hadn't the events of this morning proved to her beyond all doubt that their destinies lay with separate paths? Becky was the one he wanted, and it was only his keen sense of honour that had made him offer to escort her into what was for him a lion's den.

Honour and some small fondness, for he did care a little for her happiness. She knew that was what he had been trying to tell her this morning, but mere fondness wasn't enough. She wanted his *love*; nothing less would do.

But Kirk Thorburn wasn't prepared to offer that kind of commitment to her or any other woman.

The sight of the little town of Keswick gladdened Sophie, but she felt too uncomfortable to take much interest in the quaint old courthouse which presided over the market-place or the tiny cottages that clustered in its shadow. The ride had been marginally less frightening than she had feared, but she was frozen and aching in every limb.

Darkie's hoofs clattered against the white cobble-stones of the main street and Sophie made a mental resolve to improve her riding skills. The prejudice induced by that fall when she was a child ought to be put behind her!

'Where do ye wish me to set ye down, Miss Fleming?' Sam enquired.

'I don't know exactly,' Sophie confessed. 'But I want to hire a carriage to convey me to Stanton Hall.'

Sam sniffed, but, deciding it wasn't his place to criticise, said, 'I think they might have a gig available at the George.'

To Sophie's relief the landlord of this establishment was eventually willing to accept her word that he would receive payment when she reached her destination. His thick eyebrows had risen at her request and she had coloured as his gaze had swept over her bedraggled appearance. For one embarrassing moment she had thought he would insist on the money in advance, but Sam had indignantly vouched for her.

'Thank you, Mr Braithewaite, for all your help,' she said as the gig was brought out into the innyard with surprising speed.

Sam ducked his head in embarrassment, muttering that he was glad to oblige.

He assisted her up into the rather shabby vehicle and stood back to wave her off.

Twisting round on the hard seat to return his gesture of farewell, Sophie experienced an odd flicker of desolation. He was her last link with Watendlath!

The gig jolted along over the half-frozen roads, but Sophie was too preoccupied to notice any discomfort. For the past few days she had been putting off making a decision, but now she was rapidly running out of time.

Could she endure to marry the baronet? For if she could not, now was the time to tell him so!

It was impossible to ignore her feelings for Kirk Thorburn, but Sophie tried as she struggled to view the situation dispassionately.

She didn't love Pelham, but then she never had. What had changed was that she had lost the mild liking and respect she'd previously felt for him. Kirk's revelations had begun the rot, but Pelham's own recent behaviour was the main cause of her dissatisfaction.

On the other hand, there was Uncle Thomas to consider, and all the embarrassment of returning in disgrace to Kendal. Every malicious tongue would snigger and say the Flemings had over-reached themselves. Even worse, in her heart Sophie was beginning to wonder if the gossips were right. Perhaps she was doomed to remain a spinster, unwanted by anyone except for her enormous dowry.

Stanton Hall loomed up on the horizon and Sophie shivered. What a coward I am, she thought in despair. If only I had some proof that Pelham was the monster that Kirk paints him, then my conscience would be eased!

'Shall I drive on up to the house, miss?'

The question roused Sophie from her wretched thoughts and she nodded, sitting up straighter. It was too late now to do anything other than brace herself to face the storm ahead.

The driver brought the gig to a halt at the foot of the imposing flight of steps that led to the main entrance, and Sophie had barely alighted before the massive double doors were flung open and Sir Pelham appeared, flanked by his butler and two footmen.

Taking a deep breath to steady her nerves, Sophie began to ascend.

'Where the devil have you been?'

The baronet flung this demand at her almost before she had reached the top step.

Sophie returned his angry stare with a calmness she was far from feeling. 'I shall answer your questions in a moment, Pelham, but first pray be so good as to pay off the driver so that he may return to Keswick before it gets dark.'

'Keswick!' the baronet ejaculated.

For an instant Sophie thought he might argue, but then with a sulky glare he snapped his fingers at his butler and said, 'See to it.'

He followed Sophie into the house, but she pretended not to notice and walked across the wide marble hall towards the log fire that blazed in the massive hearth.

'Well? What have you to say for yourself, ma'am?' the baronet barked at her. 'Seeking refuge with that bunch of peasants! Did you want to humiliate me?'

Sophie continued to rub her hands before the blaze for a moment before she turned to answer him. 'I am not deaf, Pelham. There is no need to shout, unless, of course, you wish to air your grievances for every servant in the house to hear.'

The baronet goggled at her, utterly disconcerted by her unexpected insouciance. 'I had expected you would have the decency to apologise at least,' he growled at last. 'Don't you realise what a furore your ridiculous behaviour has caused?'

Sophie shrugged nonchalantly. 'I cannot think why,' she said coolly. 'I am sorry if I caused you any anxiety, but, after all, I wrote to tell you that I was safe and would return as soon as the weather permitted.'

'You wrote to your maid, you mean!' He glowered at her. 'Didn't you consider how distressing I should find it to hear such news at second hand?'

'Did you really?' She lifted her brows delicately. 'You surprise me, Pelham.'

This interview was not going in the least as the baronet had imagined. He had consoled his frustration over Sophie's disappearance by picturing the agreeable scene in which his distraught betrothed begged his forgiveness in a flood of repentant tears.

'By Hades, Sophie, your absence has not improved your manners!' His fists clenched involuntarily and Sophie experienced a flutter of fear.

He looks as if he would like to hit me, she thought, wondering if her impulse to brazen things out had been the right one. But what other choice had she? If she allowed him the upper hand now, he would ruthlessly exploit her weakness in future.

Sensing her confusion, the baronet pounced. 'And what have you been doing to yourself, my dear? Is that absurd garment meant to be a dress or a cleaning rag?'

Sophie couldn't prevent a deep blush from colouring her cheeks. 'I'm sorry my appearance displeases you, sir,' she snapped. 'My own clothes were ruined and I was forced to borrow this one from Mr Hynde's daughter.'

Sir Pelham laughed scornfully. 'Couldn't she find you anything better? You were never a beauty, my dear, but now you look like a scarecrow.'

Suddenly all Sophie's doubts vanished and her anger boiled over at his deliberate rudeness.

'Since neither my manners nor my appearance pleases you, am I to assume that you wish to curtail our betrothal?'

The hot words sprang of their own volition to her lips. For an instant she was too shocked to feel anything but dismay that she had not waited to seek her uncle's permission to break off the betrothal, but then an upsurge of joy banished her consternation and she was able to meet his astounded stare with a fiercely proud look.

'You mistake my concern for you,' the baronet muttered, his complexion turning grey. 'Pray forgive me if I have inadvertently offended; I fear I am overwrought. Your absence caused me great anxiety.' He essayed a smile. 'How can you think I wish to break off our betrothal? I desire it to continue above all things!'

Presented with such a handsome apology, Sophie could do nothing but incline her head in gracious acceptance, but she carefully refrained from reassuring him.

Instead she said, 'Please excuse me, Pelham. I long for a hot bath and a change of clothes.'

'Of course. Will I see you at dinner?'

There was a rare note of hesitancy in his tone, and Sophie experienced a flicker of triumph. Her instinctive decision not to show any weakness had been the correct one! Now all she had to do was to choose the right moment to tell him that she wanted her freedom.

'I think not. I am exceedingly weary,' she murmured, eager to see how he would react.

'Then you must rest, my dear.' The baronet smiled at her fulsomely and bowed.

Hiding her satisfaction, Sophie nodded and moved towards the stairs.

Nancy was waiting for her in her room.

'Oh, Miss Sophie, you don't know how glad I am to see you!' she exclaimed.

Sophie hugged her soundly. 'I missed you too,' she affirmed.

Nancy searched her with a keen glance. 'You've lost weight,' she pronounced with a frown. 'And what have you been doing to your hair? I've seen tidier bird's nests.'

'Don't start scolding me the minute I walk in through the door,' Sophie begged.

Nancy's gaze softened. 'Nay. I've ordered them to bring up a tray of tea and enough hot water for your bath.'

'Bless you! You cannot know how much I long to discard this dress. It was loaned to me by the dearest person, but we do not share the same size or taste!'

Nancy began to help her out of it.

'It's good material and I dare say it was cleaner before you got up to your tricks, Miss Sophie,' she commented, holding out a loose robe for Sophie to slip into.

'Do you think you could restore it? I could make

Rose a present of a new gown, but I don't want to risk offending her. She is very proud and independent, like most of the people I met in Watendlath.'

Nancy's eyebrows climbed. 'Oh, aye?'

Sophie obliged with a somewhat censored version of her adventures while she soaked in a tubful of hot water.

'When will you learn to act like a young lady, Miss Sophie?' Nancy scolded. 'Fancy cooking and cleaning like that, as if you were a. . .a kitchen-maid.'

'Now don't fuss, Nancy. I could hardly sit there and expect to be waited upon when the Hyndes were being driven distracted by the weather.'

Nancy snorted. 'I reckon there's more to it than you are letting on, miss!' She gave Sophie a sharp look. 'I wish I'd got a look at this Mr Thorburn of yours when we were in Kendal.'

'He isn't my Mr Thorburn,' Sophie replied, adding hastily, 'Be a dear and rinse my hair.'

The subject was forgotten and a few minutes later Sophie was ensconced before the fire, sipping her tea. 'Oh, it's so nice to feel clean!' she sighed luxuriously.

'Shall I lay out your cream silk?' Nancy smiled at her indulgently. 'I'll warrant you want to erase the bad impression that brown horror must have had on Sir Pelham.'

Sophie hesitated. Much as she loved her maid, she was loath to confide in her. Nancy was inclined to treat her as a child still, and she would be shocked to hear that Sophie proposed to give the baronet his *congé* without consulting her uncle first.

'No, there's no need,' she murmured at last. 'I intend to dine here in my room this evening. My ankle is aching and I feel a little weary.'

As expected, this reply brought a flurry of searching questions concerning the state of Sophie's health before Nancy announced, 'You need an early night, my girl.'

Sophie agreed with a meekness that might have aroused Nancy's suspicions had her thoughts not been on brewing a posset to revive her beloved nursling.

'You rest now until supper,' she admonished, after watching Sophie drink this concoction.

Sophie nodded, but when Nancy had quit the room she rose and crossed to the dressing-table on which resided her jewel-case. Opening it, she took out her betrothal ring and stared at it thoughtfully.

The enormous diamond winked up at her, dazzling in the candlelight. For an instant she was tempted to slide it on to her finger, but then she thrust it back into the case and slammed the lid shut.

'I'm sorry, Uncle Thomas,' she murmured softly. 'But my mind's made up!'

A long-case clock, its polished brass plate bearing the name of Jonas Barber, the celebrated clockmaker of Winster, decorated the corridor leading to Sir Pelham's study, and Sophie paused to check the time.

It wanted ten minutes to the hour. She was a little early. The baronet had answered her message asking to see him with a note saying that he would be pleased to receive her at ten.

Sophie had dressed with great care for this meeting. Rejecting all of her new diaphanous gowns, she had selected a pale lemon-coloured caraco dress. The longish jacket fell almost to her thighs over the matching petticoat and it was nipped in at the waist by a bright red sash which emphasised her slender waist.

The style was a slightly mannish one, devoid of any feminine frills, and it flattered Sophie's tall, slim figure. It also suited her mood. This morning she wanted to feel brisk and businesslike. *I won't let him accuse me of being silly or hysterical,* she vowed silently to herself. *He will have to take me seriously!*

The corridor was richly carpeted, another of the

baronet's expensive whims. Sophie smiled grimly to
herself. He'll have to find another dowry to squander
on such extravagances!

The door to her betrothed's sanctum was ajar and
Sophie could hear the murmur of male tones. Annoyance flickered through her as she recognised Simon
Conrad's voice. If Pelham was closeted with his secretary, then she would be kept waiting just when she
had screwed up her courage!

Damn Conrad, I feel like walking in on them, she
thought crossly.

'You fool!'

The baronet's angry shout made Sophie jump in
alarm, and she forgot all thoughts of announcing her
presence. Instead she cast aside her scruples and crept
closer, the thick carpet deadening her footfalls.

'I am sorry, sir, but I have done my best.' Simon
Conrad sounded harried. 'Unless you repay the sum
you owe him by the end of the month the Duke insists
he will foreclose the mortgage.'

'That's less than three weeks away!'

'He was most insistent, sir.'

'I will not lose the Hall!'

Sophie smothered a gasp and pressed her ear to the
door to catch Conrad's reply.

'My dear sir, you stand to lose everything! When I
arrived I warned you of the Duke's mood and you
promised me that you would be careful, but you lost
another two hundred at cards to old Mr Curwen the
other night.'

'By Hades, are you never satisfied?' Sophie could
have sworn she heard the grinding of teeth. 'I gave up
my mistress to suit your notions of economy and still
you lecture me, you insolent puppy!'

'But sir, you said yourself that you were tired of Miss
Hurst.'

Sophie's heart missed a beat. Had she heard aright?

'Aye, ten years is enough with any woman, and so I told Becky. God knows I need a fresh start! Maybe my luck will change once I'm wed.' The baronet laughed unpleasantly.

So *he* was Becky's mysterious lover! Sophie felt the bile rise in her throat. The hypocrite!

The sound of Sir Pelham's voice interrupted her angry reflections.

'There's only one answer if that stupid fool is going to kick up a dust. This accursed wedding will have to be brought forward. Waiting until May is too risky. We can be married here, and once I have my hands on that dowry he'll sing a different tune.'

Shock sent all thoughts of Becky out of Sophie's head.

'Will Miss Fleming agree?' Doubt edged Conrad's tone. 'I cannot help wondering if she could have somehow got wind of your debts. Why else should she run away like that?'

'Nonsense, she didn't run away. The silly wench got lost.' The baronet snorted dismissively. 'Don't forget, I kept my nose clean in Kendal. There was no difficulty in cozening her or that old fool Fleming. They think me as rich as Croesus.'

Sophie's lips tightened at the insult to her uncle, but she forced down her fury so that she could concentrate on what was being said.

'Would to God that I had been able to convince one of the society mamas in London that my fortune was still intact! I am sick of rustic simplicity. Still, I suppose I shouldn't complain. The wench might be a lanky bag of bones, but she is young and not too ill-favoured.'

Sophie's anger was increased by Conrad's answering laugh.

Oh, how dared Pelham talk about her like this?

Not trusting her temper a moment longer, she began to back away.

'Never fear, I shall tame Miss Fleming. She will do
precisely what she is told.' Sir Pelham chuckled and
then his amusement abruptly ceased. 'Speaking of
which, I expect her here in a few minutes. You may go.
We will discuss the Duke's terms another time.'

'Very well, sir, but. . .'

Sophie didn't linger to listen to the rest of the
secretary's reply, but took to her heels. Anger lent her
speed, but her stomach turned over with a sickening
lurch as she heard the study door creaking behind her.

There was no time to escape from the long corridor,
so she ducked behind the long-cased Barber clock,
pressing herself flat against the wall.

If Conrad came in this direction instead of heading
for the stairs. . .!

Sophie's heart was pounding so loudly that it was
several moments before she realised that the danger of
discovery had passed. The relief made her feel dizzy,
and she had to clench her hands together to try and still
them as she fought for composure.

The chiming of the hour startled her, breaking the
spell that held her captive.

What shall I do? Pelham is waiting for me, but he will
know something is wrong the minute he looks at me,
she thought. Ten to one, I should blurt out my disgust
and he'd know I'd been eavesdropping!

The baronet's cruel remarks only strengthened her
determination not to marry him, but something warned
Sophie that it would be most unwise to cross him in his
present mood. He sounded quite desperate, she
thought, pushing aside the unwelcome suspicion that
she'd been unwise to dismiss Kirk's advice to stay at the
farm.

I must go home, Sophie decided, all her instincts
screaming that she was in danger. But how the devil
was she to achieve such a thing, when the baronet
commanded all forms of transport?

Idiot, worry about that later, she castigated herself. First of all you must pretend you are ill, to give yourself time to think of a plan.

'Why, Miss Sophie, what are you doing back here? I thought you were seeing the baronet.'

'There's no time to explain now, Nancy,' Sophie said, rushing into the room and flinging herself down at the elegant writing-table. 'I want you to take this note to Sir Pelham, and if he asks you must say I am too sick to receive him.'

Nancy's plump face looked bewildered. 'But, Miss Sophie ——'

'Quickly, Nancy.' Sophie thrust the scrawled note into her hand. 'Then hurry back and help me to pack. We are going home.'

'Pack?' Her maid repeated the word helplessly. 'I don't understand.'

Sophie bit down hard on the impatient reply that sprang to her lips. 'Be a dear and just do as I say,' she begged, giving her maid a little push towards the door.

Nancy hesitated. 'I hope you know what you are doing, Miss Sophie,' she said doubtfully, watching Sophie snatch open the clothes cupboards that ran the full length of one wall. 'Your uncle won't be too pleased if you offend the baronet.'

Sophie shook her head wildly. 'I'll tell you everything later,' she cried, grabbing a handful of dresses and tossing them on the bed.

She peered into the bottom of the cupboard. 'Damn, where are my portmanteaus? There is only one small valise in here.'

'They were taken to one of the store-rooms, of course.' Nancy flapped her hands in consternation. 'Miss Sophie! You are creasing everything!'

'Never mind. We can't take much anyway. This will have to do,' Sophie declared, snatching up the valise and starting to stuff clothes into it willy-nilly.

'Miss Sophie, have you run mad?'

'Oh, do stop wasting time, Nancy, and please hurry with that note.'

'Oh, very well, but I don't know what on earth your uncle is going to say,' Nancy grumbled.

Even as Sophie heaved a sigh of relief there was a sharp knock at the door.

'No, don't open it —'

But it was too late.

CHAPTER ELEVEN

'WHAT? Rose, I don't find this amusing. Now where is she?'

'I told ye. She's gone, Kirk.'

Kirk stared speechlessly at Rose. He felt as if she had punched him hard in the gut.

Gone! Sophie had left him without a single word of farewell! An unbearable sense of loss seared through him.

'Of all the senseless, stupid things to do!' he roared, unable to contain the rage that filled him. 'Why the devil couldn't she wait for my escort?'

'Because she knew ye would lose your temper with Stanton and make matters worse,' Rose retorted, giving him a sharp look.

'I don't understand. She cannot still intend to marry that scoundrel!'

'Mebbe, mebbe not. But what's it to ye, Kirk Thorburn?' Rose demanded crossly. 'I reckon it's about time ye decided who comes first with ye.'

Kirk paled beneath his deep tan. 'Rose!' he growled warningly.

Rose planted her hands on her hips. 'Nay, I'll have my say, Kirk Thorburn. Ye are a friend of mine and a good man, but right now I'm ashamed of ye. Ye've been playing fast and loose with that lass, and she deserves better. I know ye owe a debt to the dead, but if ye choose your brother's memory over a girl who loves ye then ye are a bigger fool than ye look!'

Kirk glared at her. 'Damn all women,' he muttered furiously and stalked out of the cottage.

Seeking refuge at Haraldsgarth, he tried to find

237

forgetfulness in hard physical labour. Exerting the power of his splendid muscles, he cleared a satisfying pile of fire-blackened stones, but once his fury had cooled his conscience began to trouble him.

Perhaps Rose was right. Perhaps he had let his sense of duty outweigh all else. Perhaps it would have been fairer to explain to Sophie. . . Perhaps. . .oh, the devil take it!

Wishing he understood more about women, Kirk's brain whirled as he strove to make sense out of Sophie's defection.

Of course, Rose was wrong to imagine that Sophie was in love with him. Good God, they'd done nothing but quarrel! She probably thinks I'm a monster, he decided ruefully, a deep gloom settling over him.

His black mood was not improved by the unexpected arrival of Becky early the next morning.

'Will has thrown me out,' she sobbed, casting herself upon his chest in a flurry of tears, almost upsetting the easel and the drawing he was working on.

'Becky, I told you yesterday that it was over between us.' Containing his irritation, he gently loosened her grip and put her from him. 'If it's money you want, I'm happy to advance you the sum I mentioned the other day.' He stared blindly at the half-finished drawing of the new house he planned to erect. 'However, I have no wish to try and rekindle old flames.'

'You still hate me,' she wailed. 'You hate me because I ran away with Pelham.'

'No, not any more.' He shook his golden head wearily. 'But we cannot resurrect the past; too much has happened to both of us since then.'

She sniffed and gazed up at him piteously. 'You are in love with Sophie.'

Kirk suppressed a groan. 'Sophie Fleming has got nothing to do with it. I am well rid of the troublesome wench!'

'What do you mean? I asked Will where Sophie had gone, but he wouldn't give me an answer.'

Becky's face was alive with curiosity, and Kirk realised she mustn't have overheard yesterday's quarrel after all.

'It's no mystery,' he said shortly, unwilling to reveal Sophie's secret. 'She has merely returned to her friends.'

Something in his tone convinced Becky it was futile to keep on trying to lure him back into her arms. No matter how he protested, he had the look of a man in love.

Swallowing a brief pang of jealousy, Becky shrugged philosophically and decided to make the best of it.

'I'll take your money, Kirk, but only because I know you won't miss it,' she said with a return of her usual acumen.

'Where will you go?'

'Back to London. Here, there is always the possibility that I might encounter Pelham in some quiet spot, and I think I would grab the chance to knife him!' Becky's violet gaze hardened and Kirk knew that she was free of Stanton's spell at last.

Becky's expression cleared. 'Will you give me a ride into Keswick? If I remember aright, the mail-coach runs today and I might be lucky enough to secure a place if I hurry.'

'Of course,' Kirk replied, trying to hide his relief.

They made good time and found that there was one single inside seat still available.

'Goodbye, Kirk, I doubt if we will meet again,' she said to him as she prepared to board the coach after they had eaten a hasty meal.

A smile lit her perfect features.

'Perhaps it is better this way.' She patted her reticule, where his bank-draft lay safely stowed. 'I should have driven you mad.'

'You'd have been bored within a week,' he agreed with a grin.

Laughing, Becky stretched up to kiss his cheek, and he handed her into the vehicle.

Her expression sobered as she leant her head out of the window. 'Take care, Kirk,' she whispered. 'Pelham is dangerous.'

He started at this unexpected warning.

'What do you mean?' he demanded hoarsely.

'Just that I know what Pelham is like. Need I remind you I was his mistress for many years?' Kirk's expression hardened and she carried on hastily. 'Never mind my morals. Remember what happened to Ingram when he tried to cross him.'

'Do you have any shred of evidence to back your suspicions?' he asked eagerly.

Hating to disappoint him, Becky shook her head. 'He never confided in me, Kirk, so I have no proof. All I know is that just before Ingram's death he was suddenly in funds. Not that it lasted, of course.'

She paused and then added abruptly, 'Did you know he plans to wed? Some heiress who will restore his fortune.'

Kirk frowned grimly. 'Aye, I knew.'

Long after the coach had pulled away he stood there turning the problem over in his mind. . .

Sophie had rejected him, but he could not abandon her. She would brook no further interference on his part and he could hardly blame her, considering how ineptly he had handled matters in Watendlath, but perhaps she would listen to her oldest friend.

Calling for his horse to be saddled, Kirk strode across the innyard, a look of grim determination on his handsome face.

'Really, my dear, you will have to learn to be more punctual. I dislike to be kept waiting.' The baronet brushed Nancy aside, ignoring her gasp of surprise, and strolled into the centre of the room.

'I do not recall inviting you in, Pelham,' Sophie said coldly. 'Please leave.'

He shrugged. 'It pains me to have to point it out, but this is my house, my dear.'

His cold gaze turned to Nancy. 'Out.'

Nancy's eyes widened. 'Sir —— '

'Out or I'll have you whipped for disobedience, you stupid hag.'

Sophie felt her anger return in full force. 'How dare you speak to my maid in such a manner?' she snapped.

'Oh, I shall dare more than that, my dear.' The baronet laughed unpleasantly. 'Now tell her to leave or I'll have one of the footmen throw her out.'

The baronet's voice was quiet, but Sophie sensed the anger simmering in his well-fleshed frame.

'Do as he says, Nancy.'

For an instant it looked as if her maid would dispute the command, but then she nodded.

'I think we have something to discuss,' the baronet announced grimly once Nancy was gone.

Sophie ignored him. 'What is the meaning of this outrage, Pelham?' she demanded haughtily, attempting to stare him out of countenance.

He laughed shortly. 'Don't play the fool, Sophie.'

His glance fell upon the disordered bed. 'Packing? And in such haste too.'

Sophie frowned. 'I have no intention of talking to you, sir, until you apologise for your disgraceful behaviour,' she announced. 'I am astounded that you should neglect the civility you owe to me, and I demand —— '

'It won't work this time,' Sir Pelham interrupted bluntly. 'You managed to bluff your way out of answering any questions yesterday, but I will have the truth now. The fact that you were planning to leave only confirms my suspicions.' He fixed her with his cold gaze. 'What exactly did you overhear?'

Shaken by the barely veiled menace in his tone, Sophie played for time. Moving gracefully to her dressing-table, she sat down, settling her skirts slowly.

'What do you mean?' she asked, carefully avoiding his gaze. 'What should I have heard? You are talking in riddles, Pelham.'

She picked up her silver-backed hairbrush and began to rearrange her disordered curls. 'Are you angry because I kept you waiting just now? It wasn't my intention to do so, I assure you, but on my way downstairs I realised that I had forgotten my fan, so I came back to collect it.' Sophie strove to inject all the conviction she could muster into her voice. 'Unfortunately I could not find the yellow one which matches this dress, hence the mess. There is no need to imagine that I was packing! I would have kept our rendezvous if only you had waited another few minutes for me.'

'Very good, my dear. You almost have me convinced. Almost, but not quite.' The baronet laughed unpleasantly. 'Now let's try again.'

Sophie's dark eyes glared at him through the mirror.

'You have no right to question me like this,' she said hotly, trying hard to think up a plausible denial.

'Come, enough of this nonsense,' the baronet snapped. He produced a lace-trimmed handkerchief. 'I found this just now outside my study door.'

Recognising the dainty scrap of lawn he held out, Sophie paled. It must have fallen from her pocket, and she'd been too upset to notice its loss!

'What, nothing to say for yourself at last?' The baronet gave her a taunting smile. 'You were eavesdropping. Admit it!'

'Go to hell!' Sophie's precarious hold on her temper snapped. She slammed down her hairbrush and whirled round to face him, her expression defiant. 'I won't answer your stupid questions!'

'You little shrew. . .'

Before Sophie could guess his intention, he grabbed her by the wrist and jerked her to her feet with such cruel force that a shocked cry was startled out of her.

'Don't make me angry, my dear.' He twisted her wrist savagely. 'I am not an easy man to cross.'

Sophie choked back a gasp of pain. 'You want the truth? Very well, you shall have it, you bully! I wouldn't marry you if the King commanded it! You disgust me!'

'Damn your infernal impudence!' The baronet thrust her violently from him with a growl of rage.

Flung off balance, Sophie fell against a small tripod table. It gave way and she crashed painfully to the floor. For an instant she was too shocked to move, before her fighting spirit revived and she struggled to her feet.

Sir Pelham made no attempt to assist her, but stood staring at her with cold distaste.

'I had hoped to avoid unpleasantness, but since you now know the truth about my debts there is no need for pretence. Get this through your head—you are going to marry me whether you like the idea or not.'

'Never.' Sophie spat the word at him. 'You are a liar and a hypocrite.' She had guessed he only wanted her for her money, but she had never dreamt he might be Becky's mysterious lover, and she couldn't forgive him for the misery he had caused. 'You can't make me marry you.'

'Oh, but I can.' His smile was silky with menace. 'Here at the Hall I have a private chapel, so we can dispense with the necessity of a public ceremony. You will stand at the altar with me if I have to drag you there by the hair. And don't think you can defy me. There will be no guests to listen to your protests. No one will help you.'

'No parson would consent to such vileness,' Sophie

gasped. She was shaking and her legs felt like water, but she held her head defiantly high.

'You think not? Then you are a fool, my dear. Men will do anything for money, and I know a certain cleric who would be only too happy to oblige. Not that it need come to such a pass. There are drugs which I can use beforehand to render you docile.'

Sophie stared at him in disbelief. Impossible as it seemed, he really meant what he was saying!

'Oh, yes, I intend to go through with it, my dear.' The baronet smirked, amused by the look of horror on her expressive face. 'What's more, the arrangements won't take long to complete. You see, I've already taken the precaution of obtaining a special licence, so we ought to be able to hold the ceremony within the next day or two.'

He bared his teeth at her in another taunting smile.

'Perhaps you ought to choose a dress to wear for the occasion—if you can find one that you haven't crushed too badly, that is.'

Goaded by this deliberate mockery, Sophie flew at him, but he was too quick for her. He fended off her raking nails and held on to her hands, his grip savage.

'Temper, temper! You'll have to learn to control yourself better when we are wed,' he jeered, panting a little.

In answer, Sophie kicked him hard on the shins, but since she was wearing flat kid slippers she knew it did little good.

'Hellcat!' The baronet released her and, thrusting her aside, swiftly extracted the key from the door. 'You won't be needing this.' He glared at her. 'No one will come to release you, whatever happens, but if you are foolish enough to annoy me by making a fuss you'll get no food or drink until the wedding breakfast.'

The door banged shut behind him and Sophie heard the key turn in the lock. She was a prisoner!

* * *

'Mr Thorburn, ma'am.'

'Thank you, Jane.' Maria Strickland nodded dismissal to the parlourmaid. 'This is a pleasant surprise, Mr Thorburn. However, I'm afraid my sister is not here. She is dining from home this evening.'

'Actually, I came to see you, Mrs Strickland.' Kirk bowed politely.

Maria's dark brows rose. 'Pray be seated, sir. Do you wish to wait for my husband? He will be down shortly.'

Kirk shook his head. 'I think it is better I speak to you alone.' He shifted awkwardly in the satinwood chair. 'I have come to ask for your aid.'

Maria's fan fluttered in surprise. 'Perhaps you had better begin at the beginning, sir,' she murmured.

Kirk coughed. 'You may find my story shocking,' he warned.

Maria smiled. 'I am rarely shocked, Mr Thorburn.'

Kirk's well-cut mouth thinned.

'I hope not, ma'am,' he said drily.

'So you see,' he ended his explanation, 'Sophie has rejected my advice.'

Maria strove for composure. 'What you have to say is most alarming, sir.' She surveyed her satin skirts for a moment and then raised her head. 'I must admit, I have been anxious myself. Sir Pelham's behaviour while we were his guests was most odd. He showed no respect for Sophie and no regard for her wishes.'

'Then will you add your persuasion to mine and beg her to return to Kendal without delay?'

Maria's fan fluttered in agitation and Kirk's expression grew impatient. 'I know I have no right to ask you to break off your holiday——'

'My dear Mr Thorburn, curtailing our stay here is of little importance,' Maria interrupted. 'You suspect that the baronet might make Sophie a dreadful husband, and I agree with you. For that reason alone, I am inclined to think that the betrothal ought to be broken off, but I do not understand why you think there is such need for haste.'

'Once they are wed he will gain control of her fortune. I fear that he may have been cast into a panic by her absence and use the opportunity presented by her friendless state to bring the wedding forward.'

'You think he would coerce her?' Maria gasped, turning pale.

Kirk nodded, and Maria's hand flew to her mouth in a shocked gesture.

'Shall I ring for your maid, ma'am?'

'There is no need.' Maria recovered her composure. 'Pray forgive me. I am not usually given to the vapours.' She fanned herself vigorously. 'It seems fantastic to imagine Sir Pelham a murderer!'

'Whether or not you accept that the baronet had a hand in my brother's death makes no odds,' Kirk replied tightly. 'What matters is that you persuade Sophie to leave Stanton Hall before it is too late.'

Maria bit her lip. 'I do not like to interfere.'

Kirk's hands clenched on the arms of his chair.

'But in this case I think I must,' Maria continued slowly. 'Thomas Fleming entrusted his niece to my care and I must fulfil that obligation. Whether or not you are correct in your suppositions, Mr Thorburn, there is certainly cause for concern.'

She gave him a direct look.

'I am grateful to you for coming all this way to warn me, Mr Thorburn, but may I ask why you are taking such a close interest in Sophie's affairs?'

He coloured beneath her scrutiny. 'I think you have already guessed the reason, ma'am.'

Maria nodded, satisfied, and Kirk rose to his feet.

'Must you leave, sir? It is late, and I know my sister would ask you to remain as our guest for the night.'

Kirk thanked her, but refused.

'Won't you at least stay and dine with us?'

Kirk hesitated and then shook his head. 'I have already bespoken a meal at the inn at Ouse Bridge,' he replied. 'A friend of mine was kind enough to loan me his yacht to speed my arrival here. I intend to set sail on the return journey at first light and so must be up betimes.'

'In that case, sir, I shall not seek to detain you.'

Maria rose to her feet in a rustling of skirts and escorted him in person to the front door.

'You will let me know if I can be of any further assistance?' Unconsciously Kirk twisted the brim of his hat in his hands.

Maria nodded. 'Of course.' She smiled at him. 'I am sure Sophie will wish to get in touch with you herself, sir, once she is safely home again.'

Kirk politely returned her smile, but his heart remained heavy.

He should have made his feelings clear to Sophie while he'd had the chance, but he'd bungled it. The devil alone knew what women thought — *he* certainly didn't — but somehow he had the feeling that Sophie wouldn't forgive him for putting duty before love.

'Oh, Miss Sophie, my head's all of a whirl!'

Nancy gazed open-mouthed at her young mistress. 'Who would have thought it?'

'But you do believe me, don't you?' Sophie asked anxiously.

'Aye, that I do!' Nancy affirmed stoutly.

Sophie heaved a sigh of relief.

She had been kept solitary all day and once her first fury had worn itself out she had sunk into a dismal depression. Over and over again she had replayed the events leading up to her confrontation with the baronet, tormenting herself with the thought that she ought to have managed better.

Why hadn't she realised earlier that Becky's lover was the baronet? Good heavens, but it was so obvious that she must have been blind not to see it! Becky had even known that Haraldsgarth was ruined, in spite of frequently declaring that she hadn't kept in touch with anyone from Watendlath!

Yet even if I had known, would I have behaved any less stupidly? Sophie wondered dismally. Kirk kept warning me about Pelham, but I was too stubborn to listen to him. Too stubborn, too proud. . .and too desperately in love to think straight!

She had rejected all Kirk's advice, and look where her obstinacy had led! He must think me a fool and be glad to be rid of me, she thought sadly, her depression deepening.

Nancy's arrival with her supper-tray had been a welcome surprise, and Sophie's spirits had begun to lift when she realised that her maid was to be allowed to remain.

'Eat up your supper, Miss Sophie, and then we'll talk,' Nancy had insisted.

Sophie had obeyed, realising that her maid had been badly shocked and was trying her best to preserve some semblance of normality.

But as soon as the meal was finished Sophie had made Nancy sit down.

'It is time I told you the whole story,' she had confessed.

Recovering from her surprise, Nancy smiled with cheerful determination. 'Never you fret, lass. There's many a slip 'twixt cup and lip, and that villain's plans don't deserve to prosper.' She shook her greying head. 'I never thought to see a gentleman behave in such a way!'

'Do you think we should attempt to escape? It will be difficult, but what other choice is there? I feel I must at least try; I can't sit here meekly waiting for that brute to force me up the aisle!'

'That you can't, my lamb!' Nancy nodded vigorously.

'One of the footmen will come soon to bring fresh fuel for the fire,' Sophie said thoughtfully. 'Perhaps we could distract him.'

Nancy eyed the brass poker by the hearth. 'Aye, it might work at that, Miss Sophie.'

Sophie followed her gaze. A shiver ran along her spine as she realised what her maid was thinking, but she crushed her reluctance. 'We have got to get out of this horrible place!'

'Where will we go once we are free?' Nancy asked with a calm practicality that soothed Sophie's strained nerves.

'Keswick. It isn't very far and we won't get lost even in the dark if we keep in sight of the lake.'

'But won't Sir Pelham think of looking for us there?'

'I don't intend to remain in the town, Nancy. I have plenty of money — Uncle Thomas was very generous — so we don't have to rely on the stage. The landlord of the George has a carriage for hire, and there must be others. Travelling post will be both quicker and easier.'

'Oh, but I shall be glad to see Kendal again!' Nancy exclaimed fervently.

Sophie nodded, but it occurred to her that it might be safer to head for Cockermouth, where they could beg the Stricklands' protection. The journey home to Kendal was far longer, which made the risk of Sir Pelham catching up with them proportionately greater.

She felt sure that the baronet would chase after them. He is desperate to get his hands on my dowry and he dare not let me spread the story of his perfidy, she thought, but decided not to add this anxiety to Nancy's other worries.

Instead, she concentrated on remembering the road to Keswick, pouring out aloud all the details she had noticed in the hope that talking about it would enable her to recognise their way in the dark.

'Shall I see if I can sew your purse into the hem of a dress, Miss Sophie?' Nancy enquired when they had finished discussing their route.

'What a good idea!' Sophie exclaimed. None of her gowns possessed deep pockets. 'We shall have enough trouble without carrying bags.'

Nancy helped her select a redingote dress. It had a dark wine-coloured overskirt in a warm corduroy material, making it the most suitable in her wardrobe for the night ahead, but Sophie rejected the matching buckled ribbon sash.

'I don't want anything that might catch the light.'

'Then you must wear a hood over your hair,' Nancy cautioned.

Nancy swiftly completed her alteration to the gown, but Sophie decided to wait before putting it on.

'The footman might notice and think it odd I am wearing an outdoor gown so late in the evening,' she explained, and Nancy nodded, impressed by this foresight.

'I think that's everything.' Sophie's brow creased in concentration. 'Since there are no more preparations we can make, shall we go over our plan again?'

They perfected their simple scheme and sat down to wait.

The house grew quiet and Sophie began to be alarmed that she had been forgotten and that no one would come to replenish the fire.

By the time the tap came at the door just before eleven she was so keyed up that she jumped. Quickly signalling to Nancy, she grabbed her book and sat down in the armchair by the fire.

'Enter!'

The youngest of the ornately liveried footmen, a

callow youth who seemed overawed by his position, came scurrying in.

Looking up from West's *Guide to the Lakes*, she said in her most haughty voice, 'What an age you have been! Pray attend to this wretched fire at once.'

The footman glanced at the fitfully smouldering flames and then over his shoulder at the door, which he had left slightly open.

'Beg pardon, ma'am, but I was told not to linger,' he said, setting down the bucket of sea-coal which he carried.

'Good heavens, you don't expect me to get my hands dirty, do you?' Sophie demanded with a petulant pout borrowed from Becky's repertoire. 'Stop dawdling at once and get on with it, man.'

Recognising the voice of authority, the footman succumbed and knelt by the hearth. Keeping his gaze fixed on the heap of coals he was carefully placing on the embers, he said, 'Where is the poker, ma'am? I need it. . .ah!'

'Here you are!'

Nancy brought the poker down hard on his bewigged head and he slumped forward.

'For one awful moment I thought you were going to wait too long in the dressing-room,' Sophie gasped, leaping to her feet. She began to rip off her loose robe. 'Is he all right?'

Nancy bent over the footman. 'Aye. His wig helped protect him.' With deft efficiency she made him more comfortable, straightening his limbs. 'He'll suffer naught worse than a headache when he wakes.'

Sophie clambered into the wine gown and they both donned their cloaks, the plainest and darkest that Sophie owned. At the last moment she remembered to throw the hood up over her bright, revealing hair.

Their plan was to try and slip out via the servants' quarters, but first they had to traverse the richly

furnished upper halls. Sophie's mouth was dry with fear
as they crept from her room, but they saw no one.

A maze of drab passages and back-stairs led down-
wards towards the service area of the house and its rear
exits, and Sophie stood back to allow Nancy to lead the
way, knowing she would have been lost within moments
if she'd been alone.

Giving the kitchens a wide berth, they slipped into
the deserted laundry-room.

'There's a small door. I hope it's not been locked up
yet,' Nancy whispered.

It yielded to her touch and they found themselves in
the grassy plot used for clothes-drying.

'I think we go this way, through the herb and kitchen
gardens,' Nancy whispered.

Sophie nodded and they set off at the fastest pace
they could manage. Unfortunately this part of the
grounds was not as well kept as the formal areas and
Sophie cursed as her elegant leather-soled boots slipped
on the wet grass and muddy paths, unlike Nancy's
outdoor clogs. Nancy had removed them to creep
downstairs, lest the iron caulkers shod over the alder-
wood soles made a noise, but now they gave her a
secure footing that Sophie envied.

Sophie also began to wish ladies' gowns aped the
more sensible shorter length worn by servants, for her
skirts soon became uncomfortably damp and heavy as
they worked their way round the side of the house.

They were barely in sight of the long gravelled drive
when the elegantly high heel of Sophie's boot caught in
a tussock of rough grass. She slithered, wrenching her
weak ankle, and could not prevent a little gasp of pain.

'Are you all right, Miss Sophie?' Nancy asked
anxiously.

Sophie nodded gamely, ignoring the fire in her ankle.

'We'll have to head for the main gates,' she said. 'I

don't know the way through the park and we can't afford to waste time getting lost.'

'We'll never get past the gatekeeper,' Nancy objected.

'The wall is low. We can climb it.'

Nancy wasn't sure she shared her mistress's confidence.

'Eh, Miss Sophie, but I'm too old for all this gallivanting,' she muttered.

Sophie chuckled softly. 'Nonsense,' she whispered. 'You are tougher than any of us.'

Nancy gave her an answering grin, but their good humour abruptly vanished when someone shouted, splitting the silence.

'They must have discovered our escape!' Sophie gasped.

The noise increased and light blossomed from the direction of the house, illuminating the darkness.

'We cannot have more than a few minutes' lead on them; they'll catch up with us for sure.' Sophie came to a rapid decision. 'You must go on alone, Nancy. Hurry, I'll stall them for as long as I can. It's me they are after anyway.'

Nancy gazed at her in horror. 'I can't leave you, Miss Sophie!'

'You must! You have to get word to the Stricklands.' Sophie's voice was harsh with anxiety. 'Maria will help me, but I shan't be able to delay the marriage long.'

Nancy nodded reluctantly, her face crumpling. She threw her arms around Sophie and gave her a brief fierce hug.

'God keep you, my lamb!' she sobbed.

For an instant Sophie lingered, watching her melt away into the darkness. Then she turned and began to walk resolutely back towards the house.

* * *

The wind blowing across the lake struck chill as Kirk Thorburn stood at the rail of the *Western Star*. He stared unseeingly at the grey water, willing the small yacht to greater speed.

'I've made some coffee for ye, sir. Will ye come below and drink it?'

'In a moment.' Kirk smiled mechanically at the sailor, one of the permanent crew Mr Farrington kept on board.

The sailor nodded and disappeared, shaking his head over this strange passenger.

Kirk barely noticed him go.

Harry had readily agreed to loan him the boat he kept on Lake Bassenthwaite. They hadn't seen each other in years, but they had been firm friends once and Kirk had been willing to risk a rebuff to his pride in order to save time in reaching Cockermouth.

Kirk stirred uneasily, raking a hand through his tousled hair.

His visit to see Maria Strickland had been fruitful, but he could not rid himself of the disquiet which had been haunting him ever since he had discovered Sophie's absence.

'Damn it, I swore I wouldn't interfere in her affairs again!' he muttered aloud and stamped below deck to consume his coffee.

His unease grew stronger as the morning passed. Kirk ignored it. By thunder, he had his pride and he'd be damned if he'd lay himself open to any more insults from that little baggage!

By the time he left the boat his mood was foul. Electing to dine in Keswick, it didn't improve his temper to find the yard of the George deserted.

'Ostler! Ostler! What the devil is going on?' he demanded when the groom came running to take Sultan's reins.

'Beg pardon, Mr Thorburn, sir. Only there's a madwoman abadgering Mr Fletcher. She came running in here not ten minutes ago, hollering fit to burst. Mr Fletcher, he told her to go, but she marched into the parlour as bold as brass. She's demanding all manner of things, so I've heard, and Tom says Mr Fletcher is likely to go off in an apoplexy!'

Kirk grinned sourly. It seemed that the landlord, who was noted for his bull-headed character, had met his match at last.

Tossing the ostler a coin, he decided to go and watch the entertainment while he waited for his dinner.

A crowd of giggling servants clustered around the entrance to the parlour, but, recognising him, they respectfully parted.

A small, thick-set woman stood firmly planted in the middle of the room. Her greying hair hung in wild disarray and her servant's attire was torn and splashed with mud, but nothing in her dirty face suggested that she was mad to Kirk. In fact something about her plucky stance stirred his admiration, and on impulse he stepped into the room.

The landlord was shouting in an angry voice, but he fell silent when he spotted Kirk.

'Can I do anything to help, Fletcher?'

'That you can, Mr Thorburn, sir. You can tell this. . . this harridan to leave my inn before I set the law on her!' the landlord gibbered.

'Thorburn?' The woman's sharp eyes fastened on Kirk's face. '*You* are Kirk Thorburn, sir?'

Kirk nodded, vaguely disturbed by the intensity of her stare. He was just beginning to wonder if he had made a mistake in getting involved when she burst into noisy tears.

'Well, don't just stand there, man!' Kirk bellowed at the landlord. 'Fetch the lady some cordial.'

The landlord backed away in alarm.

'And you may bring me some brandy while you are about it,' Kirk called after him.

Gingerly he put an arm around the woman's shaking shoulders. 'Come and sit down, ma'am,' he invited gruffly.

'Thank you, sir,' his protégée sniffed.

To Kirk's relief, she stopped crying almost immediately.

'I'm sorry,' she said. 'I should be rejoicing that I have found you, not snivelling like a ninny.'

This remark puzzled Kirk, but before he could ask her meaning the landlord came hurrying in with the required refreshments.

His protégée took a swift sip at her wine.

'Let me introduce myself. I am Nancy Nelson, maid to Miss Fleming.' She gazed at him beseechingly. 'She spoke of you as a friend, sir, and God knows she is in sore need of a friend to help her now.'

A muscle by Kirk's well-cut mouth jerked involuntarily, but his voice remained creditably calm when he replied to this startling announcement.

'Where is Miss Fleming? I take it that she did not accompany you here.'

Nancy shook her head vehemently.

'We planned to leave Stanton Hall together, but our escape was discovered. Miss Sophie bade me leave her and fetch help. She told me to go to Mrs Strickland, but that fool of a landlord will not listen to my pleas. He refuses to hire out his gig without payment in advance, and I haven't a farthing on me!'

Kirk turned cold. 'Why did you use the word "escape"? Is the baronet preventing Miss Fleming from leaving the Hall?'

'Aye, sir. He wanted to bring the wedding forward and locked Miss Sophie up when she said she would not marry him.' Nancy quelled the sobs that threatened to rise in her throat and added in a choked voice, 'He plans to force her, you see, sir.'

'The devil he does!' Kirk's intensely blue eyes began to blaze. 'Do you know when the ceremony is to take place?'

'Today, I reckon, from what Miss Sophie told me.'

'Then it is already too late to hope Mrs Strickland can intervene.'

Rapidly Kirk explained about his mission to Cockermouth. 'But I fear they will not arrive until tomorrow, since they are travelling by road,' he finished.

Nancy chewed her lower lip frantically. 'My poor lass said she would try to delay the wedding.'

'I think it is too risky to pin our hopes on her succeeding,' Kirk answered gently.

'Oh, sir!' Nancy blinked away a tear. 'What shall I do? I should never have left her!'

Kirk patted her hand in an awkward gesture.

'You have done all you, could, Mrs Nelson,' he said firmly. 'I'm sure Sophie will be proud of you. Now you must recover from your exertions and leave the rest to me.'

'To you, sir?' Nancy shot him a hopeful look.

'To me,' Kirk repeated and rose purposefully to his feet. 'I have a score to settle with Sir Pelham Stanton, and what better time than now?'

'I won't sign.'

Sophie glared at the baronet across the width of his walnut pedestal desk. On its surface lay an impressive-looking legal document, the formal contract stating the marriage terms she had agreed to in Kendal.

Sir Pelham's thin mouth twisted in a mocking sneer.

'Very well, my dear, continue in your obstinacy. After tonight it will make no odds.' He laughed cynically. 'If necessary, I can always instruct Conrad to forge your signature. He is remarkably skilled in such useful arts.'

Sophie paled. She was very tired after a sleepless night spent pacing the floor of her gilded prison, but her voice was firm. 'You won't get away with it. My uncle ——'

'Bah! The old fool will have to accept accomplished facts. I will have the marriage-lines, and, make no mistake, I shall bed you whether you are willing or no! There will be no annulment, no claims of non-consummation!'

A shiver ran down Sophie's spine. The thought of his pale hands upon her body made her feel sick.

Her revulsion showed on her expressive face and the baronet threw down the pen he was still holding out to her with an angry oath.

'Do you think I wish to marry an ugly, ill-bred cripple?' he asked venomously. 'Believe me, I would never do so if it were not for the fact I need your dowry.'

The look of hatred in his eyes made Sophie recoil.

His nature is twisted, she thought, with a flash of sudden understanding. His over-weening pride and selfish ambition have driven out all finer feelings. He doesn't care whom he hurts so long as he gets his own way!

Fear curbed the retort that sprang to her tongue. Once he had control of her fortune, what was to prevent him arranging another little 'accident' to remove *her* from his path?

'The ceremony will take place as soon as the parson arrives. He should be here within the hour.' The baronet fixed her with a cold stare. 'Wear the cream silk gown and tidy your hair. You look like a village slut.'

Sophie was still wearing the wine redingote she had donned for her escape, and it had been stained and torn during the struggle to drag her back into the house.

'How am I to dress without the assistance of my maid?' Sophie taunted him, recovering her courage.

His frown deepened. The fact that the older woman had got clean away irked him, but he consoled himself with the thought that even if she managed to persuade anyone to believe her story it would be too late to affect his plans.

'I'll send one of the housemaids up to you, but heaven help you if you try any more tricks,' he snarled, turning to tug savagely at the bell-pull to summon Conrad, who was waiting outside the study.

The baronet conferred in a whisper with his secretary and the fleshy young man departed with an obedient bow.

'I have sent him to fetch the drug I spoke of yesterday,' Sir Pelham informed Sophie.

Her great dark eyes widened.

'It is a potent draught.' Idly the baronet pretended to examine his well-manicured fingernails, but he was watching her like a hawk. 'You'll be able to walk and talk a little, but nothing more.'

Sophie could not repress a shiver, and she stared in horror at the glass of dark brown liquid which the secretary brought in.

Coming out from behind his ornate desk, the baronet thrust it beneath her nose.

'Smells vile, doesn't it, my dear? What a pity you dislike taking medicines.' He smiled mockingly at her start of surprise. 'You see what a devoted husband I shall make, since I can remember even your lightest remarks!'

His glance flicked towards his secretary. 'Here, Conrad, hold her.'

'No!' Sophie retched. 'Take it away, for pity's sake!'

Sir Pelham laughed and set down the glass.

'Am I to assume that you will behave yourself without this little inducement?'

Sophie nodded silently.

'Do I have your word?'

Again she nodded and, satisfied, he waved Conrad to remove the sedative.

Sophie was trembling. Her reluctance to swallow his disgusting brew was quite genuine, but she had exaggerated her fear in order to convince him that she would honour her promise. Naturally she had no intention of doing so. Pelham had forfeited all rights! She would take any chance to escape that presented itself, and for that she needed to keep her wits about her.

The secretary shut the door quietly after him and the baronet said, 'Now shall we discuss the matter of wedding gifts? I'm sure you'll be able to persuade your uncle into forgetting his disappointment at missing the ceremony. I have a fancy for something generously large and splendid.'

Sophie regarded him with scorn. 'What a despicable creature you are, Pelham!'

He raised his fist to hit her and then let it fall. He would not risk marking that white skin of hers before the service. There would be plenty of time to teach her obedience once they were wed.

'Watch your tongue,' he snapped. 'I don't find insolence amusing.'

He tugged at the bell-pull again and, while they waited, delved into the pocket of his elegantly cut satin coat.

Sophie stared hard at the snuff-box he pulled out.

'It is pretty, is it not?' The baronet preened beneath her gaze and flicked open the lid. 'French, of course, in *quatre-couleur* gold. Still, I suppose you would know that. Your uncle is a connoisseur of sorts.'

Sophie's mouth had gone so dry that she could only nod.

'It is new.' The baronet's gloating expression faded

and he sighed. 'I had another, very similar, but even
finer. Unfortunately I lost it somewhere.'

'Perhaps one of the servants stole it,' Sophie managed to whisper.

'Don't be stupid!' The baronet glowered at her. 'Do
you think I would allow my staff to cheat me? I am not
so gullible! It went missing last spring after a night at
my club.' He shrugged irritably, annoyed by the
memory. 'I was celebrating my return to London. A
man must drink on such occasions, but carelessness led
to my pockets being picked on my way home.'

He patted the little box possessively. 'I shall be more
vigilant in future. It took my goldsmith months to find
this one and adapt it to my wishes.'

'Is that your initial?'

'So you have noticed it! I was beginning to think you
had no appreciation of art!' Sir Pelham threw her a
pleased look. 'It is my own design.'

The entrance of Simon Conrad saved Sophie from
having to think of a reply.

Numbly, she allowed the secretary to take her arm
and escort her to the door.

'Until later, my dear. And don't forget to smile as
you come up the aisle.'

Sophie did not hear the mockery in her betrothed's
farewell. All she could think of was the last time she
had seen that intricate golden S, when it had decorated
the snuff-box sitting on the counter of her uncle's
shop, the snuff-box that had been found in Ingram
Thorburn's dead hand.

CHAPTER TWELVE

A SUDDEN flash of movement caught Kirk Thorburn's eyes. There was someone in the marble pavilion that overlooked the flower-garden.

A faint curse escaped him. He had been counting on the fact that the grounds would be deserted at this hour. Desperately he racked his brains to think of another way of gaining access to the house, but he didn't know of any other secret entrance.

Not that it was truly a secret entrance, of course. That was just the name Ingram had christened it years ago. Its secluded door gave on to a series of passages, one of which led up a back-stair to Pelham's boyhood room. Another, if he remembered aright, branched off in the direction of the chapel.

Kirk's plan was simple. He intended to conceal himself in the chapel and, at the appropriate moment when the parson asked if anyone knew of any impediment to the marriage, he would stand up and declare that Sophie was being forced.

If that failed, well, he was armed.

A swift glance at the sinking sun reminded him that it would soon be dusk. There was no time to stand here dithering like an old maid!

Resolutely putting aside the worry eating into him that he might already be too late, Kirk decided to run the risk of being seen. Taking a firmer grip on the crowbar he carried, he slipped cautiously from his hiding-place in the shadow of the cypress hedge.

At the exact same instant a frail figure emerged from the pavilion and began to walk towards him, head bowed as if in prayer.

For a moment Kirk thought she might not see him, but then she looked up and almost staggered back in shock.

'Mrs Stanton. Don't be alarmed. I won't harm you.'

'Kirk?' she gasped. 'Kirk Thorburn!'

The old lady peered up at him. She'd been too surprised to let out a scream of fright, and now she had recognised him she knew that there was no need.

'Kirk, you must leave,' she ordered in a quavering voice. 'If Pelham discovers you are here there will be trouble.'

Kirk's mouth set in a grim line. 'The fact that you seek to warn me proves you suspect your nephew of villainy.'

The gathering shadows could not hide her guilty blush.

'Kirk, you were always a good boy. Please do as I ask,' she pleaded.

He shook his head. 'It's too late, Mrs Stanton. This time you can't prevent the truth from coming out. Pelham's gone too far.'

She hugged her fur-trimmed cloak tighter about her tiny body. 'I know,' she whispered. Tears began to trickle down her wrinkled cheeks. 'Oh, Kirk, I know about your brother!'

Kirk's fingers clenched on the cold iron of his crowbar.

'I wasn't sure at first that Pelham had been involved,' his aunt continued shakily. 'I suppose I didn't want to believe it. When I finally taxed him with it Pelham only laughed. He told me not to worry, that no one would ever find out.'

Kirk handed her his handkerchief and she dabbed at her eyes.

'I think this fever for gaming has turned his brain. I have begged him to desist until I'm hoarse, but he won't listen. He's even mortgaged the Hall.'

'So that's why he is desperate to marry a fortune,' Kirk breathed.

Mrs Stanton did not deny it. 'He has chosen a Kendal heiress, a Miss Fleming. She is a sweet girl.'

Kirk's heartbeat quickened.

'Have you spoken to her recently?'

Another sob shook the old lady. 'Pelham will not let me see her. He says she is willing for the ceremony to go ahead this afternoon, but Kirk, I fear he is lying!'

'I know he is,' Kirk replied grimly. 'That's why I'm here. You see, Miss Fleming is a friend of mine and I'm going to put a stop to this wedding one way or another.'

Her eyes flew to the sword he wore.

'Do you intend to tell Pelham I'm here?'

His demand made her tears fall faster, and Kirk felt a fleeting pang of sympathy for her predicament. She had always adored her nephew.

'I cannot condone what he has done,' she whispered. 'I came out here into the peace of the garden to pray for guidance, and God has sent you to me. My nephew has become a monster; he must be saved from himself before he hurts anyone else.'

'Then we must hurry,' Kirk said, taking her arm.

They approached the door.

'I have the key. There is no need to use that thing,' Mrs Stanton informed him with a shudder.

Once inside the house, Kirk had additional cause to be grateful for the old lady's assistance. The twists and turns of the numerous passages were more complicated than he remembered, but with Mrs Stanton's help he swiftly found himself outside the chapel.

'I think it would be better if you waited out here until the service is under way,' Pelham's aunt announced thoughtfully. 'There is little concealment in the chapel for a man of your size.'

Kirk nodded. All eyes would be on the altar; no one would notice him slip in later.

'Will you attend the ceremony?'

'Pelham requested my presence, and in his present mood I did not dare refuse him.' She glanced at the diamond-encrusted little watch which decorated the sober neckline of her gown. 'It is almost time.' She wiped her eyes with a resolute gesture. 'I must go in and take my place.'

Her hand crept timidly to find his sleeve.

'I know I have no right to ask it of you, but say that you will not hurt him!'

He removed her hand gently.

'I'd be a liar if I made you any promise,' he answered quietly. 'I have sworn to bring your nephew to justice and, if Pelham resists, then be it on his own head!'

Her shoulders sagged and she turned away without another word.

Kirk watched her go and frowned. Could he trust her not to betray him or would the habit of protecting her nephew prove too strong?

Shrugging the thought away, he took up the position Mrs Stanton had suggested behind one of the thick, ornately carved pillars that decorated the archway leading to the chapel doors.

After a few moments he heard the sound of approaching footsteps.

'My aunt must have already gone inside. Her maid said she left her room some time ago.'

The baronet's voice sounded unnaturally loud in Kirk's ears and his jaw clenched involuntarily.

Another man answered in mellifluous tones.

'Indeed, go on ahead, sir. You must wish to familiarise yourself with the altar. I shall join you in a moment when my secretary arrives with Miss Fleming.'

The other man, who was obviously the parson, quipped, 'What? Will you risk bad luck by seeing your bride ahead of time, Sir Pelham?'

'*I* am not superstitious.' The baronet's tone was reproving.

His remark provoked a flurry of apology, followed by the sound of the heavy chapel door shutting.

Kirk tensed. It was so quiet that he could hear Stanton breathing.

Suddenly all the frustration of these long months of inaction came boiling to a head, and Kirk knew he couldn't endure to wait another moment. Without pausing to consider, he stepped out of his place of concealment.

'A word with you, sir.'

Stunned, the baronet stared at him, his mouth falling slack with disbelief. 'Thorburn! What. . . How. . .' He stammered over the words, his shock rapidly turning to dismay.

Kirk slowly unsheathed his sword. The long, fine blade glinted in the candlelight that illuminated the corridor.

'You murdered my brother,' he said softly.

'Prove it!' The baronet had turned a sickly grey colour.

'Don't worry, I shall.'

'Hah, there is no proof! You are bluffing, Thorburn. No magistrate will believe you.'

Kirk took a step nearer, raising his blade.

'Let's go and find out if you are right, Stanton.'

The baronet's eyes rolled wildly.

'Don't be absurd, man. I'm not going anywhere. In a few moments I am going to be married.'

'Wrong again, Pelham.' Kirk shook his head.

A look of fury replaced the fear on the baronet's face.

'The little bitch! *You* were the one she met in Watendlath!'

'Leave Miss Fleming out of this,' Kirk replied tersely.

'Ah, I see. Smitten by her rustic charms, are you? Or

is it her dowry that impresses you, Thorburn?' The baronet gave a jeering laugh.

'Don't judge everyone by your own low standards,' Kirk retorted. 'Unlike you, I have no need of Sophie's money.'

Sir Pelham blanched, and it was Kirk's turn to laugh.

'The game's up, Pelham. I know all about your debts, and I'm not the only one. Soon your disgrace will be on everyone's lips.' His smile hardened, his blue eyes cold. 'Still so sure that the magistrates won't believe me?'

'Fiend take you!' The baronet had begun to sweat. 'You'll never carry this off, Thorburn. I've a dozen servants——'

'But none within earshot,' Kirk interrupted. 'You gave them all leave to make merry in the servants' hall.'

'How the devil did you know that?'

'Your aunt told me.'

This simple reply seemed to rob the baronet of any further speech, and in the sudden silence they both became aware of the sound of footsteps.

Automatically, they both turned. Simon Conrad was approaching. At his side, her face as pale as her silk gown, walked Sophie. In her reluctant hand hung a posy of hothouse flowers, a bridal tribute.

'Conrad! Here, to me!' the baronet cried desperately, backing away from Kirk.

The iron grip on Sophie's arm slackened and she wrenched free.

'Kirk!'

She began to run towards him, but the secretary grabbed her, hauling her back.

'Never mind her, you fool!' Sir Pelham screamed. 'Get Thorburn!'

Obeying, Conrad flung Sophie to one side and advanced on Kirk, drawing his light dress sword.

After one agonised look to check that Sophie had not

suffered any harm, Kirk tried to concentrate his attention on this new threat.

The secretary was surprisingly good for a man of such fleshy appearance. Kirk had the superior reach, but his swordsmanship was of the plain variety; he preferred pistols. Unfortunately, never dreaming how matters would turn out, he had left his behind when he'd set out to escort Becky to Keswick.

He had borrowed this sword from the landlord of the George, who had acquired it in payment for a debt. It was a fine blade, but within moments Kirk realised that he had never learnt the dirty tricks that the secretary had mastered. Only his quick wits and natural strength enabled him to counter the flashy sword-play employed against him.

Sophie watched anxiously as he was gradually forced back, her joy at his miraculous arrival turning to fear for his safety.

'Don't worry, you'll be a bride yet!'

Unnoticed, the baronet had crept to her side, and Sophie flinched as he pinched her arm, emitting a vicious little laugh.

'You miserable swine!' With all her strength, she slapped his face, and his squeal of pain caused the distraction Kirk needed.

Abandoning the niceties, he lashed out with his fist, catching Conrad unawares. The blow landed directly on his jaw and the secretary crumpled into an untidy heap and lay unmoving.

'My dear sir, what is the meaning of this outrage? Have you no shame? How dare you brawl on the doorstep of the house of the Lord?' cried a mellifluous voice.

The noise of the fight had filtered into the chapel, bringing the parson and Mrs Stanton hurrying.

Ignoring them, Kirk whirled to face the baronet, but Sir Pelham had already seized his chance.

'Let her go, damn you!'

The baronet laughed shrilly and tightened his savage grip on Sophie, who was struggling frantically to free herself.

'Keep still, you bitch!' Sir Pelham snarled, burying his free hand in Sophie's curls and yanking viciously.

Tears of pain spurted from beneath Sophie's eyelids, and with a growl of rage Kirk hurled himself towards the baronet.

'Come one step nearer, Thorburn, and I'll break it,' he warned, forcing Sophie's arm up behind her back.

Kirk halted, and a thin little smile touched the baronet's mouth.

'That's better,' he gloated.

'Pelham, please! Don't do this!' His aunt began to sob.

He glared furiously at her. 'Be silent, ma'am!'

He tugged at Sophie's arm. 'Walk!' he ordered.

'No!' Sophie spat the word at him, but when she tried to resist he increased the pressure on her arm.

'Do as he says, Sophie.'

Kirk's anxious voice seemed to reach her through a mist of pain, and she nodded giddily.

Sir Pelham began to back away down the corridor. Half dragged along in his wake, Sophie sought frantically for a means of escape, but the baronet's grip never wavered.

Kirk followed, careful not to cause alarm by coming too close. He did not trust that wild look in those cold hazel eyes. One wrong move and Stanton would panic, forgetting everything but his own fear, and he had Sophie!

They had reached the grand staircase, and for the first time the baronet halted, uncertainty flickering over his narrow face.

A glimmer of hope lit up Sophie's distress. He's worried now that there's room for Kirk to spring on him. He can't defend himself and hold on to me at the same time!

'Let her go, Stanton,' Kirk said quietly.

'Not until it suits me!' cried the baronet, but his voice quivered.

'Let her go and I'll leave here quietly.'

'No!' Sophie protested, unwilling to be the cause of Kirk's defeat.

'Be quiet, Sophie,' Kirk pleaded. 'Release her and I give you my word that I will allow you a clear start of three days before I come after you.'

'How do I know I can trust you?'

'The parson here can bear witness.' Kirk gestured to the cleric, who had followed them at a discreet distance, accompanied by Mrs Stanton. 'All I ask is that you let Sophie come away with me now.'

'Pelham, do as he suggests.' The old lady spoke up. 'Be sensible, boy! The truth is bound to come out. This way at least you have a chance. Don't make things worse.'

The baronet hesitated, and in that instant his grip on Sophie's arm eased.

Seizing the opportunity, Sophie drove her unfettered elbow into her captor's ribs as hard as she could. Sir Pelham gasped, involuntarily slackening his hold on her other arm.

Instantly Sophie wrenched herself free and took to her heels.

'Good girl!' Kirk flung a comforting arm around her shoulders and gave her a quick hug before turning back to face the baronet.

'Come on, Pelham,' he murmured softly. 'Let's see how you defend yourself now you can't hide behind a woman's skirts!'

'Get away from me!' Gibbering with fear, the baronet stepped backwards.

'Look out, you fool!'

Kirk's warning came a second too late.

In his panic the baronet had forgotten where he was standing, and one high-heeled shoe slid over the edge of the top stair, throwing him off balance. His arms wheeled up as he tried desperately to regain his footing, but it was no use.

His elegantly clad body tumbled backwards and, bouncing from marble step to marble step, came to rest spread-eagled on the cold stone below.

'Miss Fleming! A word if I may.'

Sophie reined in her newly acquired chestnut mare.

'Mrs Birkett.' She acknowledged Caroline's greeting with a slight nod.

'Will you dismount and enter?' Caroline gestured towards the house a little further down the street. 'We could take tea together.'

'No, thank you.' Sophie eyed the parcels Caroline held. 'I would not wish to interrupt your shopping.'

'I have just finished.' Caroline smiled. 'It is such a warm day; I'm sure a little refreshment would not come amiss.'

About to refuse, it occurred to Sophie that Caroline must have other matters than the unexpectedly mild April weather on her mind.

'Very well, but I cannot stay long. My uncle expects me home from my riding lesson,' Sophie explained.

The groom, whom her uncle insisted attend her at all times, helped Sophie dismount.

'My servants will show you where to go,' Caroline murmured to him, beckoning Sophie to follow her into the neat terraced house that was her home.

After the glare of the streets, the little parlour seemed deliciously cool.

'Pray remove your hat and sit down,' Caroline invited.

While she rang for tea Sophie cast a surreptitious

glance around her. It was a very feminine room, charmingly decorated in the exact blue of Caroline's eyes.

A wry smile touched Sophie's generous mouth for an instant.

'You look a little pale. Would you like something stronger than tea to revive you? Some sherry perhaps?' Caroline asked solicitously.

Sophie shook her head and refused politely. Her uncle had purchased a horse for her, a pretty little chestnut mare named Jasmine, and she'd had several lessons. She was still rather nervous, hence her lack of colour, but she was determined to succeed in becoming a good rider, as she explained to her hostess.

'I see,' Caroline answered. 'Only I couldn't help wondering if you were still feeling the effects of your shocking tragedy. After all, it is only two weeks ago that Sir Pelham met his death.'

Sophie gritted her teeth.

'I am perfectly well, thank you.'

Her evasive answer caused Caroline to hesitate, but after their refreshments had arrived she said bluntly, 'Forgive me if I offend, but you don't seem in the least bit broken-hearted.'

Sophie tensed. 'I find public displays of grief distasteful,' she announced with perfect truth.

Caroline set down her tea-cup.

'Of course. Everyone must deal with bereavement in their own way, but I'm surprised you are not wearing mourning.' She eyed Sophie's riding-habit, a dashing affair in fine royal blue cloth, its severe lines softened by military-style gold frogging. 'And you left Stanton Hall before the funeral.'

'I. . . I longed to get home,' Sophie stammered.

'And Mr Thorburn escorted you, did he not?'

Sophie nodded unwillingly.

It had been a dreadful journey. Old Mrs Stanton's

screams seemed to ring in her ears long after they had left the Hall behind and rejoined Nancy.

Maria's arrival at the George Inn had helped Sophie recover from the shock, but they were not free to leave Keswick until they had given evidence about Pelham's death to the local magistrate. Despite the fact that everyone involved, for varying reasons of their own, had agreed to say the baronet's fall was a sheer accident, Sophie found the interview a dreadful ordeal.

She had still been feeling shaken when they finally reached Kendal. Uncle Thomas, appalled by the news and distressed by Sophie's wan appearance, had ordered her off to bed, and when she had awoken the next day it was to discover that Kirk had already left.

The disappointment had been crushing. The brief letter he had left behind for her had merely stated that he had several urgent matters to attend to. Even worse, it made no mention of when he would return.

'It must have been terrible to actually witness the accident.'

Caroline's probing remark broke the awkward silence that had fallen.

Sophie agreed warily. Her uncle had cautioned her to say nothing about the true events that had taken place at Stanton Hall.

'Whether the truth comes out is up to Kirk, lass,' Mr Fleming had announced. 'I know he has to think of his brother, and I won't try to hide the facts if I'm asked, but there's nothing to be gained by letting the world know what an old fool I've been!'

He had shuddered, heaving a deep sigh. 'When I think of the danger you were in! Eeh, lass, but the gossips will have a field-day if they ever find out Stanton had you imprisoned in that palace of his! I could kick myself when I think of the damage this whole business might do to your reputation! Won't you wear black at least for a few weeks? It might stop some talk.'

Sophie had shaken her bright curls. 'I will not play the hypocrite, Uncle,' she had said flatly.

He had heaved another sigh, too worried to try and persuade her. 'Stanton's treachery has brought it home to me how much you need a proper husband to look after you, lass. I'm getting too old for the job.'

Sophie had denied it, adding, 'I'm not sure I want to marry anyway, Uncle.'

'Hey, now, what's this? You've had a bad fright, lass, but you are only young yet. There's plenty of time to find the right man.'

Sophie had coloured, and something in her expressive face warned him that his niece had already done so.

'So it's young Thorburn you've set your heart on, eh?'

Sophie's blush had deepened.

Thomas Fleming had stroked his chin thoughtfully, but to Sophie's relief he hadn't pursued the subject.

She had been too grateful at not having to explain about her tangled relationship with Kirk to wonder at his lack of curiosity, but, thinking about it now, it occurred to her how odd his attitude had been. It was almost as if he knew all about it, and yet that was absurd!

'And your betrothed's death coming so close to the wedding!' Caroline's voice was continuing relentlessly, forcing Sophie to abandon her thoughts and concentrate on the present.

'It must be hard for you not to dwell on the fact that the ceremony should have taken place next month.'

Sophie repressed a shiver. She had ordered Nancy to burn the cream silk gown she had worn that fateful day, but her memories were not so easily eradicated. Nightmares still haunted her sleep.

'More tea?'

Caroline reached out to refill her cup, but Sophie shook her head.

'I heard a rumour the other day that you had returned
your betrothal ring to old Mrs Stanton. Didn't you wish
to treasure it as a keepsake?'

'What are you hinting at, Mrs Birkett?' Sophie
demanded, tiring of the inquisition.

'I'm sorry.' Unexpectedly, Caroline apologised. 'I
know I shouldn't ask, but what I am trying to discover
is whether you truly loved the baronet or not.'

'Loved him? I detested the man!' Sophie snapped,
innate honesty getting the better of discretion.

'Thank goodness for that!'

'I don't understand.' Sophie gazed at her in
confusion.

'I will try to explain in a moment, but first I think I
owe you an apology. You once accused me of being in
love with Kirk Thorburn and I denied it, but I was
lying.' Caroline chewed her lower lip. 'I would never be
unfaithful to my husband, but I find Kirk very
attractive.'

Jealousy seared through Sophie, but she managed to
say levelly, 'Your private emotions are none of my
concern. You don't have to justify yourself to me.'

'But I do. Unless I miss my guess, you love Kirk, and
I fear my infatuation has done him a disservice!'
Caroline fixed her limpid blue gaze earnestly on
Sophie's face. 'Kirk is not attracted to me. I think he
would be horrified if he realised how I felt! He is
entirely blameless!'

'Why are you telling me all this?' Sophie asked.

Caroline sighed faintly. 'Kirk came to pay a brief
courtesy call on me before he returned north. I could
tell that he was unhappy. He would not discuss it, but I
think he is in love with you. However, I sensed there
was something causing a rift between you.'

Sophie tasted blood as she bit her lip. Bitterly, she
reflected that Caroline was right. No matter how he felt
about her, it was Becky Kirk had chosen!

'I just wanted to make it clear to you that I am not your rival,' Caroline continued doggedly. 'Even if I so far forgot myself as to disregard my marriage vows, Kirk would never consent to betray James.'

'You must care a great deal for Kirk's happiness to risk telling me this,' Sophie murmured.

'Above all else, Kirk is my friend.' Caroline nodded. 'That's why I wanted to know how you felt about the baronet. If you had been in love with Stanton. . .well!' She shrugged expressively. 'I don't want to see Kirk hurt.'

'The boot is on the other foot!' Sophie cried hotly. 'Kirk must have guessed how I feel, but he left Kendal without a word.'

'Then you *are* in love with him?'

Sophie couldn't deny it.

'I hope things sort themselves for you,' Caroline said awkwardly. She paused and then added in a rush, 'Will you keep my secret?'

'I won't breathe a word to anyone,' Sophie affirmed, and Caroline let out a gasp of relief.

'I must go.' Sophie rose swiftly to her feet, anxious to be on her own so that she could think over what Caroline had said.

'So soon?' Caroline prepared to escort her to the door. 'I was hoping that perhaps we might start to become better acquainted.'

'I should like that, but my uncle will worry if I don't return. He is even more nervous about my riding than I am!'

Caroline acknowledged this remark with a smile, but then her expression grew serious.

'There is one other thing I ought to confess. When Kirk first came to Kendal I'm afraid I rather exaggerated the extent of his fortune.'

'But I thought his plantation was to bring in an enormous profit?' Sophie exclaimed.

Caroline coloured. 'Kirk told me in confidence that its value would be affected by an attack of chenille bug, which apparently lowers cotton yields. I ignored him. It seemed to me that people would take more notice of his claims if they thought him to be a rich man.' She shrugged defensively. 'I did it for the best.'

Sophie refrained from making the obvious comment that Caroline's meddling had placed Kirk in an awkward position.

'I'm sorry, I seem to have made a complete hash of things,' Caroline sighed, leading the way into the hall.

Once upon a time, not so long ago, Sophie would have thrown Caroline's apology back in her face, but recent events had taught her not to be so hasty. She would always be hot-tempered, but she had acquired a little more tolerance, and kindness wasn't to be despised.

'I never thanked you for attempting to warn me about Pelham,' she said slowly. 'It was good of you to try, especially as I behaved like a spoilt brat.'

Caroline's face brightened. 'You have changed!' she exclaimed.

Sophie smiled faintly. 'So my uncle informs me,' she replied with a humourous inflexion in her voice that made Caroline laugh and say,

'Come again soon.'

Sophie promised to do so and they parted on good terms.

On the ride home Sophie's thoughts were in a whirl.

She had assumed that Kirk had left Kendal in order to return to Becky's side, but Caroline's assertion seemed to contradict that idea.

But why had Kirk left in such a hurry? Could the dread of being thought a fortune-hunter have driven him away? He was a proud man, and Sophie knew he would hate being tarred with the same brush as Pelham.

It was another reason to hope that the real facts about the baronet's villainy never got out, but Sophie was aware of the flaw in her argument. If Kirk didn't broadcast the truth, which included Pelham's motive for marrying an heiress, of course, how was he to avenge Ingram's murder?

Sophie bit her lip. Was Kirk worried about her reputation? He had once accused her of being spoilt and selfish, but surely he couldn't think that she would rate gossip more important than a debt of honour?

Oh, why had he left without a word? If only she could have spoken to him she could have reassured him that she was prepared to endure the spiteful talk his revelations would undoubtedly bring.

She was on the point of dismounting from Jasmine's back when it suddenly occurred to her that her uncle was the last person to have spoken to Kirk before he left. Uneasily, she remembered how concerned Uncle Thomas was about the possibility of gossip, and he was very old-fashioned. . .

'Oh, no!' she breathed, almost breaking her neck as she scrambled down.

Leaving her groom tut-tutting his disapproval, she ran into the house. Pausing only to cast her whip and hat on to the hall table, she marched into the parlour.

'Uncle Thomas, I want to —— Oh!'

Kirk Thorburn uncurled his great length from the armchair and rose politely to his feet.

'Your uncle is in the wine cellar,' he informed her.

Sophie nodded wordlessly and collapsed on to a red-velvet-cushioned settle.

'May I join you?' Before she could frame a coherent reply Kirk had sat down next to her.

Recovering her breath, Sophie demanded, 'Why didn't you let us know you were coming?'

'I did,' Kirk replied coolly.

'But. . .but my uncle said nothing!' Sophie gazed at him in bewilderment.

'Ah, I'd rather hoped he might have changed his mind.'

There was a rueful note in his deep voice, but Sophie scarcely heeded his cryptic remark. Her first astonishment over, a fierce joy had taken possession of her as her starved senses drank in his nearness.

He looked immaculate, in a smart grey coat over his pale lemon silk waistcoat. Cream-coloured pantaloons encased his long legs, their fashionable tightness defining the strong muscles in his thighs, and his boots were so highly polished that they almost glittered.

Sophie's mouth went dry. How blue his eyes were! They were smiling at her with that devastating charm she remembered so well, setting her pulses racing!

A little shiver ran through her. Suddenly every nerve in her body seemed to have come alive. She wanted to lay her head against his broad shoulder. . . She wanted to twine her fingers in the thick mass of guinea-gold curls that clustered at the nape of his neck. . . She wanted to feel his lips on hers. . . She wanted. . .oh, dear God, she wanted *him*!

'Did you receive my note, the one I left for you before I departed?' Kirk asked carefully.

Sophie's euphoria vanished in a twinkling.

'Indeed I did, sir.' She glared at him. 'Thank you for sparing me so much of your time when you were obviously in a hurry.'

To her surprise Kirk merely grinned at her.

'Do you know,' he said in a conversational tone, 'I was beginning to think I had come to the wrong house, but now I feel at home.'

Sophie flushed. Her gaze dropped to survey the somewhat dusty hem of her riding-habit. Damn, she had meant to keep her unruly tongue under control!

'Oh, Sophie, don't start aping those polite little

drawing-room manners.' Kirk tipped up her chin with a gentle hand. 'I prefer you the way you are.'

Sophie's heart skipped several beats, but she managed to say coolly, 'And pray, what is that, sir?'

'Truthful, courageous and loyal,' he replied with a sincerity that shook her to the core.

She swallowed hard. 'Kirk, I —'

'No, wait. Let me finish.' He touched one long finger to her lips. 'There are many qualities about you that I find endearing, Miss Fleming, but most of all I admire your honesty.'

A blur of tears almost blotted out his smile, and Sophie had to sniff hard before she could say, 'You are very kind, sir, but sadly mistaken, I fear! I'm not in the least bit honest. If I possessed even a quarter of the attributes you so flatteringly accredited to me just now I would never have accepted Pelham's offer, which would have saved everyone a great deal of bother!'

Kirk suppressed a groan. 'Must we discuss Stanton right now?'

'Yes!' Sophie almost shouted the word at him, her composure in shreds.

Kirk hesitated. He ached to enfold her in his arms and finish what he was trying to tell her, but a sense of caution prevented him. Her unguarded expression of delight on seeing him was encouraging, but he had no right to take her love for granted.

'Very well. I suppose you want to know what happened when I returned north.'

Sophie nodded. 'I won't have any peace until you tell me,' she said simply.

'I went to see old Mrs Stanton. The Hall is mortgaged to the hilt, but everything else is to be sold to try and pay off his debts.'

'I guessed as much,' Sophie breathed. 'Does she have anywhere to go?'

'She has a small income from her late husband,

barely enough to live on.' Kirk coughed awkwardly. 'I offered her one of the properties I own in Cockermouth, but she has decided to live with a cousin in Derbyshire. That's where the Stantons originally hail from, if you remember.'

His generosity made Sophie want to hug him, but the expression on his handsome face curbed her impulse.

'Kirk, what else did she say?'

'I should have known I couldn't fool you,' he muttered.

'She pointed out that there would be a scandal when Pelham's guilt was revealed, didn't she?' Sophie persisted.

Kirk regarded the toes of his leather boots. 'Aye,' he admitted at last.

The old lady had been vehement.

'My nephew is dead, sir! What good will it do to rake over old grievances now?'

Clad in black, she had faced him across the resplendent grandeur of the gold salon, her lined face ravaged by tears, but her head held defiantly high.

'Without your interference, Pelham would still be alive. Oh, I know he deserved punishment, but must you pursue him beyond the grave? It won't bring Ingram back. All it will do is cast a shadow over the reputation of Miss Fleming.'

Kirk had stared at her, unable to deny her angry claim.

'Can't you be satisfied with the fact that he is dead, Kirk?' she had continued more quietly. 'You never used to be unreasonable. You were always a kind boy.'

She had paused and then added, 'Stanton Hall and all its treasures will be sold. The house in London is already on the market. There is nothing left! Soon everyone will know that my nephew died a ruined man.'

When Kirk still hadn't answered she had fixed him with a stern eye.

'You owe me something, Kirk Thorburn. Against every family feeling, I helped you that day. Promise me that you won't hound Pelham now! Revenge is a bitter dish and you'll rue ignoring my advice, believe me!'

Kirk had refused to give his promise, but as he had ridden away from the Hall he had pondered her words.

If he revealed Pelham's guilt the scandal would rock society, and the gossip would reach new heights if he then went on to marry the baronet's betrothed!

Old Mr Fleming had been cool when Kirk had approached him. He would run a dreadful risk if he exposed Stanton, but was honour satisfied by the mere fact of the baronet's death?

This dilemma had given Kirk sleepless nights, but, gazing down into Sophie's vivid little face, all his doubts suddenly vanished. He couldn't face the prospect of losing her. She meant more to him than anything in the world!

'You're right, the old lady did warn me,' he said, finally answering her question. 'However, I don't intend to reveal Stanton's guilt.'

Sophie's eyes widened. 'But why, Kirk?' she breathed.

'Because of the way I feel about you,' he said abruptly.

For a moment Sophie couldn't believe her ears.

'Me? But what about Becky?' she demanded.

'Becky?' Kirk's brows drew together in a puzzled frown. 'What the devil has Becky got to do with it? I haven't spoken to her in weeks. In fact I doubt if we'll ever see her again.'

Sophie gulped as the truth hit her. 'Oh, Kirk, I've been such an idiot!'

'You didn't imagine that I had fallen under her spell again, did you?' Kirk demanded indignantly.

'You were very kind to her,' Sophie countered.

'I felt sorry for her!'

Realising he was shouting, Kirk took a deep breath and unclenched his hands.

'Sweetheart, don't let's start quarrelling!' he begged.

Sophie began to giggle helplessly. 'We always do so! Oh, Kirk, I'm sorry, but she told me. . .well, never mind what she said. I should have heeded Rose's warning and remembered that she was skilled at manipulating people.'

'Rose sends her love.' Kirk carefully steered the conversation away from the tricky subject of Becky. 'And she asked me to thank you for the gift which accompanied the return of her dress.'

A smile touched Sophie's mouth. Choosing that pretty rattle for Rose's baby had been one of the few pleasant moments in the last couple of weeks.

'I'm glad Rose was pleased,' she murmured. 'I like her.'

'She would be one of your neighbours if you came to live in Watendlath.'

Sophie swallowed hard. She hadn't misunderstood him!

'Work has started on the restoration,' Kirk said quickly, afraid of her silence. 'But we wouldn't have to live at Haraldsgarth. I own several other properties. You could choose whichever you preferred.'

Astonishment made Sophie blurt, 'Other properties? You mean you are wealthy in spite of what happened with your plantation?'

'My father invested in several diverse schemes. I inherited a tidy sum.' Kirk suddenly grinned at her. 'I can still afford to keep my wife in comfort, if not the luxury she is accustomed to!'

Sophie blushed. She had misunderstood Caroline's confession! 'I thought you would be worried about being taken for a fortune-hunter,' she admitted.

'That idea did cross my mind,' Kirk replied drily.

'Did my uncle say anything to you before you left

Kendal?' Sophie asked, plucking nervously at her skirts.

He nodded, looking faintly uncomfortable. 'I asked him if I might pay my addresses to you and he told me to go away while he thought things over.'

'Oh, I knew it!'

'Sweetheart, don't fly up into the boughs!' Kirk caught her restless hands and held them. 'You can't blame him for being cautious. I don't give a damn if he wants to have my finances investigated.'

'He said that?' Sophie gasped indignantly.

Deciding there was nothing to be gained from this conversation, Kirk drew her firmly into his arms.

'Darling Sophie, how much longer do you intend to make me wait for an answer?'

Sophie's hands slid up around his neck.

'I wasn't aware that you had asked me yet, sir,' she retorted with a saucy grin.

'Minx!' Kirk's grip tightened. 'Damn it, do you want me to go down on one knee like some milksop?' he growled.

'Of course,' Sophie laughed.

Kirk gazed down into her dark eyes, and his answering grin faded.

'My darling girl, I adore you,' he whispered hoarsely. 'I know I am no good with words, but I think I fell in love with you that evening in Maria Strickland's conservatory. It wasn't just because Stanton was a rogue that I hated the thought of his marrying you. I would have felt the same if he'd been a saint! I want you for my own!'

His golden head dipped to hers.

'Say you'll marry me, beloved!'

In answer Sophie sought his mouth, and as their lips met a joy more intense than any she had ever known shot through her.

I've died and gone to heaven, she thought incoherently, the thud of her heart loud in her ears.

The tenderness of his kiss slowly deepened into passion and waves of exquisite pleasure swept over her, intensified by the deliciously familiar masculine scents of his body and the forceful strength of his arms.

'Oh, Kirk,' she breathed when at last he released her. 'I'll marry you tomorrow if you like.'

They gazed into each other's eyes and desire sparked between them anew.

'The sooner the better, I think,' Kirk agreed with a gruffness that couldn't conceal his feelings.

Sophie shifted to rest her head on his shoulder with a sigh of pure happiness, and he held her tightly for a while in silence.

'Are you really sure about your brother?' Sophie said, stirring in his embrace as her conscience pricked her. 'I have positive proof of Pelham's guilt, you know. He had another snuff-box decorated in exactly the same way as the one found in Ingram's hand. I saw it.'

'The man I had on the trail in London wrote a few days ago to tell me he had found the jeweller who engraved them both,' Kirk admitted.

'Then we could go to the magistrates. I wouldn't mind the gossip, truly I wouldn't.'

Kirk shook his head, his expression sombre. 'No, Sophie. Old Mrs Stanton was right: there is a difference between revenge and justice. Pelham paid for his crimes with his life.' His mouth twisted. 'Anyway, I suspect people will remember how Ingram claimed he'd been cheated once it gets out that Stanton died a pauper, and they'll wonder about the fire. But I won't heap further shame and sorrow on that old lady's head.'

A faint sigh of relief escaped Sophie. 'I'm glad you have changed your mind,' she confessed.

'My debt to Ingram has been paid.' Kirk's deep voice was firm. 'It's time to put the past behind us. My brother was a kind, gentle man. He would have been the last person in the world to want to sour our happiness.'

He gently turned her to face him.

'You once told me that I put Ingram's memory above my feelings for you. It may have been true then, but I swear to you that it will never happen again. I love you more than anything, Sophie. More than honour, more than my life!'

Gazing into his vivid Viking eyes, Sophie realised he spoke the truth, and as he enfolded her into his embrace she knew that their future together would be all that she could hope for. They would quarrel and fight — that was inevitable — but nothing would ever divide them again.

'And I love you, Kirk,' she replied simply, her dark eyes shining.

Their lips met in another tender kiss and, lost in a world of their own, they didn't hear the door opening.

Thomas Fleming hesitated, the bottle of champagne in his hand.

Then, with a little smile, he quietly withdrew.

An irresistible offer for you

We'd love you to become a regular *Legacy of Love* reader. And we will send you 4 books, a cuddly teddy bear and a mystery gift absolutely FREE.

You can then look forward to receiving 4 brand new *Legacy of Love* romances every month for just £2.50 each. Delivered to your door, along with our regular Newsletter featuring authors, competitions, special offers and lots more. Postage and packing is FREE!

This offer comes with no strings attached. You may cancel or suspend your subscription at any time and still keep your FREE books and gifts. It's so easy. Send no money now but simply complete the coupon below and return it today to:-

Mills & Boon Reader Service, FREEPOST, PO Box 236, Croydon, Surrey CR9 9EL.

— — — — — — **NO STAMP REQUIRED** — — — — ✂

YES! Please rush me 4 FREE *Legacy of Love* romances and 2 FREE gifts! Please also reserve me a Reader Service subscription. If I decide to subscribe, I can look forward to receiving 4 brand new *Legacy of Love* romances for just £10.00 every month - postage and packing FREE. If I choose not to subscribe, I shall write to yo within 10 days and still keep the FREE books and gifts. I may cancel or suspend m subscription at any time simply by writing to you. I am over 18 years of age.

Please write in BLOCK CAPITAL!

Ms/Mrs/Miss/Mr _____ EP60M

Address _____

_____

_____ Postcode _____

Signature _____

mps MAILING PREFERENCE SERVICE